A GEN[...]
MASC[...]

Sally Blake

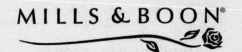

MILLS & BOON®

First published in Great Britain 1999
Harlequin Mills & Boon Limited,
Eton House, 18-24 Paradise Road, Richmond, Surrey TW9 1SR

© Sally Blake 1999

ISBN 0 263 81511 0

Set in Times Roman 10½ on 12 pt.
04-9903-75706 C1

Printed and bound in Great Britain
by Caledonian International Book Manufacturing Ltd, Glasgow

Chapter One

'Now that you're properly settled in after your journey, I want you to meet everyone who's anyone, my dear,' Lady Hartman said expansively, 'and especially the Connors boys.'

There was a smile in her voice as she and her niece took an informal mid-day lunch in the sunny conservatory, as she unwillingly admitted to herself that she was already becoming mildly exhausted by the girl's high spirits.

Truly, Lauri was a delight, but she was also as overexuberant as Lady Hartman had been led to believe all Americans were. But why should she not be, she thought next, when everything about this lovely coastal area of Devon was so new to her? And it must be so relaxing after the stuffiness of Boston and the long sea voyage to England.

Though, eyeing the curvaceous shape and flushed cheeks of her niece now, Helen Hartman wasn't so sure that peaceful relaxation was what necessarily appealed to an inquisitive and healthy girl of twenty summers.

'Oh, I want to meet all your friends, Aunt Helen,'

Lauri said eagerly, in the crisp, transatlantic accent that was not at all unpleasing to her relative's ears. 'But what is it that's so special about the Connors boys?'

She hid a small smile, wondering who these people could be. Some schoolboy scamps, perhaps, whom her aunt and uncle thought suitable companions for a young lady just out of her private tutor's clutches, who needed a little fun.

Your elders never thought you were grown up, she mused, even though she had never met these particular British relatives before. But she was thankful that the instant affection seemed to be mutual on both sides.

Her aunt laughed at her question. 'You'll find out very soon, my love,' she said mysteriously. 'We're all invited to Connors Court for dinner this evening.'

'Is that the large estate along the coast that we passed on the way here?' Lauri asked with interest, guessing that it was probably the place, since it was the biggest property in the vicinity.

'That's the one,' Lady Hartman nodded.

'Then if it's going to be so grand, I had best think of something suitable to wear.'

'Whatever you wear, you'll look a picture,' her aunt said, with a wistful glance at the girl's youthful bloom.

Once, long ago, she had looked like that…before her delicate constitution had changed the roses in her cheeks to parchment pallor. She saw her niece stretch her long legs, so elegant in the stockings that bore the unmistakeable New York flair, and anticipated the next question on Lauri's lips.

'Would Uncle Vernon allow me to borrow one of

the motors to do a little exploring on my own, do you think? I promise you I'm able to drive. Father encouraged me to learn!'

'You must ask him yourself, Lauri, but I doubt that there will be any problem. I rather think he was expecting the request, and even hoping for it.'

Her blue eyes twinkled as she spoke, and for a moment, Lauri glimpsed the lovely woman she had once been before she became so frail. Her uncle was the blood relative, but such clear blue eyes were a trademark of the Hartman family, she thought now. Her parents had had them, and so did she... She walked around the small table and gave her aunt a quick hug.

'I'm so glad I came to England,' she said with her usual candour. 'My father always wanted me to meet you—'

She stopped, and they both knew she was remembering that it was her father's legacy that had enabled her to make this trip, and Helen spoke briskly.

'I know he did, Lauri, and you're welcome to stay with us as long as you wish.'

Lauri's eyes were bright as she moved away, not wanting emotion to cloud these lovely first days of her visit here.

'You're a darling, Aunt Helen, but you know my passage home is already booked for April 10th, so I intend to see as much as I can of your lovely Devon countryside before then.'

'Well, no one could deny you the excitement of travelling back to New York on the maiden voyage of the *Titanic*,' Lady Hartman admitted. 'If my health permitted, I could almost wish I was coming with you. But if you ever felt you wanted to settle here, you know you'll always have a home with us.'

As she fetched a wrap to protect her shoulders in the March afternoon air, Lauri couldn't help thinking how blessed she was to have found two such delightful relatives. After her father's death, and completing her education with the tutor as he had wished her to do, she had simply decided to travel for a while before deciding what to do next.

And where better to begin, than in the glorious Devon countryside of her father's own youth? She was an American girl, through and through, but her roots were here, and these darling people had made her so very welcome...

She made her way to the outhouses now, where her uncle was forever tinkering. Though 'outhouses' was an impossibly down-to-earth name for the grand garages that housed her uncle's beloved motors, Lauri thought with a smile.

It reflected the man himself. He was down to earth too, for all his wealth and status in the community. And he was as unlike her own father as it was possible to be. The one brother had been a serious-minded scholar, having taken a research post in one of America's prestigious universities, where he had met and married Lauri's mother in due course, while the other brother was never happier than getting his head beneath the hood of a car, and getting his hands dirty in the process. But he had become rich in the process, Lauri admitted, with his flair for all things mechanical and being shrewd enough to patent his innovative ideas.

'Well now, my love,' Lord Hartman said, straightening up from his task with a pleased smile as he saw her approach. 'So which of my little beauties do you want to try out?'

Lauri laughed. 'You must be reading me like a book, Uncle. But aren't you going to raise any objections? Most people guard their motors jealously, and I'd be quite happy to bicycle around the lanes,' she added artlessly.

Vernon Hartman laughed back. 'And I know that you're just dying to try out one of my toys! You have the same eagerness I recognise in myself, when I'm longing to get behind the wheel and feel the power of the motor beneath me.'

'I'm not sure that makes me sound too feminine,' Lauri teased, but knowing it was exactly the way she felt.

Her father had taught her to drive, allowing her to practise in his precious Buick. And it had been so exhilarating to feel the wind in her hair and smell the salt spray in her nostrils as they had jolted along the New England coastline...

'No one could ever accuse you of not being feminine!' her uncle commented, and Lauri felt herself blush at his admiring glance. She was tall and elegant, and her hair was a natural, stunning blonde. She attracted attention wherever she went, whether she wanted to or not, and that wasn't always as comfortable a situation as people might suppose.

Sometimes she just wished she was small and mousy and anonymous...but only sometimes!

'Well, then,' Lord Hartman went on, as if realising he had stared at his brother's beautiful daughter for long enough. 'I suggest you take Mr Henry Ford's pride and joy, since I suspect it will be the type most familiar to you.'

Lauri eyed the Model-T with its sleek businesslike lines and grey leather upholstery, and nodded. One of her father's friends had had one just like it, and it held no fears for her. She climbed inside the motor, breathing in the smell of the leather and running her hands around the wheel in a gesture that was almost sensual. She truly loved driving, and exploring unknown countryside would be an added adventure.

'I'll take great care of it, I promise,' she told her uncle as he cranked up the steering handle, and she felt the engine throb into life beneath her. 'I want to go along the coast a little way and take a proper look at the sea.'

And she was also curious to take another peek at the property she now knew as Connors Court. It had looked quite dark and austere on the day she arrived, when the sky had been dull and overcast. But today was warmer and sunnier, with a real hint of spring around the corner, and just the day for exploring the highways and byways of southern Devon.

'Go towards Sidmouth,' her uncle advised her, showing her the place on the map. 'You'll find some tea-rooms there if you want refreshments later in the afternoon.'

Lauri said that she would, knowing it was exactly the direction she intended to take. Connors Court was marked prominently on the map, about ten miles from their own comfortable home.

She drove away from the confines of the Hartman property sedately, conscious that her uncle would be watching her, but once out of sight, she got up a good head of steam, as her father used to say, bowling along the rough roads and breathing in the scented air with a feeling akin to rapture.

Spring truly came early in this lush, southern part of the country, with the hedgerows already burgeoning with tiny blossoms and a latticework of fresh green leaves. England was beautiful, Lauri thought, when she had gone several miles. Little lanes crisscrossed this area of open land, and it was all just as breathtaking as her father had always told her. And the people she had met so far were just—well, just darling, she thought again happily, and so friendly.

She squeezed the rubber ball of the horn, just for the hell of it, and then she squeezed it again, laughing aloud at the quaint, dull sound.

'What the devil do you think you're doing?' she heard an angry voice yell at her.

Almost before she had time to think, or to take her foot off the accelerator, she was aware of something huge and dark rearing up in front of her, and she quickly braked, screeching the car to a halt.

A very large horse was snorting and lathering alongside the car now, its hooves pounding the turf on the grass verge, its bit tugging at its mouth where it was being restrained by the man sitting arrogantly astride the animal as if he owned the world. He glowered down at her. He was a good-looking man, Lauri registered weakly, but his rugged looks were completely lost in the scowling fury he was displaying now.

'God knows where you came from, but whoever thinks he taught you to drive needs his head examined,' he yelled.

'I'm sorry—I didn't see you—' Lauri began shakily, knowing she had been completely in the wrong.

'Really?' He was full of sarcasm now. 'Then you

obviously need spectacles as well, if you can't recognise a horse when you see one, and you certainly shouldn't be driving at all if you can't observe the country code.'

'Look, I've already said I'm sorry!' She found her temper beginning to rise at this oaf's rudeness. 'I'm sure no real harm's been done, has it? And I'll be more careful in future.'

Especially in keeping well clear of spoiled young men who could do with learning a few manners, she thought keenly.

She became aware that the man was looking at her more thoughtfully now, and that his eyes had narrowed. Her hands were still gripping the steering-wheel—her well-manicured, pink-tipped hands—and as she felt her mouth tremble, she knew that the brief incident had shaken her up more than she had at first realised.

'This is one of Lord Hartman's cars, isn't it?' the man said abruptly. 'Then you must be—'

Lauri squared her shoulders and glared back at him. Not for the world was she going to admit her identity, even if he thought he knew it. Let him think what he liked. She spoke as sarcastically as he had done.

'I guess I must be an automobile thief, and I've just taken possession of this little beauty. So if it will make your day a happier one, please don't let me stop you from reporting to Lord Hartman where you've seen me heading!'

The man leaned back in the saddle, a sardonic smile on his lips now. 'I might just do that,' he said.

Lauri pressed down on the accelerator again and as the car shot forward, she prayed that he wouldn't come riding after her. And also that he wouldn't do what she had so foolishly suggested, and go reporting to her uncle that some mad young woman was driving off in one of his precious cars.

But when she glanced back, Lauri could see that he was already riding across the fields and not in the direction of the Hartman property.

Feeling humbled now, she slackened speed, wondering how she had come to antagonise someone so quickly and unintentionally. She prided herself on being a good driver…but she acknowledged that she wasn't used to these narrow roads, nor the sudden criss-crossing of even narrower lanes and tracks.

She drove more steadily, and thankfully met no other people or vehicles, which allowed her nerves to settle down before she reached a small coastal hamlet, some miles from the larger town of Sidmouth.

Lauri took in the scene with delight. This was the England of which her father had spoken so often. The sea rippled in, silvery and smooth now, with no hint of storms or shipwrecks, and boats bobbed about idyllically in the harbour. There were fishermens' cottages and a small gift shop; a ship's chandlery, a waterside inn, and a church perched on a hill. Along the curve of the bay she could see a boatyard and hear hammering, and the scent of wood chippings was strong on the air, mingling with the salt. And there were tea-rooms offering Devonshire cream teas.

It was all too perfect, Lauri thought, parking the car near the harbour's edge. It was the stuff of dreams—American dreams, anyway—whenever they thought of England. She pushed open the door of the tea-room, hearing the bell jangle overhead as she did so. A woman came through a bead curtain from a back room, almost before Lauri could take in the quaint red-checked tablecloths with their cheerful pots of early spring flowers, and the paintings of boats and country scenes on the walls. The curtains at the windows matched the red gingham of the table-cloths.

She realised the woman was waiting for her to order, and she gave her a swift smile.

'I'm sorry to be so slow. It's just so pretty here, but I'd love a Devonshire cream tea, please.'

'For one?' the woman said unnecessarily.

'Just for one,' Lauri said, realising that the woman was assessing every inch of her, from the top of her blonde head, to her soft blue wool suit and elegant black buttoned shoes, and back again to those pink-tipped fingernails.

She gave another encouraging smile. 'I'm a stranger around here—'

'Thought so. From America, I daresay.'

'Why, yes. How clever of you to detect it.' The annoying man on the horse hadn't done so as readily, she thought. The woman nodded towards the gleaming car parked a little way along the harbour road.

'Thought I recognised one of Lord Hartman's cars, and knew he had his niece coming to visit. Cream tea for one, it is, then.'

She was gone behind the bead curtain again before Lauri could say another word.

The cream tea was a long time coming, but Lauri didn't mind. The last few months of her life had been so hectic, and even though it wasn't in her nature to be still for very long, she was more than happy to wind down for these first few days, and this was certainly the place to do it.

She would have liked to engage in conversation with the woman in the tea-room, but after a brief exchange about the area, it seemed she wasn't going to hear anything more.

'Not much ever happens around here,' the woman said finally. 'If it's excitement you're wanting, you need to go to the town.'

Lauri hid a smile at her snort, which implied that anyone going to the town was heading for damnation.

'Oh, I don't think so. I'm here on a mission to meet my relatives and get to know them.'

'You're a *missionary*?' the woman exclaimed, eyeing the girl's expensive outfit, and Lauri laughed out loud at her disbelieving look.

'Good Lord, no! It's just an expression.'

She saw the woman purse her lips and swish back to her kitchen, and she was left strictly alone, feeling as if she had committed some almighty sin in teasing a stranger with her American phrases. Weird, thought Lauri. Definitely weird.

Later, she drove towards Sidmouth, but she had lost her appetite for exploring any further. Besides, the huge property known as Connors Court was far more interesting. Towns were just collections of streets and buildings, however quaint, but a real live mansion that resembled a small castle was something out of Lauri's experience.

She parked the car on the grass verge from where she could look down the undulating hillside to see the lake in the foreground of the property, and beyond it the broad pile of weathered stones that made up the house. In its setting of parkland and shrubberies, it gleamed in the sunlight now and was breathtakingly beautiful. It spoke of money and heritage and breeding.

The young Connors boys were so lucky to have known all this, Lauri thought. She had never envied anyone anything before. It wasn't the American way. If you wanted something, you strived for it and earned it...but there was something to be said for heritage that went back generations...

She became aware of a chugging sound behind her, and it broke the peace of the afternoon.

The large man in the workmanlike vehicle that had pulled up behind her wore goggles and a driving cap and she couldn't see his face properly at all. Despite the fact that he was driving, the car wasn't an impressive one like her uncle's, Lauri observed, and he was probably an employee.

'Are you lost?' he called out.

She was glad she hadn't stopped the engine, realising she was miles from anywhere, and that this person was a stranger. He might be a perfectly respectable one, but he was still a stranger to her.

'Not at all,' she called back coolly. 'I was just admiring the view, but thank you for your concern.'

'Are you the Hartman girl?' He sounded suddenly sharper. 'My apologies if that sounded rude, but we've all heard about the famous American niece of the Hartmans, and your accent rather gives you away.'

'I'm hardly famous, and I didn't realise I would stand out quite so obviously—'

'I assure you we don't see many like you around

here, and Lady Hartman had enthused about you so often to her friends, we'd begun to feel we knew you already.'

Lauri wasn't at all sure she cared to hear all this. She had no idea who the man was, and after her earlier unnerving encounter with the horseman, she was beginning to feel isolated and vulnerable at his quickening interest.

'I'm sorry, but you must excuse me,' she said, and drove quickly away without further explanation.

She put both men out of her mind with a determined effort—the one uncouth and scowling, the other more considerate, but still far too probing for her peace of mind.

It wasn't like her to feel that way, and a mild flirtation never hurt anyone... Not that the small exchange of words had been anything remotely like that...and she decided that it must simply be the newness of it all that was making her more sensitive than usual.

'Are there ghosts around these parts?' she asked her aunt and uncle when they were finally on their way to Connors Court for dinner that evening. Her uncle was driving them now in his prized yellow Wolseley.

Lord Hartman was poker-faced as he replied, 'Of course. What respectable old house doesn't have its share of ghosts and hauntings? It would give the local people less to tease the visitors with, if there were no tales of apparitions wandering the passages of the stately houses hereabouts.'

'But not at Hartman House, surely?'

'Don't let him tease you, Lauri,' her aunt said.

'There are no ghosts here, though there's certainly a grey lady reputed to wander the passages of Connors Court.'

'Oh, now *you're* teasing me! Why does everyone go on so about ghostly grey ladies—?'

'I assure you I'm not teasing, dear, and there have been plenty of sightings of her, though only to unhappy, restless souls, I understand. I doubt that Steven comes into that category, as his feet are far too firmly on the ground. As for Robert, well, if he ever saw a ghost, he'd never admit it.'

'Are those the Connors boys?' Lauri asked, not having heard their names before, and wondering why her aunt always referred to them collectively. She was doing it herself now, she realised. 'I would have thought they'd have had a high old time teasing people about their ghost. Children love that kind of thing, don't they?'

Lord Hartman agreed. 'They certainly do. But their father saw the lady several times before he died, and considered it a kind of premonition.'

'Vernon, please let's talk about something more cheerful,' his wife said sharply, and Lauri knew she was tactfully reminding him not to talk about death.

Her own father's demise had been barely a year ago, and the realisation could still catch her painfully unaware at times, when she found herself almost turning around to tell him something, and he wasn't there.

She turned to her aunt. 'You've told me very little about these Connors boys, and I certainly didn't know they were fatherless. Their mother is still living, I hope?'

Otherwise, they would be poor little orphans…

Having been brought up on a diet of Charles Dickens's tales, Lauri's mind immediately placed these boys in the similar, exploited situations of his wretched characters. But she revised such foolish thoughts immediately, since the Connors boys lived in the palatial surroundings of the estate they were approaching now.

Orphaned or not, they would be pampered and cossetted, and might have turned into the most precocious little snobs… At the thought she chided herself quickly. It wasn't always sensible to speculate on such things, and certainly not to expect the worst of people before you had even met them!

'Their mother died some years ago,' Lord Hartman told her, confirming her idea of them being orphans.

Which was exactly what she herself was now, Lauri thought, never having put it into words until that very moment, and not caring to dwell on it at all. She had something in common with these two young boys, even if it was something she was hardly going to converse with them about.

'Perhaps I should warn you, Lauri—' she heard her aunt begin, and then the car jolted as the wheel hit a stone in the road, and for a few moments they all clung on to their seats as Lord Hartman fought to control the steering-wheel again.

'I'm sorry about that, my dears,' he said cheerfully. 'But no harm's been done, and we've a solid vehicle beneath us. Do you know anything about Wolseleys, Lauri?'

'For pity's sake, Vernon,' his wife exclaimed. 'Just because the girl enjoys driving, don't expect her to know the mechanical workings of the vehicles the way you men do. Lauri is a young lady, and it's hardly the way to go about attracting a husband by talking about engines and cylinders—and valves, and things,' she finished vaguely.

Lauri laughed. 'I assure you I'm not seeking to attract a husband, Aunt Helen, but you've obviously learned enough about Uncle Vernon's passion to know a few motoring terms.'

'One can hardly help it, my dear,' her aunt said drily, 'since it's often his sole topic of conversation.'

But the glances that passed between them were so clearly affectionate and tolerant, that Lauri found herself envying them their closeness. She had no one in the world who was close to her now, and her few liaisons with the young Boston bucks had simply fizzled out. They had seemed so immature and, despite her own exuberant nature, she had been brought up in a moderately serious and academic household.

She ignored the small gloomy feeling, and the uneasy notion that perhaps she was over-critical of male attentions. But she reminded herself that she was single and fancy-free, as the saying went, and for the moment she was happy to be so.

'We're nearly there,' her uncle observed, and Lauri could see the outline of the beautiful Connors mansion ahead of them now. The nearer they approached, the more magnificent it looked, and her heart was beating fast with the thrill and expectation of seeing it all at close quarters. She simply couldn't imagine how it must feel to live there, though she supposed that when you had lived there all your life, it would be perfectly normal.

'What were you going to warn me about, Aunt Helen?' She murmured, leaning forward with her mouth parted and her blue eyes glowing like sapphires in her excitement.

'Oh, it doesn't matter now, dear. I think it's best that you see everything for yourself,' her aunt replied.

'Are there secret passages or something?' Lauri said with a grin. 'They go with the ghostly territory, don't they?'

'Wait and see,' her aunt said mysteriously, intriguing her all the more.

Lord Hartman brought the Wolseley to a halt with a great flourish and scattering of gravel on the driveway in front of the house. Almost at once, the imposing front door was opened, and a butler came out to greet them.

'He's so much grander than the boys,' Lady Hartman said in an aside to Lauri. 'It's a strange fact of life that servants so often are, as you've probably discovered.'

Snooty was the way Lauri would have described one or two of the staff at Hartman House…

'The gentlemen are awaiting you in the drawing-room,' the butler said, and Lauri wondered just how many people had been invited to dinner this evening. She had presumed it was just her family, but perhaps it was to be a social occasion.

She followed her aunt and uncle into the great house, glad that she had dressed in a simple black dress shot with silver threads that oozed elegance and class and wouldn't disgrace anybody.

Around her neck she wore a long string of pearls that had been her father's eighteenth birthday gift, and her hair was piled high on top of her head, showing off the elegant line of her throat, and accentuating the delicacy of her heart-shaped face. She felt confident enough to meet anyone, however grand.

They were shown into the drawing-room, with its Chinese carpet and costly furnishings, and where a maid stood waiting with a silver tray of drinks to offer to the guests and their hosts.

And Lauri felt her eyes widen, her gaze fixed on one of the two gentlemen in the room who was walking towards the visitors now, and not bothering to control the slightly sardonic smile on his face.

'So we meet again, Miss Hartman,' came the voice of the horseman she had encountered earlier. But he had discarded his riding gear now, and was dressed as formally and impeccably as her uncle. 'My apologies for not revealing my identity to you at once, but after our rather unfortunate meeting earlier, I didn't want to spoil this moment.'

If his words mystified her aunt and uncle, they didn't mystify Lauri. What he meant was that he was thoroughly enjoying her discomfiture at having to make small talk with the oaf she had met earlier, however dashing he looked now.

As the maid began to offer the drinks, Lauri took one automatically. And then, as she tore her gaze away from the irritating horseman, the second man came into her focus, and she almost dropped the glass.

'We've met too, and I would have introduced myself to you then, Miss Hartman, but you drove away at such speed that I didn't have a chance to do so.'

And now her uncle would surely think she had been reckless in the extreme with his precious Model-T, Lauri thought, chagrined. She looked from one man to the other, and knew her jaw must have dropped open. She clamped it shut, feeling very foolish to be behaving so naïvely, as if she had never seen twins before, as these two must surely be, or at least, brothers very close in age…and she felt a sudden dark suspicion at her uncle's teasing smile.

'I know we shouldn't have kept it from you, Lauri, but it was too much to resist, especially when you somehow got the idea in your head that the Connors boys were juveniles. So let me introduce them to you properly, love. This is Robert—and this is Steven.'

'But you say you've already met them both!' Lady Hartman exclaimed. 'How is that possible?'

And is this the American way, to make acquaintances so casually without proper introduction? Lauri could almost hear her outraged thoughts.

'I rather think it serves you right for keeping them such a secret from me, Aunt,' she told her drily, aware that she was talking about the men as if they weren't there.

But she found it hard not to stare, for they were so very alike…although, if they were twins, they were not identical. There was a definite difference in their facial expressions. And she was already sure that if she met them separately again, she would know the sardonic smile of the one, and the more open smile of the other, now that she could see it properly without his goggles and driving cap. And she had taken him to be a *workman*, she thought, feeling her cheeks tinge with colour.

'I met your niece while she was driving your Model-T, Lord Hartman,' Robert said coolly, relieving her from answering further. 'Though it might be more accurate to say that she and my horse almost made a closer acquaintance.'

'How very ungallant of you to remind me, sir,' Lauri said at once. 'I shall take far more care in future who I encounter in country lanes.'

'And I merely asked if you were lost,' Steven put in, covering the small *frisson* of tension between them, 'and missed out on the opportunity of making your acquaintance properly before this evening.'

'I'm afraid I was too busy getting my bearings to feel overly sociable,' she said. 'I enjoy time on my own, and forming my own impressions about people and places.'

'So, brother,' Robert put in, 'you may have missed your chance, but life's full of wasted opportunities, isn't it?'

'So they say,' Steven said shortly.

It might be a true observation, thought Lauri, and she could see that there was another, very obvious one here in this room. There was no love lost between these two brothers. She could see it in the disagreeable look on Robert's more dissolute face, and the sudden sparkle of anger on Steven's stronger one.

But Lauri had enjoyed listening to the verbal tussles between her father's academic friends and the students who came to the house, for too long to let any hint of an atmosphere spoil an evening. In fact, her spirits rose, thinking that this might turn out to be a more interesting dinner party than she had supposed. Especially since she had been expecting to be entertained by two young scallywags...and the Connors boys were anything but that...

Chapter Two

The third member of the Connors household was an elderly great-aunt who spent most of her time resting in her room and listening to her companion read to her. But before dinner that evening, the lady was introduced to Lauri as Miss Freda Connors. Lauri could see the family likeness in the frail woman's face, though the strong features so evident in the gentlemen were creased and pale by comparison in hers.

Freda Connors seemed almost of another age, which indeed, she was, Lauri realised. And her old-fashioned, Victorian style of dress made the newcomer feel instantly over-dressed and modern, but she exuded old-fashioned courtesy as well.

'I've been hearing all about you, my dear,' the lady said. 'It must be very pleasant to be in England, after the hustle and bustle of America, but I hope you won't find us all too dull.'

'We shall do our best to see that she doesn't, Aunt Freda,' Robert drawled. 'Isn't that right, brother?'

Steven turned to Lauri. 'We had thought we might take it on ourselves to escort you around the country, if you would permit us, Miss Hartman. I'd also like to show you around the Connors shipyard. We're in the business of providing some of the best craft in the area to special order.'

'Really? I didn't know—but then, how could I?' Lauri said, hastily covering her surprise, having assumed that if both brothers were not exactly privileged idlers, then at least they enjoyed the indolent life.

But remembering the workmanlike appearance of Steven earlier that day, she knew she was in danger of making too many assumptions. It had always been one of her faults. A quick mind didn't always produce the correct results, especially when it was accompanied by hasty verbalising.

She found it easier to respond to Steven than to Robert. He really was a handsome young man, she thought, feeling her heart give a little leap. Despite their similarities, and his obvious business head, he had less of a ruthless look about him than his brother...and she immediately reminded herself that she had better not let her heart get the better of her in the relatively short time she was here.

It was Steven who had a mocking smile on his face now. 'Oh, Miss Hartman, I suspect you've already labelled my brother and me as the idle rich, isn't that so? And never willing to do an honest day's work for our crusts?'

Their *upper* crusts, Lauri added silently. But it was near enough to her own thoughts that she felt herself blush.

'I never thought any such thing,' she said, so airily that they all knew that she had. 'So, where is this shipyard you're going to show me?'

But as she recalled the fragrant scent of wood

chippings and the frantic whirr and buzz of saws, and the sounds of hammering, she guessed. She had been quite near to it that very day. And if only she could have persuaded the tea-rooms woman to open up a little more, she might have discovered it for herself.

'It's not far from here,' Steven said. 'Are you interested in ships, Miss Hartman?'

'Well, it was a ship that brought me here, and I'm planning to return home on the greatest ship of all time—so, yes, you could say I'm interested in ships!'

'You're travelling back on the *Titanic*?' he exclaimed, and just hearing the words sent a little thrill running through Lauri's veins.

It was going to be such an adventure…and the culmination of her father's dream for her to come to England. As she nodded, Robert spoke more scathingly.

'Well, don't expect to see anything of that nature in Steven's shipyard, will you?'

The *frisson* of antagonism was there again, Lauri thought. She was always quick to pick up an atmosphere, and there was definitely a sense of rivalry between these brothers. She supposed it was inevitable, and even more so with twins, even unidentical ones… She had already surmised that Robert was the elder of the two…and she didn't like him much.

'Isn't it your shipyard, too?' she asked, and then spoke more hastily. 'I'm sorry. I know I ask too many personal questions, and I guess I was just born inquisitive.'

'My niece takes after her father in that respect,' Lord Hartman put in, seeing her reddened cheeks. 'It was a necessary requirement in a research professor, of course.'

But not in a visitor...although she couldn't think what she had said to put the frown between Steven's brows. She had merely assumed that the brothers were joint owners of the shipyard.

'My brother has always been more interested in wider horizons, Miss Hartman,' he told her now. 'He's widely travelled, although he has not crossed the Atlantic yet, as you have.'

'Perhaps I should book a passage to New York on the *Titanic* to visit those unknown shores,' Robert put in. 'What would you say to that, Miss Hartman?'

'I would say you are almost certainly too late,' Lauri said crisply. 'I'm sure every passage has already been booked. And won't you please both call me Lauri? Miss Hartman sounds so stuffy.'

She prayed that this wasn't being too frivolous, but, for heaven's sake, she wasn't used to such formality. And if she implied that they were stuffy too, she didn't mean to... Thankfully, dinner was about to be served, and when Steven assisted his great-aunt, it was Robert who offered Lauri his arm, and whose side she was pressed lightly against as they went into the candlelit dining-room.

'You're a refreshing change from some of the young ladies in the district, Lauri,' he said, under cover of the general chatter as they were shown to their places.

'Oh, surely that's no more than a natural reaction to a stranger?' She was deliberately cool. She'd heard enough flattery like this not to be unduly charmed by an educated English voice. But they obviously hadn't spoken quietly enough, because she heard Steven laugh.

'I think you'll have met your match here, brother.

Our American cousin won't be as gullible to your charms as some of your Spanish señoritas.'

Lauri looked at them both with interest. They each had a healthy outdoor look, as though they spent much time out of doors, and it seemed as if it wasn't all due to horse-riding or racing around the country-side in motor cars in the pursuit of pleasure.

'Have you travelled to Spain then, Mr Connors?' she asked Robert quickly now, realising she had been staring from one brother to the other.

'Frequently, Miss Hartman, and if you expect me to call you by your delightful first name, then please return the compliment. There's no need for friends to stand on ceremony.'

From his voice, Lauri couldn't tell whether or not he had spoken generally about the whereabouts of his heart, or if there was a more significant meaning to his words.

'My brother is more interested in the viticulture of that country than in the more mundane activity of Devonshire shipbuilding,' Steven told her.

'I'm afraid you've lost me completely now,' Lauri said. 'I'm not familiar with the word. Would you mind explaining?'

And if she sounded dumber than she should to these fine folk, it didn't bother her. American children were taught to question freely what they didn't understand, and to feel no embarrassment in doing so.

In answer, Steven picked up his wine glass and raised it slightly to her across the dining-table.

'The culture of the golden grape and its produce,' he said. 'Spain is famous for its wine production, and Robert brought back several cases of a fine vintage from his most recent travels. His interest in fine wines is just one of the reasons that draws him back to the country, although he's having a brief respite from its charms just now.'

Robert laughed. 'I'd say my affection for the country's charms is more of a passion than a mere interest, brother.'

There was an undercurrent of innuendo between them now, and Freda Connors evidently decided that this was enough levity for one evening, and asked Lauri politely if she played the pianoforte, and if so, if she would care to play for them all after dinner. She was *definitely* of another age, Lauri thought, when young ladies were expected to display all their accomplishments to the assembled company.

'Sadly, the instrument is something I never cared to learn, being rather keener on book-learning—'

'Gracious, how modern,' the old lady murmured.

'Not really, ma'am,' Lauri said. 'At least, not in my home. My father encouraged me to do the things I enjoyed, and music was never one of my fortes, although I like hearing others play.'

Her uncle put in a word for her. 'My niece is a product of her time, Miss Connors, as we are of ours. It would be a pity, if not a tragedy, if none of us moved with the times, would it not?'

'Well, you certainly have, sir,' the old lady said pithily. 'I hear those noisy automobiles of yours from time to time, polluting the atmosphere with their fumes, and disturbing the natural wildlife of the countryside—'

'Oh, Aunt, you know you enjoy a spin in my motor as much as anyone,' Steven said sternly, 'so don't pretend you don't.'

'But you're a sensible driver, and you don't go speeding about the country like some of them do,' Freda added, not prepared to give in easily.

Lauri didn't look Robert's way, hoping he would make no comment to her near-brush with his horse. Instead, she felt her glance clash with Steven's at that moment, and she caught her breath as her pulses jolted.

'So how long do you intend to stay in this country, Miss Hartman?' Freda went on, unaware of any kind of tension between the younger members of the party.

'She's already told you, Aunt,' Robert said with ill-disguised impatience. 'She's travelling back to America on the maiden voyage of the *Titanic* in April.'

'I can understand your excitement at doing so, Lauri,' Steven said. 'But it's a pity you can't stay longer. We're planning to hold a masked ball in May for our joint birthday celebrations, and it will be a very lavish affair. I'm sure you would enjoy it.'

'Oh, I'm sure I would too! But my ticket is booked, and there it is,' she said, with half-regret. But who in their right minds would give up the chance of travelling on the maiden voyage of that wonderful ship for the sake of a masked ball! It would take something, or someone, very special to make her give up her ticket.

This time, she didn't meet Steven Connors's eyes, because the last thing it would be sensible to do would be for her to form a real attachment to a young man, this one or any other. A mild flirtation was one thing, but falling in love was something else that

wasn't on Miss Lauri Hartman's agenda, when she
was only here for a certain amount of time.

Besides, nobody fell in love to order, at an allotted
time of their life. And she simply didn't believe in
pre-ordained meetings and soulmates and the like...
Even if she knew to her cost that there was a strong
streak of dreamy romanticism beneath her feisty ex-
terior, she had no intention of letting it get the better
of her until she was good and ready for it. And only
on account of the right person.

By the time the Hartman family left Connors Court
that evening, Lauri had been given two vague invitations. Robert had offered to teach her to ride, and
Steven wanted to show her all the intricacies of the
shipbuilding business.

'Steven's idea might be very dull for you, Lauri,'
her aunt remarked when they were on their way
home. 'You'll have seen by now that both boys get
very enthusiastic about their passions, but I hardly
think a shipyard is going to be very interesting to a
young lady.'

'On the contrary! I rather like the sound of learning how a craft is put together. You forget that my
father put the notion of *finding out* into my head from
a very early age, Aunt Helen. And I'm not sure I
shall be as keen on horse-riding as Robert seems to
think.'

'Ah, yes, Robert,' her uncle ruminated.

Lauri looked at him sharply. 'That was a very
enigmatic comment, Uncle. Is there something I
should know about Robert that's not altogether to
your liking, perhaps?'

If there was some intrigue about the brothers, she

would definitely be interested in knowing it. Such background information always put spice into any relationship, however superficial. And it occurred to her that she had annoyingly forgotten to ask a single thing about their reputed ghost!

'I never like talking out of turn about a neighbour, love,' her uncle replied. 'But perhaps in this case—'

'For goodness' sake, don't tease the girl so,' Helen Hartman exclaimed. 'Robert has a bit of a reputation, Lauri. He's always been a wanderer, an adventurer, if you like, and one hears that he's also been a womaniser as well, especially in foreign parts where he's not so well known as he is here. How much truth there is in these wild stories, I don't know, but it's as well to be pre-warned.'

'Well, if that's the case, then I truly thank you for telling me, Aunt!' Lauri said steadily.

Privately, she thought that Robert Connors wasn't going to scare her one little bit. But she knew her aunt was only being anxious for her welfare.

'And neither of them is married, obviously?' she asked casually next. The question was redundant, of course, for there had been no wife present at dinner that evening.

'Nor promised,' her uncle said. 'Robert's kept well clear of that little trap, and I doubt that Steven will even think of marrying until the right person comes along. He's far too involved with his business.'

'And what of this viticulture thing that Robert's interested in? I presume he has to go to Spain for that. There are no grapes grown around here, are there?'

'Not for centuries, anyway, although Robert's been looking into the possibility. He's been back in

England for some months now, but that's the reason for his many sojourns to Spain. Or so we're led to believe.'

'And you don't believe it?' Lauri queried. She had never met two such contrasting and interesting brothers in an age.

'Your uncle has a theory that it's just a blind to mask what he really does when he's away,' she said vaguely. 'Playing in the fields, is what I believe you young people call it nowadays.'

'Something like that,' Lauri said with a laugh. 'But why shouldn't he enjoy the company of several ladies, if he has no other ties? Presumably there's no shortage of family money.'

She knew she was being far too modern and nosy again. The Connors family coffers were certainly none of her affair, and the mere sight of that beautiful house and grounds were enough to let her know that what they had between them was a serious amount of money. Any girl who married either one of them would presumably want for nothing. Providing she married him for the right reasons.

She veered her thoughts away from such things. Thinking about marriage wasn't why she was here. All she wanted was to absorb the atmosphere of this lovely corner of England that her father had loved so much, and to meet these refreshingly eccentric relatives.

'And what about Steven? Since it seems he's determined to show me around the county, does he have some bad points that I should guard against?' she went on.

'None to speak of,' her aunt said. 'Unless you call an obsession with his work a bad point in his favour.'

'I don't. I think it's admirable. I liked him enormously, and he didn't seem as volatile as his
brother.'

Helen laughed. 'Oh, don't be fooled, Lauri. Steven
has inherited his father's ruthlessness every bit as
much as Robert. They just show it in different ways,
that's all—and Steven controls it better.'

Lauri decided to stop showing such an interest in
the pair of them, before her aunt started matchmak-
ing.

'Have you been to London, Uncle?' she asked.

'Several times, and I wouldn't care to live there.
Once you've breathed clean English country air, this
is the only place you'd ever want to be, and in glorious Devon in particular,' he added, smiling.

Apparently Robert Connors didn't feel the same
way, Lauri thought, if he spent as much time away
from Devon as possible, while Steven was so clearly
in love with his birthplace and his work. The brothers
might be physically alike, but in temperament and
character, she guessed, they were poles apart. And
she was still thinking about them, darn it.

'I'd like to go to London, though, to see all the
famous buildings my father spoke about. Would it
be possible, do you think? Could I take a train or a
bus and stay in an hotel for a couple of nights?'

'Not on your own, Lauri!' her aunt said at once.
'It would be far too dangerous for a young girl.'

'I'm very independent, Aunt Helen. And if I could
travel across the Atlantic Ocean on my own, I don't
see what harm could come to me in London.'

She tried to keep her voice even, and to hide her
impatience. But it was a long time since anyone had

clamped down on her movements, however endear-
ingly, and she didn't care for it now.

'We'll all go some time soon,' her uncle said.
'You wouldn't object to two ancient monuments
showing you the sights, would you, Lauri?'

'Of course not!' she said warmly. 'And anyone
less like an ancient monument than yourself, I can't
think—nor you, Aunt Helen!' she added hastily.

For a moment she thought she might really have
offended them, and it was the last thing she wanted
to do. She had been here over a week now, and the
days stretched ahead blissfully. And so far she had
been content to inspect every nook and cranny of
Hartman House and the surrounding area of this
lovely coastal part of Devon. But she was far too
restless to spend all her time idling, and the urge to
look further afield was becoming stronger all the
time.

Her chance came a few days later, when a small
car that she recognised came roaring up to the house.
She and her aunt were inspecting the glass conservatory with its exotic flowers and shrubs, and enjoying some freshly made lemonade during the warm
afternoon. And through the glass they could see the
owner of the car unwinding himself from the driving
seat, before coming inside the conservatory and
bringing a breath of salt air with him.

'Good day, ladies,' Steven said breezily. 'I can see
that you're both well, and I hope you'll forgive the
informality of this visit. But we're launching our
newest vessel in a couple of days' time, and I thought
Lauri might be interested in seeing it, and sharing in
the champagne celebrations afterwards.'

'My goodness, yes, I would indeed! It all sounds terribly exciting!' she exclaimed.

He showed his delight at her uninhibited reaction. 'It doesn't always happen like this, I assure you. Most of our work is very mundane. This time, the client is a member of Parliament and he's bringing his family down from London to see the launch of his seagoing yacht before the fitting out is completed. So, on his instructions, we've booked a room at a local hotel for the small party afterwards.'

Lauri's blue eyes sparkled. 'How marvellous. And I'm honoured that you've invited me to see how the other half lives.'

As Helen Hartman asked Steven mildly if he would like some refreshment, and poured him a glass of lemonade, they both looked at the lady as if they had forgotten she was there. And Lauri immediately wondered if her aunt felt slighted that she hadn't also been invited. But presumably there was a limit as to how many extra people even a member of Parliament would want included on the guest list.

'You don't have any objections to my accepting private invitations, do you, Aunt Helen?' she asked hastily.

'Of course not, providing they're from reputable sources. And Steven has my approval on that score. You must feel free to do anything you like while you're here, love.'

As long as it wasn't travelling to London on her own, Lauri thought drily. But Steven would have had her father's wholehearted approval too, she realised at once.

He had just the same kind of enthusiasm and energy for his work as her father had had. Even though

Miles Hartman's work had involved the head rather than the hands, the pleasure the two men derived from it was clearly the same. No wonder his personality appealed to her.

She found herself looking at Steven's hands. They were large and capable, but far from coarse. Whatever he did, he was still a gentleman, but a gentleman who obviously enjoyed the physical activity of his work. His fingers were very strong, and she felt herself flush, imagining their touch...

'Well, then,' she said brightly to cover her sudden confusion. 'You'd better tell me which day, and at what time all this begins, Steven, before my social calendar gets completely filled up!'

Though as yet, she had only done the rounds of a few afternoon teas with her aunt's acquaintances. Yet, pleasant and welcoming as all those older folk had been, this boat-launch celebration promised to be far more interesting.

And meeting a member of Parliament, no less. How her father would love to hear all about that...

Her eyes suddenly prickled, as they always did, when she momentarily forgot that he was no longer around to hear all about her latest jaunts or escapades. It was foolish and somehow heartbreaking to think she could forget, even for a moment, but some psychologist or other would probably tell her it was far preferable to remember him as if he was still here, than to dwell on the fact that he wasn't.

She realised that Steven was still talking to her, while she had been dreaming.

'I asked if you would you care to take a spin this afternoon, Lauri, to see how the shipyard operates?'

'Right now, you mean?'

She heard herself sounding so stupid and inane, when she had always prided herself on being reasonably sophisticated and self-reliant, and very much in control of herself.

'Why not?'

Helen Hartman took command of a situation that seemed oddly to be going nowhere.

'For two people who obviously want to do the same thing, you seem to be walking right around the bush to get there. Go and enjoy yourself, Lauri. When you bring her back, join us for dinner this evening, Steven. We're quite informal here.'

'That's very kind of you, and I accept.'

Lauri was glad her aunt hadn't felt obliged to include Robert in the impromptu invitation. But just because the brothers were twins, it didn't mean they were joined at the hip, she thought inelegantly. She spoke quickly.

'Then if you'll wait just one moment, Steven, I'll fetch my jacket.'

Her heart was beating faster than usual as she went into the house and ran up the stairs to her room for her linen jacket. She told herself it was no more than a natural reaction to an unexpected diversion to liven up the day, and she didn't want to admit that it could be more than that. She already liked Steven Connors enormously, but she didn't really know him as yet, and she had rushed headlong into love before now, and lived to regret it when it all turned sour.

There was something to be said for the old Victorian values of the past century, she thought, to her own surprise. Young girls, then, were chaperoned and guarded, and led towards suitable attachments, instead of living in the sometimes bewildering new freedom that existed now—especially on the side of the Atlantic where she had been raised.

She gave a small shiver, adjusting the collar of her jacket and seeing her eyes darken in her dressing-table mirror. Her brief fling with a student, the hero of her father's college sports team, had been more passionate than she had expected, stirring up feelings and emotions in her that she hadn't known existed.

And when he had wanted more than she was prepared to give, he had turned swiftly to a more obliging girl, and left Lauri heartbroken. She didn't intend getting caught up in that kind of trap again, however charismatic the fellow was. Even if she had to deny her own quicksilver nature, she intended taking things slowly when it came to romance.

She turned away from the telltale face in the mirror, knowing she was fooling herself, and that you couldn't stop falling in love any more than you could stop the tide ebbing and flowing. The fact that it was a seagoing analogy that filled her head didn't escape her either, and she left her room quickly, determined not to fall in love with either of the Connors boys.

'So, how are you enjoying Devon? Is it everything you expected?' he asked, as they rattled along the leafy lanes towards the coast.

'It's exactly as my father described it,' she told him. 'It all feels so familiar to me—which probably makes me sound like a crazy woman!'

'Not at all,' he said. 'It sounds just the way I would expect someone to react on coming home.'

She stared at him. 'That's an odd thing to say!'

'I suppose it was.'

'No—what I mean is…that's just how my father

described it to me. He said that if I ever managed to come to Devon it would feel like coming home, because the place was in my blood.'

'So maybe you were meant to stay,' he said easily.

Lauri shook her head vigorously. 'I told you last night. This is no more than a trip, and my passage home is booked—'

'Oh, yes. On the famous *Titanic*. But you could always change your mind. I thought that's what young women were famous for,' he said, half-mockingly.

'Then you shouldn't lump all of them together,' she answered smartly, 'because nothing would induce me to do such a thing. Why would I want to give up such a chance, anyway? Would *you*?'

'That would depend on why I wanted to stay. You might just find that the lure of your birthplace is too much to resist, after all—or whatever you find in it.'

Lauri decided that the conversation was taking a far too personal turn.

'Can we please talk about something else? It's not very fair of you to disturb my peace of mind, when it's been one of my dreams to be on the maiden voyage!'

'It probably isn't,' he agreed. 'So what do you think of us Devonshire yokels so far?'

Her face relaxed into a grin, because anyone less like a Devonshire yokel than Steven Connors she couldn't imagine. Nor his brother.

'If you're fishing for compliments, then all I'll say is that I'm very happy to be here and made to feel so welcome. Will that do?'

'I suppose it will have to, for now. And you didn't leave any attachments back home?'

'Now you're really fishing, aren't you?'

'No,' Steven said coolly. 'Just making sure I don't tread on anyone's toes when I tell you you're the loveliest girl I've ever seen. So, am I?'

It would be very easy to fob off any unwanted attentions from Steven, or anyone else for that matter, to confirm what he asked. It was very tempting to say there was a beau waiting for her the minute she stepped off the ship in New York to whisk her back to Boston. And it was just as unlikely that Lauri Hartman would ever resort to such subterfuge.

She shook her head and spoke airily.

'You're not treading on anyone's toes, as you put it. But neither am I over here looking for flattery, or a husband—'

'That's all right, then. Because I wasn't actually proposing,' he answered smartly.

She looked at him quickly, seeing the firm set of his jaw, and his unsmiling face. And as she wondered if she had offended him in some way, the look changed, and he was laughing at her suspicious glance.

'I'm *teasing* you, Lauri, but I'm not about to confess an undying love from the minute I saw you, either. You're not looking for a husband, and I'm not looking for a wife, so does that suit you, ma'am?' he added, mocking her accent.

As he spoke he reached across and squeezed her hand for a brief moment. The contact only lasted seconds, but all the way down to the coast and the bustling shipyard, Lauri was still aware of the touch of his hand. And the fact that it had sent her pulses racing quite ridiculously simply filled her head with all kinds of warning bells.

Chapter Three

They covered the same route as Lauri had driven in her uncle's car, but she admitted that it was more fun to have someone pointing out the various aspects of the countryside to her, without having to concentrate on driving an unfamiliar vehicle. It was more fun to be with Steven, period, she thought.

There were cliffs on the far side of the small hamlet where she had discovered the tea-rooms, and Steven drove right along them and parked on the scrubby moorland, where they could look down at the glittering water far below.

'It looks so wonderfully tranquil today,' she said, breathing in the clean air as they left the car and stood on the cliff-edge. 'But I remember my father telling me how rough it can get here at times, and about all the ships that have been wrecked along the coast, in Cornwall especially. But I can hardly imagine it now.'

'Oh, it happens all right,' Steven said. 'Cornwall isn't the only county with its share of wrecks, though I concede that it's the worst.'

Lauri gave an involuntary shudder, imagining

nothing more terrible than being on board a ship that was heaving about in bad weather and splitting to pieces on treacherous rocks...

'Your business isn't in building huge ships, though, is it, Steven?' she said, willing away the imagery.

He shook his head. 'We cater for many types of boats to order, but we're not equipped for the heavy stuff. We leave that to the big commercial yards in Liverpool and elsewhere.'

'There must be a lot of satisfaction in seeing a boat come alive from just plans on paper and specifications,' she commented.

'There is,' Steven said. 'And it's sweet of you to pretend to be interested in men's work. Not many young women can be so concerned.'

'That sounds a mite patronising—why shouldn't I be interested? Women travel by sea as well as men, don't they?'

'But not all of them care about the nuts and bolts of the craft they're travelling in. There are plenty who take an ocean voyage with the sole purpose of finding a wealthy husband, and little else enters their heads.'

Lauri was outraged at this chauvinistic attitude, and her Boston accent sharpened.

'I think you do women a disservice if you think that's the only thing they have on their minds, Steven! Present-day women aren't so dependent on men that they have need to simper around them begging for crumbs!'

'Good Lord, I seem to have really hit a nerve, don't I?' he said, as she paused for breath. 'I didn't mean to offend you, and I must say it's good to meet a woman with a mind of her own. And now I suppose I've done it again, by implying that every other one I've met is—what did you call it?—simpering around, begging for crumbs?'

But she realised that he was baiting her again now, and she knew she had taken offence where none was intended. They were from different cultures, no matter how similar the language, and although she guessed by his accent and demeanour that he was well educated, the American female sex always seemed that much more liberated. Or so she thought.

The lighter skirt she had worn that day whipped around her legs as it was caught by the fragrant moorland breeze now, and the tangy salt air teased her nostrils.

It was far too glorious a day to be arguing, though she had to admit she thoroughly enjoyed a good argument or debate, or however you cared to describe it…and that was the American way, too…

'All right. Let's call it quits, shall we? So now you know I've got a mind of my own, and I'm not afraid to use it—and I'm sure every other woman around here is perfectly capable of doing the same,' she told him.

'I think you'd better meet Alice before you go making rash statements like that,' he said, as they walked back to the car.

She perked up at once, wondering if there was any significance in the way she detected a smile in his voice.

'And who is Alice?'

'She's Aunt Freda's companion, and she'd have joined us for dinner the other night if she hadn't had a bad cold and decided to stay in her room.'

Well, that changed any opinion that she might have been Steven's paramour, thought Lauri. She sounded a real milksop if anybody did, but she generously gave the poor woman the benefit of the doubt in not wanting to pass on her germs.

'Is she as elderly as your aunt?'

'Hardly! She's not that much older than you, but I must say there's a world of difference in you both, which is undoubtedly due to your upbringing.'

'Is that so? And which of us comes off worse, in your considered opinion?'

She couldn't stop the sarcasm creeping into her voice now, knowing he was really enjoying this. And so was she, she thought, unsurprised, despite laying herself wide open to criticism by the question. But no Englishman would be so ungallant as to censure a visitor from overseas...

'Regardless of anything else, if I reiterated that you were the most beautiful and exciting and interesting woman I've ever met, you would probably think I was being far too forward on such short acquaintance,' he said. 'So if you prefer, you can just forget I said it.'

Lauri was taken completely off-balance by the crispness of the words. And of *course* it was far too soon... They had only met a few days ago, but while they stood on the cliff edge, momentarily suspended in time, she realised that he had been in her thoughts for much of that time. But she had met so few young men here as yet. Only Steven, and his brother...

She felt that *frisson* of fear again, sensing that she could be plunging towards something over which she had no control. And she had always kept such firm control of her life and didn't want any complications in it...

Without thinking, she took a step backwards, as if to put some distance between them. Even though they weren't physically touching, she felt as though his senses reached out to hers and held them captive, claiming her...and her own senses spun in response...and such feelings had no place in the world of the feet-on-the-ground Boston sophisticate that she was...

'For God's sake, be careful, Lauri,' Steven said sharply. and now she knew that the touching was very real, as he pulled her away from the dangerous cliff edge.

She was necessarily pressed close to his chest, and she could feel his heartbeats, as rapid as her own. She could breathe in the texture of his skin, and see the deepening brown of his eyes. If she let her fantasies roam where they would, she could swear she saw the beginning of love...

She gave an awkward laugh, moving swiftly out of his arms, knowing she had to lighten this charged moment for her own sake.

'I think we had better get on with our drive, Steven, otherwise we're in danger of being seen in a compromising position by any passing motorists, however innocent it is.'

They both glanced around, aware of the isolated moorland where they might have been the only two people in the world.

'What are you afraid of?' he asked. 'Of being hurt? I would never hurt you—'

'I really wish you wouldn't talk this way,' she said jerkily. 'I'm glad to have you as my friend, but I'm not looking for any complications in my life at this time.'

He laughed shortly. 'I've been called many things, but never a complication, and if I've upset you, then of course I apologise unreservedly. Though I assumed that you weren't the kind of girl who was afraid to face new experiences. It took a lot of courage to take a long sea voyage alone.'

'That was different.'

That hadn't involved any romantic emotions or any major decision as to how to live the rest of her life—and she had no idea what direction the rest of her life was going to take as yet.

She suddenly thought about the companion that Steven had spoken about, and gave a small shiver. Being a lady's companion was something from another era and the woman called Alice would probably find another post when Freda Connors died. It seemed a pretty dismal prospect to Lauri, to be always living on the fringe of someone else's life, and definitely not the way she wanted to live hers.

'Are you all right?' Steven asked.

'Of course. So shall we do what we set out to do, and go to see this shipyard of yours?'

'Right away, ma'am,' he said crisply, copying her accent again and making her smile.

She admitted that she liked him. She hardly knew him, she reasoned—but reason didn't come into it when there was a rapport and an empathy between two people. And, for now, she was quite determined to leave it at that. She didn't know Robert yet, either, the thought occurred to her, and when he wasn't bellowing at her from the back of a horse, he might be very pleasant company!

'We're not far from Plymouth,' Steven went on. 'Being as smart as you are, I'm sure that you're well aware that it's where the *Mayflower* set sail from for the New World in 1620.'

'Oh, *really*?' she said mildly, and then she capitulated with a laugh as she caught his incredulous look. 'Oh, of course I know! It was one of my earliest history lessons. My father had fond memories of Plymouth and the Sound.'

'Then I'll take you there one day.'

'Look here, Steven, I don't want to be a nuisance to you, or to take you away from your business. Besides, my uncle may well want to show me around my father's old haunts—'

'I wouldn't want to overstep the mark with your uncle, of course, but what's the sense of being a boss if you can't take time off when you want to?' he said. 'I don't work all the time, and it will be my pleasure to take you as long as he approves.'

And she had the feeling that whatever Steven wanted, Steven got. She reversed her passing opinion from that first evening, when she had thought Robert Connors was the stronger of the two. He was different—more aggressive, more brash—but Steven had a ruthlessness of his own. It wasn't unattractive. It all depended on the way you used such a trait, she thought, but she liked the fact that in no way was he overshadowed by his brother. They weren't like two halves of the same coin at all. And she liked that too. She liked it very much.

'What does your brother do when he's not travelling to Spain? I understand he's not involved with the boat-building business,' she asked curiously, as the car began its descent over the rough tracks towards the small village she now knew was called Kingscombe.

'Robert has his own pursuits and we don't interfere with one another. I know he's been making enquiries about growing grapes in the area, but I'm not sure it will be a success. Not that English wine is anything new, as a matter of fact.'

'Really?' she said, in genuine surprise now.

'The Romans introduced vines to this country and taught us how it could be transformed into wine. Many monastery vineyards flourished after 1066, until dear old Henry the Eighth abolished them, and it all ceased.'

'You're very knowledgeable, aren't you?' she observed.

'Oh, yes. Despite living in the sticks, some of us are,' he said, tongue-in-cheek, and Lauri felt herself blush.

'Anyway,' he went on, 'I daresay Robert will divulge anything he wants me to know in due course, but he usually keeps his plans close to his chest until he's ready.'

She was right in her early assessment of the brothers in one way, Lauri decided. There was little love lost between them—though, as in all family relationships, she wouldn't mind betting that if a disaster occurred, they would stick very closely together. And why such an inane thought should enter her head at that moment, she couldn't think.

But she gave up trying to analyse the relationship between the Connors brothers, however simple or complex it might be, and concentrated instead on enjoying the panorama of the village setting ahead of her. It really was so pretty… It was just the way her father had so often described a Devon village, with the little thatched cottages set so higgledy-piggledy in the cobbled streets, and the lingering old-world appearance.

'It's so beautiful that it makes me wish I could paint, so that I could take the images back home with me,' she exclaimed as they drove past the centuries-old stone-built church, the tea-rooms she remembered, and the village pub.

They passed a small sandy cove, where the fishermens' boats were hauled up high on the sands now, and drove along the bank of a narrow river, to where it opened out to the sea in a wide series of inlets and creeks.

The location of the shipyard was in one of the larger creeks near the village. The sign of Connors and Sons was emblazoned across the gates, evidence of a long-established family business.

As they got out of the motor, Lauri was glad to stretch her legs from the bone-jolting ride down from the moors. They walked towards the industrious sounds of sawing and hammering, and the scents of sawdust and glue and paint.

From the reception from the workmen, it was obvious that Steven was well respected and well liked, as he pointed out the boats in various stages of production, and allowed each craftsman to explain its progress to her.

'And now you must see our pride and joy,' he told her, with barely disguised enthusiasm. 'This is the one we're building for Sir Gerald Hawkes that I told you about.'

'The Member of Parliament,' Lauri murmured.

She wasn't normally overawed by the thought of meeting anyone, but she had to admit that eminently titled people weren't exactly two a penny where she came from.

'That's right,' Steven said, unaware of her small attack of stage fright. 'You'll like him. He's rather like your uncle, in fact, big and bluff and outspoken.'

They were walking now towards a quay, where a sleek and very large sailing boat was tied up in the dock. Lauri didn't know much about boats, but it wouldn't take a genius to know that this was clearly going to be someone else's pride and joy, as well as Steven's.

'It's magnificent,' she breathed. 'I'm filled with admiration, Steven.'

He laughed, but he was openly pleased at her reaction.

'It's not all due to me, I assure you. We have skilled workmen here who all love the work that they do.'

'That's the real secret of success, isn't it? My father used to say the same thing.'

He held out his hand to invite her on board, and she stepped gingerly over the gangplank to stand on the deck. She knew it wasn't yet fitted out, but it was a privilege just to stand here and share in his pride.

'You loved your father very much, didn't you?' he said.

'Doesn't everybody?'

'Not everybody,' Steven replied. 'Some fathers can be tyrants and hold the purse strings so tightly it almost ruins all that the sons hold dear.'

'What a profound thing to say!' She tried not to betray how very intriguing she found the statement, but dearly wanting to hear more. 'But I presume this has some personal and private bearing so I won't pry.'

'You may as well know, since it's common knowledge, and I suspect your inquisitive little brain would soon find a way of discovering it from your uncle.'

'Please don't make me feel like a busybody! I'm naturally interested in my relatives' acquaintances—'

'Is that all? I hoped you might be more interested in one of them in particular, and not just as an acquaintance.'

Lauri's heart jumped at the words, and as if to avert any hint of closeness between them again, her voice was shorter than usual.

'You were going to tell me something about your father, I believe, but please don't, if you'd rather not.'

Steven shrugged, and the more intimate moment passed.

'Why not? He always wanted both his sons to be involved in the shipyard. But Robert never had the same interest as himself, and intended travelling where he pleased rather than settling down. So my father arranged for the business to be controlled by a consortium, with myself as managing director, to come into effect after his death five years ago. We knew nothing about his plans until then, and according to our lawyer, there's another little surprise to come after our birthday in May.'

Lauri could tell by his voice that he bitterly resented his father not telling them of his plans. And he was understandably bitter, she thought. It seemed a particularly cruel thing to do, when one so loved the shipyard so much, and the other would appear to have a far more feckless nature.

'Did Robert resent all this?' she said, trying not to sound censorious.

'Why should he? He does nothing except reap his share of the profits every quarter. But I didn't bring you here just to hear about our family squabbles, Lauri. What do you think of our masterpiece?' he said, running his hand over the smooth wood of the deck-rail.

'I think it's fit for a king, and anyone would be proud to own it,' she said honestly.

Steven nodded. 'Let's hope Sir Gerald Hawkes feels the same about it. He's not quite royalty, but the most prominent client we've had so far and his name as a patron will definitely add to our prestige.'

By the time they had traversed the entire shipyard, and Lauri had been introduced to some of the craftsmen, it was time to return to Connors Court for afternoon tea.

'So where is your brother today?' she asked, as they motored away from the shipyard and headed back inland.

Steven gave her a brief smile. 'You've mentioned him frequently this afternoon. Are you coming under his spell, like every other female he meets?'

'I most certainly am not,' Lauri said crossly. 'And I'm not the kind of *female* who falls for every good-looking man she meets, thank you very much. I was merely wondering if I'm to meet him again today.'

They sparked off one another, she thought, but it was the kind of banter that added a heady spice to any conversation. And Lauri was very aware of how quickly she and Steven Connors were developing an easy friendship.

'*So?*' she asked, more aggressively, not wanting her thoughts to go in that particular direction.

'So, no, you won't be seeing Robert today, or for however long he intends staying away this time. Spain seems to have temporarily lost its attraction, and he hasn't been back there for six months, but he'll never lose his wanderlust. I've no idea where he's taken himself off to now. But maybe that facet of his nature appeals to you, being a traveller yourself?'

Lauri recognised the edge to his voice now, and he didn't bother to disguise it.

'It doesn't, as a matter of fact,' she said carefully. 'I admire anyone for wanting to explore and widen their knowledge of the world, but I wouldn't want to spend my entire life wandering the globe. It sounds so—so rootless.'

'Then I'm relieved that we agree about one thing,' Steven said. 'So why don't we forget about Robert?'

'All right. Tell me instead about your birthday in May. You implied that it was going to be a very special occasion, and I'm interested to know more, even though I won't be here to share in the celebrations.'

'Oh, I think that's best left to another time,' Steven said to her surprise as they reached the outskirts of the Connors estate. 'Maybe you'll even change your mind about going back to America before we've hardly had a chance to get to know one another properly. I promise you I intend to do my best to persuade you to delay your return.'

'Well, I wouldn't advise you to put any wagers on

it,' she retorted, refusing to see anything in his remark other than a predatory male assumption that meant nothing.

But who would give up the chance to sail on the maiden voyage of the greatest ship ever built? With his own love of ships, Steven must know that it would have to take something very special to make anyone change their minds on such an important issue. Something as special as being in love…and she certainly wasn't.

The motor stopped outside the front door of the mansion, and once he was out of the vehicle, Steven held out his hand to assist her and she put her own in his without a second thought. And just as before, the touch of his hand remained with her long after the polite contact ended.

'Allow me to introduce you to Miss Alice Day,' Steven said, when they reached the drawing-room. There was an innocence in his voice now that didn't fool Lauri for a minute.

She took the proffered hand of the elegant, dark-haired woman who sat sketching, while her employer dozed in an easy chair near the long windows. Hiding her surprise as best she could, Lauri thought that Alice Day was nothing remotely like the way she had imagined an elderly lady's companion to be.

'I'm delighted to meet you, Miss Hartman,' Alice told her in an educated accent. 'Miss Connors has mentioned you several times, and I would be quite interested to hear something about your country sometime.'

'It will be my pleasure, although America is so vast that you'll realise I'm only acquainted with a very small part of it, Miss Day. But the eastern part of it is rich in history, of course—'

'Oh, history is of no concern to me at all! I'm more interested in the people and their habits.'

'My goodness, then perhaps I should try to dissect myself for you,' Lauri couldn't help saying.

Instantly, she knew she didn't like this woman. She was attractive, and probably attentive to the aged Freda Connors, but there was no warmth about her at all. It was her eyes, Lauri decided. Her mouth smiled, but her eyes were cold and calculating... Lauri immediately wondered if she had set her sights on one or other of the Connors boys—and if she saw the newcomer from across the Atlantic as any threat to whatever plans she harboured.

She must be going crazy, Lauri thought, to be letting her imagination run away with her like this. But she had always trusted her own intuition, and it had rarely let her down.

Her employer began to waken at the sound of voices, and Alice spoke to her at once.

'Here's a visitor to see you, Miss Connors,' she said brightly. 'Steven's brought Miss Hartman along to join us for afternoon tea. I'll ring for it, shall I?'

Yes, an out-and-out sycophant, Lauri decided. With one sentence, Alice put herself in the role of prospective lady of the house.

She couldn't seem to stop such thoughts flitting in and out of her head, and for all her intuition, it wasn't like her to be quite so suspicious of anyone so soon. It wasn't even as if it mattered a fig to her. Presumably Robert would marry some day, and his bride would become the lady of this beautiful house. And if he was to continue roaming the world in his bachelor state after his brother married, then Steven's wife would have virtual control of it. And which one of them was Alice really angling for? Lauri wondered interestedly.

'I said, how is your aunt, Miss Hartman?' she heard Freda Connors say now, and she started, realising she had been staring into space for a few moments.

'I do beg your pardon, ma'am,' she said hastily. 'My aunt is tolerably well, thank you, apart from her cough.'

'We all have our troubles, Miss Hartman,' the old lady said drily. 'And one of yours will be the dry old sticks you've been obliged to meet since your arrival, I daresay.'

'Ma'am?'

She heard Alice give a tinkling laugh. *Yes, definitely a sycophant,* thought Lauri again.

'You'll have realised that my employer is of an age where she doesn't mince words, Lauri—may I call you Lauri?'

'But she's not so old that she can't speak for herself, girl,' Freda reprimanded her sharply.

She turned away and spoke directly to Lauri, ignoring her companion's darkening face.

'Come closer, my dear, and tell me what you've made of Devon so far. Are we all the yokels that you expected?'

Lauri laughed out loud. Old she might be, but Freda Connors was a delight, and as Alice swished off to ring the bell for tea, she sat on a tapestry stool near the old lady.

'Not in the least! My father spoke about it so often that I felt as if I was truly coming home. He was very nostalgic for Devonshire, and I think if he hadn't met and married my mother he might have had second thoughts about remaining in Boston all those years. He spoke in just the same way as everyone around here—though maybe his accent had gotten a little slicker over the years,' she conceded.

'Yours is very much slicker than many people are used to hearing,' Alice put in, coming back to join them.

'Well, that's because I'm an American, and proud of it. We're all a product of our environment and upbringing, aren't we, Miss Day?'

She turned back to Freda Connors. 'I must say that everyone has been very pleasant to me since my arrival, and I know I shall be sorry to leave.'

'Do you still have some family in Boston?'

Lauri shook her head. 'My mother's family live in Illinois. There was never much contact between us, and it virtually ceased when she died. And then my father—'

She looked down at her hands, swallowing for a moment, and then spoke more brightly. 'So you can see why I was so eager to connect with my English relatives and re-establish the links between us.'

'I know they're delighted that you did. And now let's all have some tea,' the lady added as the maid brought in the tray.

It was obvious that Alice was going to pour, and moments later Steven joined them and took his cup and saucer from her hands with a smile.

Did he feel any warmth towards her? Lauri speculated idly. Was he even aware of any special nuances in her voice when she spoke to him? Maybe when the older son was away, she was content to play up to the younger one...

Lauri was suddenly annoyed with herself for all these speculations, but it was just a game, no more. She was an observer of life, or so her father had so often told her, and it was a good and healthy thing to be, as long as it didn't mean standing on the sidelines for ever, and letting the rest of the world pass you by.

She could almost hear him saying the words now... *Don't forget to live your own life, darling, while you're busy observing everyone else's...*

By the time she and Steven left to return to Hartman House for dinner that evening, it was with a distinct feeling of relief on Lauri's part. Such life-observations as she had made that afternoon were normally a source of interest, but there was an antagonism emanating from Alice Day that was quite undeserved, and it dulled any pleasure Lauri might have derived from trying to form an instant analysis of her character.

'You're very quiet,' Steven said. 'And I know you're about to scold me for not warning you that Alice wasn't in the least like the stereotypical spinster companion.'

'Not at all,' Lauri said coolly. 'Actually, I'm getting rather used to the deviousness of the British mind. Did you know that, before we met, my aunt referred to you and Robert as the Connors boys, and I almost brought you each a plaything on that first evening?' she elaborated. 'How foolish would that have made me look?'

Steven laughed. 'I'm sure I would have accepted

it graciously if you had done so. I can't answer for Robert, of course. His sense of humour is sometimes suspect. But seriously, are you very annoyed that I didn't tell you Alice was the way she is?'

'Before I answer that, I'd like to know what you mean. What way is she?'

'Well, she's hardly the ancient crone that you might have been expecting to see. Her family once had money, until her father gambled it all away, and she resents everyone else who still has it, while knowing that she has to earn a living. But I apologise for teasing you, Lauri.'

'Please don't bother your head about it,' she said again. 'I doubt that Miss Day and I will come in contact very often.'

And not at all, if Lauri had anything to do with it, she thought keenly. Anyone she was less likely to want for a confidante she couldn't imagine. And nor could she explain exactly why she felt the way she did. It wasn't as if Steven had shown any regard for the lady, and even if he had, Lauri had no cause for feeling jealous. He was nothing to her, except a friend.

Chapter Four

In a very short space of time, Lauri felt as if she really belonged in England. One of the highlights, she admitted, had to be the day her uncle drove her to Connors Court, where she transferred to Steven's motor, and accompanied him to Kingscombe for the launch of Sir Gerald Hawkes's yacht.

The gentleman was just as Steven had told her—he was the same physical type as her Uncle Vernon, big and bluff and jovial. As well as his wife, he brought his two young daughters and a gangling son.

Lady Hawkes was openly fascinated by Lauri's accent. Once the yacht had been safely launched, and the party had adjourned to the local hotel for the champagne reception, Lady Hawkes was keen to show hospitality to the American girl.

'We often meet visiting tourists in London, Miss Hartman, and we always find Americans such delightful people. If you should ever come to London, please do call on us. But do tell me, are you and the dashing Mr Connors courting?'

It was obvious that, Member of Parliament's wife

or not, she dearly loved a bit of gossip. Lauri answered quickly.

'Oh no, not at all! He's just my aunt and uncle's neighbour, and he very kindly invited a stranger along to join in these celebrations.'

The lady laughed. 'Well, perhaps that's how you see it, my dear young lady, but it's obvious to another woman that he has eyes for you, Miss Hartman. I'm never wrong in such matters,' she said archly. 'And I've been told that you're travelling home on the *Titanic*, is that correct? What a thrill that must be for you.'

'It most certainly is, ma'am. I can't imagine how large a vessel she is, and I'm simply dying to take my first look at her. I'm sure the voyage is going to be something I'll remember all my life.'

'And it's something we're all trying to persuade her not to do,' Steven put in from the far side of the table. 'She should stay in England much longer so that she can get to know us all properly.'

'You see, Miss Hartman?' Lady Hawkes murmured in the style of a conspirator. 'And there's only one person that young man wants you to get to know properly!'

Thankfully, Steven didn't hear her, Lauri thought fervently, but he went on speaking in a mock-mournful voice. 'As it is, if she persists in returning home in April, we shall have to be content with driving to Southampton with her relatives to wave her off. But it won't be the same at all.'

'Oh, Steven, for pity's sake, do stop,' Lauri protested with an embarrassed laugh. 'You'll be giving Sir Gerald and Lady Hawkes the wrong impression—'

'Not at all, you sweet young thing,' the Member of Parliament boomed, in what Lauri guessed was the kind of House of Commons voice that would quell any opposition arguments at a stroke. 'Any young fellow with a gel like yourself would want to keep her with him, and be mad with jealousy when she went away, especially with all those shipboard tales of romance and intrigue ahead of her!'

'But it's not like that at all,' Lauri began feebly, feeling for once in her life that this Hawkes couple, so different in style and yet so very forceful in their own ways, were in danger of taking her over. 'Steven and I are good friends, and nothing more.'

'I understand.' Sir Gerald leaned forward with a chuckle and a wink, pressing her hand briefly. 'But just remember that good friends often make the best of liaisons, Miss Hartman.'

Lauri let out the breath she hadn't realised she had been holding. But for one awful moment she had thought he was going to say that good friends often make the best of lovers...and that would *really* have been embarrassing.

Their company was heady and exciting, but she felt rather saner when they had all gone back to London in Sir Gerald's expensive motor.

'So, what did you think of our city folk?' Steven asked when they were driving back to Hartman House.

'Well, since I'm a city girl, too,' she reminded him, 'I liked them—'

'And they certainly liked you. Did I hear Lady Hawkes inviting you to stay at their town house in London if you could spare a few days?'

'Well, she didn't exactly say that, and I hardly think it's likely. I do want to go to London, but my uncle won't let me go alone, and he and Aunt Helen will accompany me if it's possible. But I'm sure I could make a point of calling on Lady Hawkes while I'm there.'

She gave an unexpected giggle, and Steven asked what was so funny.

'It's just hearing myself being so blasé about calling on such important people, that's all!'

'You're just as important—'

'Oh, yes, to my family and friends, maybe, but not in the same way as these grand people are!'

'We're all the same under the skin, Lauri. I thought it was part of your American belief that all people were created equal. Isn't that right?'

'And you're so clever to remember part of the Constitution. For an *Englishman*,' she added facetiously.

He laughed, mimicking her again. 'Honey, I'll do my best to live up to your image of the weak-chinned Englishman, if you prefer.'

'I don't. I like you just the way you are. And before you get swollen-headed over that statement, I mean—well, I mean just what I say. I like my friend.'

'And I like mine,' Steven said with a smile in his voice, and not looking at her.

She glanced at his profile now. He wore his usual goggles and motoring cap that had formed such a useful disguise when they had first met. Not that it had been intended that way, but it meant that Lauri hadn't immediately connected him with his brother. But the accoutrements certainly didn't detract from the firm jawline and very masculine features, and in no way could he be called a weak-chinned Englishman…

'Good God, look who's turned up again, like the proverbial bad penny,' Steven exclaimed, as they both saw a horseman riding at breakneck speed across the fields.

Lauri's heart jolted. There was something about Robert Connors, sitting astride a horse with his coat-tails flying, that could stir the heart of any susceptible woman, and even though she wasn't physically attracted to him, she was not completely unaware of the sensuality of the man.

'You must have known he'd be back some time, I presume,' she murmured now.

'Of course. But all too frequently he brings some sort of upheaval with him, and that's putting it mildly.'

He brought the car to a stop as Robert reached them, leaning over to greet them and ignoring the way the horse was lathering and snorting.

'So, brother, you've been taking advantage of my absence, I see, to further acquaintance with the lovely Miss Hartman!'

'I wasn't aware that you had any priority over her movements,' Steven said coldly.

'But now that I'm back—'

'Now that you're back, *I'll* say whether or not I want to further my acquaintance with you or anyone else, Mr Connors!' Lauri said, annoyed that the two of them were talking about her as if she wasn't there.

Robert laughed arrogantly. 'Of course. But you promised to let me teach you to ride, and I'm holding you to it. Borrow one of your uncle's cars and drive over to the Court tomorrow afternoon about three o'clock, and I'll have the nag saddled and ready for you. If you've got no riding gear, there'll be some at the stables.'

Before Lauri could utter another word he had pulled on the reins and twisted the horse's head around, and was galloping away from them. He was outrageous, she thought angrily, and for two pins...

'You'll be there, of course,' Steven said.

'*Will* I?'

She drove to Connors Court the following day in the same Model-T Ford she had borrowed before, and on a number of occasions since that first encounter with Robert and his horse. She was very familiar with the car by now, and also with the Devonshire lanes, where it was prudent to drive cautiously.

Today she was going horse-riding...and she had to admit that the prospect didn't thrill her overmuch. Generations of well-bred English countrywomen had ridden horses, and played musical instruments, and excelled at all of those things, and she did none of them.

It didn't make her any less of a person, Lauri thought defensively, and she had other skills. Though she conceded that a quick brain and a penchant for absorbing historical facts might not be considered great attributes for a wife of the landed gentry. But since such a prospect didn't apply to her, she could just as cheerfully disregard it.

Helen had produced a riding jacket and breeches they had bought for a young girl they had fostered for a while, and were still in their packing tissue. They were a reasonable fit, despite Lauri's long legs, and she preferred to be fitted out in this way than to borrow anything Robert Connors might supply.

But she mustn't resent him…she had to give him the benefit of the doubt that he was a decent, upright person who was being kind to a visitor, the way Steven had been…

She still had her doubts about him though. He was brasher than Steven…more adventurous than Steven…and she knew that many women would say he led a more exciting life than Steven, but that didn't make him any more admirable.

She drove the last few miles to the Court, determined not to be so darned analytical about things as she usually was, and to take this day for the outing that it was.

'Well, the gods certainly smiled on me when they sent me such an elegant pupil,' Robert remarked as soon as he saw her at the stables. 'My only regret is that something I have to do that's unavoidable prevents me from taking you, so Steven has volunteered to do the honours instead.'

His eyes assessed her slowly, from the top of her stunning blonde hair that she had pinned up into a tidy topknot today, down over the well-fitting green jacket, and the beige jodhpurs and leather boots. Such blatant appraisal of her shapely figure made her nervous, and when she was nervous she spoke sharply.

'I'll be quite happy to go with Steven, thank you, and I look the part then, do I? I'll *do*?'

Something about the way he looked her over made her feel vulnerable and defensive, and she didn't care for that feeling either. What *was* it about him that bugged her so?

'You'd look the part, whatever you wore—or didn't wear, Miss Hartman,' he said with deep innuendo in his voice.

Now she knew what it was. They might be brothers, and twins at that, if un-identical ones, but Robert had none of Steven's finesse. Steven wasn't averse to mocking, but Robert liked to shock, and not always in a pleasant way. For all his background breeding, he was uncouth. And if Alice Day had set her sights on him, she was welcome to him.

'So where is Steven? Or are we going to stand here looking at one another all day?' she said at last.

'I think it would be a more pleasurable experience to do the latter, but he'll be here in a moment or two,' he said with a grin. 'Every English lady should know how to sit on a horse properly, and thank God we can forget all that old-fashioned side-saddle nonsense.'

Such genteel activities seemed to define the difference between the background and status of these people, and her own modern upbringing, thought Lauri, when all she had wanted to learn was readily available in books and her father's extensive library.

'This is your nag,' Robert said now, as a doe-eyed, piebald mare was brought out of the stable. It wasn't a big animal, but up close it seemed enormous to Lauri, and she knew that another attack of nerves was coming on. The mare was already saddled, and the young lad was inviting her to step onto the mounting-block.

To her relief, as soon as Steven appeared, Robert bid them good day and strode off on his own.

'I'm not at all sure about this, Steven,' she began.

'Don't tell me someone who's cruised the ocean

between two continents is nervous of this little beauty! Molly wouldn't hurt a fly, would you, girl?'

He palmed the mare's mouth as he spoke, and the animal nuzzled his hand. She certainly *looked* docile enough, Lauri thought dubiously, and seeing the challenging look in Steven's eyes, she knew she couldn't back out.

'Let's get on with it, then,' she said.

He explained how to hold the reins and pull on them when required, and when to press her heels gently into Molly's flanks to make her trot and go faster. And all the time, Lauri was conscious of the power of the beast beneath her, however gentle it might seem to an experienced rider, and she prayed that she wouldn't make a complete idiot of herself.

She watched as Steven swung easily into the saddle of his own sleek brown horse. He and his mount were well suited, she thought. They were both large and powerfully made, reeking of breeding and strength. In that respect the brothers were certainly alike too, she conceded.

'You won't make me gallop, will you? I'll be terrified of falling off if you encourage Molly to race, and I'd prefer to get back in one piece, if you don't mind.'

Bravado made her imperious, and he laughed as they cantered slowly away from the stables. But once they had struck out towards the open fields and he coaxed her to go a little faster, she began to relax. Almost before she realised it, they had reached the coast and a long stretch of sand, and he suggested that she let Molly have her head, just to feel the exhilaration of it.

'What are you afraid of, Lauri? I don't imagine

there are many things in life you aren't curious to try.'

She couldn't miss the undoubted question in his voice and his eyes now, and she felt her face burn. She was no little ingenue, no wide-eyed kitchen-maid of a previous age, destined to be seduced by the son of the house in some lonely spot…but nor was she fast or promiscuous, just because she came from a different and aggressively progressive culture… He insulted her by hinting as much.

Without thinking what she was doing, she dug her heels hard into Molly's flanks, and the mare surged forward in response. Lauri screamed, clinging tightly to the reins as Steven shouted at her to hold on tight and she'd be fine…

'What do you think I'm doing!' she screamed back as the wind tore some of the pins out of her fine hair and sent it streaming away from her shoulders. Sand was whipped up into her eyes and made them sting, and she frantically tried to calm Molly down by leaning low over her neck, and tried not to notice how harshly the animal was breathing.

And then Steven was alongside her, reaching out and grabbing Molly's reins and pulling her expertly to a halt in a flurry of sand. Controlling the animal, and laughing…

Unbelievably, and to her fury, he was *laughing* at her…and she quickly revised her opinion of his sense of humour!

She slid from Molly's back, and almost fell over, discovering that her legs seemed to have turned to jelly in the last few minutes.

'I suppose you thought that was funny!' she yelled, all her usual aplomb deserting her.

'From where I was sitting, it was, rather,' he said. 'But you brought it on yourself by digging so hard into her flanks and implying that you were ready for her favourite gallop along the sands. But you did it so fast you scared her—'

'*I* scared *her*?' she spluttered. 'What the devil do you think she did to me? She was completely out of control!'

'Nonsense. She would have slowed down the minute you stopped prodding her with your heels. Wouldn't you, girl?'

He had dismounted by now, and began to cradle the mare's head between his hands, talking soothingly to her, before feeding her some sugar lumps from his pocket.

All his concern was for the animal, Lauri seethed, and although it was creditable that a gentleman should be kind to animals and children, she wasn't sure that she appreciated being made to feel the scapegoat for Molly's madcap race across the sands.

She turned away from him, folding her arms across her chest, and looked defiantly out to sea while she got her breath back and recovered herself. And then she felt his arms around her, and her heart leapt as she felt the heat of his hands on her shoulders.

'You must forgive me if I wasn't as attentive towards you as you had every right to expect, Lauri. But nothing was hurt except your pride, and the animals are valuable—'

'And I'm not,' she snapped, starting to feel rather ridiculous now after such a display of panic.

'Oh, I wouldn't say that, my dear girl,' Steven said.

She was instantly aware that they were alone in this isolated spot...and before she could think of anything smart or witty to say, he had twisted her around to face him, and the next moment he had fastened his mouth over hers in a long, sweet kiss. One hand had moved upwards to capture the silky strands of her hair in his grasp, and the other one had slid downwards to her slender waist, so that she couldn't move...

She wrenched away from him, wondering if this had all been planned. Bringing her here...not warning her of how eagerly Molly would respond to a gallop in her favourite place...or did he just think all American girls were easy? Such a thought depressed her instantly.

'What do you think you're playing at?' she asked angrily. 'Do you think my aunt and uncle would be anything but scandalised to know you were trying to compromise me?'

And, oh Lord, how *stuffy* that sounded! But Steven's impatient response did nothing to alleviate the feeling.

'Compromise you? God help me from a pious female who can't accept a spontaneous bit of affection. And don't tell me those Boston fellows didn't take every advantage of kissing a pretty girl when they got the chance.'

'Maybe some of them did,' she said coldly. 'And some of them waited until they were invited to do so. I'd have thought an English gentleman came into the second category. And do we continue with this ride, or was that the end of the lesson?'

Her eyes dared him to argue, and he gave a careless shrug. 'Of course it wasn't the end, and if you promise not to suspect me of seduction if I unavoidably have to touch you, I'll help you to remount.'

Once she had crammed her hair back into a reasonable twist with her remaining pins, she let him help her back into Molly's saddle. Only then did she realise how scared she had actually been when the mare had taken control. She didn't want to be here at all, and she decided there and then that horse-riding definitely wasn't for her.

'I can see now that Molly's too small for you,' Steven stated. 'Robert was stupid to suggest her, and you would probably have been more comfortable with a larger mount—'

'Well, neither of you need trouble yourselves over any future one, because I don't intend repeating the experiment,' she told him.

'That's a pity,' he said, as their horses trotted along the sands. 'You have a very attractive seat.'

Lauri glared at him, but he was looking straight ahead, and she couldn't tell whether or not he was being serious about her riding posture, or completely outrageous. And she wasn't going to provoke an unwanted answer by asking.

But she gradually relaxed as they cantered at a more gentle pace over the moors and fields and back towards Connors Court. And she found herself thinking of two things. One was that she was fervently grateful that no one else had witnessed her stupidity. And the other was the memory of that kiss…

'Did you enjoy the ride?' her uncle greeted her, when she drove the Model-T back into the yard with a flourish. She stepped out of it stiffly, thinking longingly of a hot bath.

'Well, Steven certainly did!' she replied feelingly. 'But it didn't take me long to discover that horse-riding exercises muscles you didn't even know you had, and I definitely prefer to have four wheels beneath me.'

Vernon Hartman laughed. 'Funnily enough, so do I, my love. But if you've had enough jaunting for today, you might go and cheer up your aunt. I think she's feeling rather under the weather.'

'She was perfectly well when I left,' Lauri said. 'It's nothing serious, I hope.'

'I hope not too, but I shall ask Dr Vine to come and take a look at her tomorrow. Her cough is very persistent, and it exhausts her so when it goes on for a long time.'

Lauri felt a sudden alarm at his words, sensing the anxiety behind them. Even though it was a year ago, she was only just coming to terms with her beloved father's death. Now she had found these delightful English relatives, the thought of something being seriously wrong with Aunt Helen was something she couldn't bear to contemplate.

'I'll go and see her at once,' she said, all thoughts of taking a luxurious bath going straight out of her head. She walked hurriedly towards the house and straight into the drawing-room where her aunt was gazing out of the window.

Perhaps she was being extra perceptive at that moment, but there was such a pinched, white look about her aunt's face now that Lauri felt her heart turn over.

'Uncle Vernon tells me you're unwell, Aunt Helen,' she said at once. 'Is there anything I can do for you?'

Helen smiled ruefully. 'Not unless you can turn

back the years, my dear, and not even a miracle worker can do that. But don't look so anxious. What ails me is no more than is brought on by the march of time, and none of us can escape that.'

'Uncle Vernon says the doctor should see you,' Lauri said, feeling rather like a parrot as she repeated his words. And not too sure whether she was supposed to tell her or not, but quite sure that her uncle was right.

'He fusses too much. He'd smother me with affection if I let him, which is why I tend not to worry him too much with my foolish woman's troubles.'

Even as she spoke, the spasms began again, and it was a good few minutes before she could get her breath back. By then, Lauri was alarmed to see how the colour drained from her face, leaving it parchment white. She stood by helplessly, not knowing what to do, but finally her aunt spoke hoarsely.

'Just leave me be for a while, Lauri, and I promise it will pass. It always does. Don't you fuss over me as well, dear.'

'Then, if you're sure, I would like to get out of these riding clothes and have a hot bath.'

'Of course. Ask Maisie to see to it for you,' Helen said vaguely, sitting back in her chair and closing her eyes.

Lauri left her and went to find the maid. And once the girl had begun to run the bath in the splendid new bathroom her uncle had installed, she quizzed her about her aunt.

'How long has my aunt been having these attacks, Maisie?' she asked. 'You'll understand that I'm concerned for her.'

'Oh yes, miss, and so are we all,' the girl said

earnestly. 'It's been a while now, more'n a coupla years, I'd say. The doctor comes to see her fairly regularly, but he don't do much for her, 'cept to give her more linctus.'

'I see. Well, thank you for telling me.'

'That's all right, miss. Your towels are on the shelf there. Is there anything else?'

'Not a thing, thank you,' Lauri said, noting the maid's envious eyes on her slender, shapely figure. Both the Connors brothers had made it plain that they appreciated it too, and she shivered, pushing them resolutely out of her mind as she undressed and sank into the soft, warm water.

But, try as she might, Lauri found it difficult not to keep a surreptitious eye on her aunt from then on. All through that evening, she found herself registering how often Aunt Helen coughed, or tried vainly to disguise the fact. But her concern didn't go unnoticed, and Helen finally spoke in an exasperated tone to her niece while they were taking their coffee in the drawing-room.

'Lauri, dear, please don't pay me quite so much attention. I'm really not about to expire!'

'I'm sorry, Aunt Helen,' Lauri said contritely. 'It's only because I'm worried about you.'

'And I've told you, there's no need. Doctor Vine will come to see me tomorrow, and a new bottle of his famous brew will put me right in no time.'

As if to defy what she was saying, a sudden spasm caught her unawares, leaving her coughing and gasping, and her husband began thumping her in the small of her back.

'For pity's sake, Vernon, stop it,' she croaked, her

eyes watering. 'I shall be black and blue by the time you've finished with me, and it does no good at all.'

But the little scene alarmed Lauri considerably. She couldn't get it out of her mind when she went to bed that night, and while she fretted over the possible causes for the persistent coughing she resolved to have a private word with the doctor if it was at all possible.

Doctor Vine wasn't due to arrive until the afternoon, by which time Helen was robustly telling everyone that it was a lot of fuss about nothing, and she was perfectly well now. She certainly *looked* better, Lauri conceded, unless it was all for show, so as not to alarm the rest of them. And maybe she was just seeing things that weren't there, she told herself…like that grey lady ghost she had still forgotten to ask the Connors boys about…

She turned her thoughts to that interesting fact, and tried not to worry too much about her aunt. But she still caught up with Dr Vine after he had finished his visit with her aunt, and spoke to him outside the house.

He was an elderly, bespectacled man, who obviously had no time for new-fangled machinery and motors and had arrived in a conventional pony and trap, which gave him a certain air of country solidity.

'I would be obliged if you would tell me honestly, Doctor, if there's any cause for concern over my aunt's condition?' she asked him.

The doctor answered abruptly.

'And what makes you think I may not have been honest with the lady herself, young woman?'

Lauri flushed, but she was nothing if not direct.

'Because I know how physicians work. I have had much experience with them at one time or another. Out of kindness to the patient, they frequently say one thing and mean another. Isn't that so?'

She kept her gaze rivetted on him, knowing she might well have gone too far. Doctors didn't like their methods questioned. They were a breed unto themselves, but this one's eyes suddenly twinkled, and he spoke more lightly.

'I can see the lady would have an excellent nurse in you, should she ever need one—'

'And *will* she?' Lauri demanded, with no intention of being put off, however charming the man might be.

To her alarm, his face became graver. 'It could happen. But then it could happen to us all in time—'

'I think you're prevaricating, Doctor,' she said boldly, 'and I wish you would tell me the truth. I do have some experience of illness.'

He eyed her more thoughtfully. 'I'd say Mrs Hartman has as many good years left to her as anyone else with a weak chest and a tendency to ignore it. It will never get completely better, or worsen unduly, but there's a limit to how much a doctor can do if the patient's own nature decrees otherwise. Does that answer your question?'

'Not entirely, but I suppose it will have to do for now.'

'Then enjoy your time here, Miss Hartman, and keep your anxieties to yourself. Your visit is the best tonic my patient could have, as she told me herself,' he added.

After he left the house, Lauri stared after the receding dust from the trap's wheels for a good few minutes. She was certain the doctor hadn't been using a kind of emotional blackmail in saying that her visit was the best tonic for her aunt. But she knew it was true. She also knew, by now, that her aunt's dearest wish was for Lauri to remain here longer than her allotted time.

But it wasn't her plan. It had never been her plan to make this an extended visit, or a permanent one. The thought of that had never entered her head. It was one of the reasons she was also determined not to let friendship with any young man turn into something deeper, when there was no future in such a relationship. How could there be, when she would be thousands of miles away in Boston, and Steven was here…?

She drew in her breath, not having intentionally thought of him at all. The very thought that she had done so alarmed her. He was her friend, nothing more, even if she also knew by now that she was infinitely more attracted to him than she could ever be to his brother.

But remain here in England for a while longer, after all her plans…? She toyed with the tiny idea of it for no more than a minute. This was just a delightful visit, and the fulfillment of a dream. But home was Boston, where her roots and her friends were. Yet, even as she thought it, she knew that without her father there, home might as well be anywhere.

She banished the sad thought from her mind, wondering if she was becoming spineless. Of *course* she was going home when her visit was over. Her passage was booked on that wonderful ship, and her aunt would get well once the summer sunshine arrived.

You had to believe in the positive things of life, Lauri told herself determinedly. You had to be an optimist in this world, otherwise you might just as well curl up and die.

Chapter Five

As the days grew warmer, Lauri made herself believe that her aunt was getting stronger, and that her own theory of sunshine being the best tonic of all was helping the situation. Helen was certainly no worse, and made no attempt to curtail the determined round of visits to introduce her niece to the county. Lauri began to have doubts, though, about the hoped-for trip to London. But Steven was shortly to take her on the promised visit to Plymouth.

He arrived on the appointed day, looking less than pleased, and bringing his Aunt Freda to spend the day at the Hartmans'. The pair of them looked highly agitated, but although nothing was said immediately, Lauri turned to Steven the minute they got in his car and set off from the house.

'Are you going to tell me what's wrong, or do I have to sit looking at your grumpy face all day?' she demanded.

'You don't mince words when you want to know something, do you?' he countered. 'I was going to tell you anyway. Maybe you haven't heard the story of our reputed ghost…'

'Yes, I have, and I meant to ask you more about it some time. Don't tell me it's materialised again.' She couldn't help a smile, hardly able to believe that Steven would be taken in by such romantic nonsense.

'Three nights ago Alice swore she saw it wandering the corridors, and it scared her out of her wits.'

'What?'

Lauri couldn't help feeling even more sceptical, remembering the calculating Miss Day, and wondering if this was no more than a simple pretence of nerves, to enable her to rush into some obliging young man's arms… Who was being the cynical one now? she thought.

'Has she upset your great-aunt very badly by telling her?' she asked swiftly, remembering the story of how Steven's father had seen the grey lady shortly before he died, and taken it as a grim premonition.

'She told everyone, and got the entire household at fever pitch with nerves. And then she packed her bags and went off without a word to anyone. Robert's furious, since it transpires now that he and Alice had taken a shine to one another. And Aunt Freda's incensed since it looks as though the girl helped herself to some of the old darling's money and jewellery.'

'Oh, no!' Whatever else she had thought of Alice, Lauri wouldn't have labelled her as a thief, even if she had fallen on hard times. 'You've called in the police, of course?'

'Naturally. The house has practically been invaded by constables for these past few days. I was glad to get Aunt Freda out of it for today, now that they've left us to follow up some leads, as they say, but I

doubt that they'll trace the girl. By now, she'll be
long gone from here.'

'Oh, Steven, I'm so sorry. It must have been an
awful ordeal for you all, and especially for the old
lady.'

'If Alice was a thief, we're obviously well rid of
her. But nobody can be sure whether or not she really
did see the grey lady, or made up the whole thing to
send the household into a state of panic, which it
certainly has done, although Aunt Freda's starting to
scoff at it now. But if Alice did see the ghost, then
should we give any credence to the old story, that it
foretells a death? More importantly, whose death?
Tell me the answer to that, if you can.'

Lauri hadn't thought that far ahead, but she could
see that Steven, for all his common sense, still had
a nagging respect for a supernatural tale that was part
of his family heritage. She supposed one would, if it
was in the family...

'Is that what your Aunt Freda thinks?' she said
carefully. 'That it foretells a death?'

And presumably she would think of it as her own.
In the natural order of things, the older members of
a family perished before the younger ones. In the
natural order of things, at least...

'Oh, she skirts all around the subject, and so does
Robert, though I know very well he doesn't forget
my father's dire prediction about his own death. And
that came true.'

'It could have been nothing but a coincidence—'

'And it might not.' He glanced at her pale face.
'But I shouldn't be bothering you with my family
troubles, and I wish I hadn't done so on our day out.'

'You had to tell me. If you hadn't, Aunt Helen

would have done so, since I dare say the two ladies are getting their heads together over it right now.'

And maybe they were also eyeing one another up, and trying to gauge which one of them was the most likely to be at the mercy of the Grim Reaper…

At the thought, Lauri felt her heart stop in shock for a moment, before it raced madly on.

The visitation of the Connors ghost would surely have nothing at all to do with anyone outside the family, and there was no reason why it should affect Aunt Helen at all. But Helen was the one who was ill and under a doctor's care, while Freda, for all her pallor, was probably in the rudest of health and would go on for years yet. Lauri felt the most appalling sense of fear as her imagination leapt ahead of her, until she had her aunt well and truly dead and buried…

She hardly realised that Steven had stopped the car on the roadside. She hadn't even realised how much she was shaking until he put his arms around her.

'Perhaps we should postpone this trip until some other time, Lauri,' he said quietly. 'Neither of us is in the mood for sightseeing any more, and I can see that I've upset you far too much. It seems I have a habit of doing so.'

'It's not you. I've upset myself,' she muttered. 'I'm worried about Aunt Helen, and all this talk of death—'

His face was very close to hers, and before she knew what he was about to do, he had placed his lips gently on her cheek.

At least, that was where it started out, and it was Lauri herself who moved a little jerkily, unwittingly twisting around so that their mouths met, and clung, and remained together for a long, sweet moment.

It was as different from his earlier kiss as it was possible to be. It was different from any kiss she had known before, and if the analytical Miss Hartman had ever thought that a kiss was just a kiss, then she knew differently now.

Steven spoke slowly, still holding her.

'Forgive me for that, Lauri. You looked so lost, and I couldn't bear to see you looking that way.'

'There's nothing to forgive,' she said, in a strangled voice. 'It's just that—well, I've tried to make it plain to you, Steven, I'm not looking for any romantic attachments in the short time I'm here.'

'That's all right, then. Neither am I,' he said calmly.

She felt a small shock, and then he laughed at her incredulous face.

'Now I've probably offended you again by my clumsiness. What I mean is that since our time together is so limited, I entirely agree that it would be the height of foolishness to let ourselves fall in love. Wouldn't it?'

'The absolute height of folly,' she said steadily.

She moved out of his arms, where she realised she was still so pleasurably content to be. But, clearly, Steven had the same sensible thoughts as she did. It would be madness to fall in love when they were so soon to be parted. Absolute, reckless folly...

They decided to continue on their way, and Lauri tried to think about other things, especially the despicable Alice Day, knowing she had been right in her intuitive mistrust of her. It must be a terrible upheaval for the family, and she wondered just how involved Robert had really been with her.

He struck her as a man who would fall in and out of love easily, so maybe no real harm would have been done. Not to his heart anyway. His pride was another matter.

But once they reached Plymouth and the Hoe, and she had marvelled at the wonderful expanse of water that made up the Sound, she took pleasure in absorbing Steven's knowledge of the many and varied boats that jostled on the water. She learned even more about the history of the place her father had told her so much about, and finally, when she was feeling quite exhausted, they retired to an hotel for lunch.

'I do appreciate your bringing me here, especially today, Steven,' Lauri told him, when they were seated overlooking the river. She wriggled her toes, glad to flex them after all the walking.

'It's my pleasure as much as yours,' he said abruptly. 'I wasn't fooling when I said I wished you could stay longer.'

'You know I can't.'

'Why can't you? What is there to prevent you? You could easily stay for the whole summer, and your relatives would love it if you did.'

The waitress brought their food then, saving her from making any comment. Saving her from thinking too deeply about the question that had surged into her mind at that moment.

And would you love me, too?

'Think about it, Lauri. I know your circumstances, of course. What have you got back in Boston now?'

She had a number of friends and acquaintances…but no one of her own. No one to love her, or to love in return…

'I'll think about it if it makes you happy, but don't bank on it, will you?' she said lightly as she began to tackle her meal of locally caught succulent fish and tiny, minted potatoes.

But she didn't mean it seriously, and giving it a passing thought was all she was going to do. It was a dream, no more. It wasn't part of her reality, any more than falling in love and marrying the second son of an English county landowner was.

'What are you smiling at now?' Steven demanded.

'You wouldn't want to know. I was just daydreaming about impossible things.'

'I was always told that nothing's impossible if you want it badly enough, and you can put any interpretation you like on that. You'll do so, anyway.'

She smiled again. 'Do you think you know me so well?'

'Yes, but not as much as I'd like to if the circumstances were different.'

Lauri drew in her breath. He was going too fast…too impossibly fast…but she knew now that it was all a harmless flirtation, because he had made it plain that he had as many reservations as she did, knowing she was only here for this short time.

'Shouldn't we be getting back soon?' she asked, oddly deflated at her own thoughts. 'I'm sure you're anxious to see that your aunt is fully recovered from her scare.'

It wasn't at all like the confident and perky Miss Hartman to be so nervous, but somehow she couldn't help it. Nothing was as cut and dried in her life as it had been before coming here. It *should* be, but she knew very well that it wasn't. Steven Connors had already put a complication there that she hadn't anticipated.

And she was being absurd, she told herself angrily.

'I'm quite sure Aunt Freda is perfectly well by now,' Steven replied. 'She's made of hardy stock.'

'Hardier than my Aunt Helen, I think,' Lauri murmured. 'I really am quite worried about her.'

'So you should be.'

She stared at him. This wasn't the answer she wanted, or expected. 'Well, that's not much reassurance, I must say!'

'I had the feeling you'd far rather hear the truth than false platitudes that never did anyone any good. I'm no doctor, of course, but I know your aunt pretty well. She's definitely improved since your visit, and she'll probably deteriorate again once you've gone.'

'And that's just about the lowest form of blackmail to try to get me to stay that I've heard yet!'

He shrugged. 'And I assure you I didn't mean it in that way. If it seemed so, then I apologise unreservedly.'

He sounded so sincere that she couldn't doubt that he meant what he said. But if he knew her aunt that well, he must have seen the change in her.

'Has she really improved since I've been here?' she said uneasily. And, if so, then what on earth were these ghastly coughing fits like before?

'I shouldn't have said anything, but I know your uncle has had serious thoughts of taking her to London to see a Harley Street man. It won't have escaped his thinking that your wish to see the city could coincide very conveniently without putting too much pressure on your aunt's objections.'

'*Does* she object?' Lauri asked, thinking that he seemed to know far more of her family's affairs than she did herself. Which was not unlikely, since she had only known her aunt and uncle for a short while, and the Connors had lived in the area for generations.

'My guess is that she doesn't want to admit that there might be something seriously wrong, and once she thinks it necessary to see a top man about her condition—'

He left the rest to Lauri's imagination.

She felt mounting alarm. It was *his* aunt, not hers, who had come to the house that morning in a state of agitation, but now the tables seemed to have turned, and she was filled with anxiety about Aunt Helen. And ironically, she found herself resenting Steven for being the one to put these worries into her mind.

'I'm sure you're wrong,' she almost snapped.

'Then let's hope your feminine intuition is better than that of a mere male,' Steven retorted.

She glared at him, realising they were almost coming to verbal blows in a public place. She didn't want this kind of atmosphere between them, but she couldn't deny how freely they seemed able to discuss things, in the way friends who had known one another a long time did. Such friends could even argue heatedly, on occasion, without it invading the solidity of their relationship one iota.

She shivered, knowing that too many disturbing emotions were taking hold of her since coming here, far more than she had ever envisaged. It had been intended to be the trip of a lifetime, to meet her family, and then to return home to pick up her life again. She hadn't anticipated just how delightful and welcoming she would find her relatives, nor how anxious she would become about her aunt's undoubtedly worrying health. She hadn't anticipated meeting the Connors boys, and she certainly hadn't anticipated falling in love. Which she certainly wasn't, and didn't intend to be.

'You've got that aggressive look on your face again,' Steven said lazily. 'Methinks the lady doesn't like being put in her place by a mere male. Does this independence come from your exclusive private schooling, or is it more fundamental?'

'Probably both. And I'm not in the least aggressive, I assure you. Maybe just a little on the determined side.'

Each of them caught the gleam in the other one's eyes at that moment. Relaxing, they laughed simultaneously as Steven reached out and caught her hand in his.

'You can say that again, ma'am,' he said, in a pseudo-American voice. 'But I like a girl with spirit, and you've got plenty of that.'

Lauri felt absurdly pleased at the small compliment. She'd heard plenty that were far more flowery and insincere.

By the time they left Plymouth and headed for home, she knew how much she had enjoyed seeing her father's old haunts. It was almost like having him near again, and sharing his memories.

She dismissed the small shadow that came over her mind whenever she thought of how much she still missed him, knowing the last thing he would want would be for her to waste her time here in maudlin self-pity and mourning.

But inevitably, the nearer they got to her uncle's house, the more she thought about the two ladies there, wondering how they would find them when they returned. It was quite feasible that Freda Connors had become quite ill after being betrayed so badly by Alice Day, and that she would have dragged Aunt Helen into the doldrums with her.

Lauri knew she was letting her imagination get the better of her, but she honestly half-expected to see the doctor in attendance when they drove up to the front entrance. Instead, when they alighted from Steven's car, it was to see the two dowagers sitting in the garden, chattering like magpies.

'You see?' Steven murmured, just as if he could read her mind. 'Tough as couch grass, both of them.'

It certainly seemed that way as far as Freda was concerned. She was a very resilient old lady, thought Lauri, already declaring that Steven could advertise for another companion for her forthwith, and *this* time it had to be someone of mature years, with a plain dumpling face, and no thoughts of chasing after rainbows or young men.

'It's a blessing that Robert had enough sense not to notice her making cow-eyes at him,' Freda said keenly, and Lauri avoided Steven's eyes, knowing what she did about the brief attraction that had supposedly been between them.

It would have been too awful if their attachment had been more intense, and if Robert's wanderlust had sent him chasing after Alice...

And why on earth any of their doings should be of the slightest interest to her, she couldn't think. Except that neighbours were always interesting, and she had never known neighbours quite like the

Connors boys before…alike enough in looks, though far from identical, and so very different in temperament and personality.

It was enough to intrigue anyone, let alone anyone with the kind of enquiring nature that Lauri Hartman possessed.

Later that evening, Lauri found herself watching her aunt covertly, until Helen became aware of it, and once dinner was coming to an end, she spoke in an exasperated tone.

By then, much of the talk had been about the recent doings at the Connors's house, and Lauri had thought she was being fairly subtle in trying to gauge Helen's feelings on the subject. She discovered that she wasn't.

'If you think I'm taking any notice of the Connors ghost tale, miss, you're quite wrong,' Helen said crisply. 'And I've no intention of letting it upset me in any way.'

Lauri felt the sudden heat in her face, and knew she must be crimson with embarrassment.

'I'm sorry. It's just—'

She stopped. How could she say that she had had an unpleasant glimpse of her aunt's mortality, and couldn't bear the thought of losing her so soon after finding her! No one could be that insensitive, not even the outspoken modern girl that she prided herself to be…

To her surprise, her uncle finished the sentence for her, belching ever so gently at the end of his meal.

'It's just that you've been wondering precisely who the ghostly apparition came to warn, me dear, is that it?' he said with a chuckle. 'My guess is that it was no more than a clever and calculated diversion with no substance at all—if you'll pardon the pun! The news would have thrown the whole household into such turmoil at the thought of the ghost walking among them, that the robbery wasn't discovered immediately, and by then the wicked Alice had safely made her getaway.'

Helen laughed, seeing the astonishment on Lauri's face at this summing-up.

'You'll see that your uncle has a fine way of dismissing anything so frivolous as ghostly warnings, Lauri, and so must you. It's a pretty tale, no more, and his explanations quickly reassured Freda.'

'And as everything that the woman stole was well insured there's no real harm done,' Vernon added.

Lauri couldn't let that go without comment. 'I'm sure that's a purely male point of view, Uncle. Miss Connors may not have been concerned over the loss of the money, but I'm sure some of the jewellery would have been precious. And if some of it had had great sentimental value, then that's something that can never be replaced, surely.'

'Such things become less important as you grow older, Lauri,' Helen said now. 'And good health is more important than all the crown jewels.'

'So we've come to a decision,' her uncle put in, and Lauri found herself looking from one to the other of them as if she was watching the players in a lawn tennis match.

She had noticed how often close couples behaved in that way, verbally bouncing off one another and completing one another's thoughts and sentences.

'What decision is that?' Lauri said with a smile.

'We're all going to London for a few days at the

end of next week. I'm insisting that your aunt sees
a Harley Street man just to reassure us all that her
cough is not a symptom of something more serious.'

It was all happening just as Steven had said, Lauri
thought faintly, wondering if he was clairvoyant…

'Please take that troubled look off your face,
Lauri,' Helen said. 'The visit to Harley Street is no
more than an excuse. Your uncle is really dying to
show you the sights, and if you insist on returning
home in April, we decided we had best make our
plans now.'

'Oh, Aunt, you know I have to go back—'

'We don't know any such thing,' Vernon Hartman
said stoutly. 'You're a perfectly free agent, and we'd
love to have you staying here with us for as long as
you like. You bring a breath of fresh air into this
stuffy old house. And if you wanted to make it a
permanent arrangement, nothing would please us
more.'

Lauri laughed, but she felt her throat sting, because
they were such lovely people, and she was so glad
to know them and be a part of them.

'There's nothing in the least stuffy about this
house, or the people in it, Uncle! But I thank you for
the offer and the compliment.'

'Then think about it,' he persisted.

'Perhaps,' Lauri said, wishing he had never
brought up another subject that echoed Steven
Connors's words.

For a moment, she let down her determined guard
and allowed herself to dream. Did she really want to
go back to Boston? And if she didn't go, would she
really fit in here as the niece of this so-very-English

couple? A visit was one thing, but permanency was something else.

They liked her and welcomed her for her freshness and her air of independence, and her outlook on life…but the freedom that she so enjoyed—being able to make her own decisions, and without the out-moded trappings of chaperones—wasn't necessarily the English way, and perhaps in time they would tire of her. She was new, a novelty, and everyone knew that novelties eventually became commonplace.

'Do tell me about London,' she said quickly, real-ising that her usual confidence was taking an oddly downward turn.

And that wouldn't *do*, as her father used to tell her.

'Let's go into the drawing-room and discuss it,' Helen said. 'We've got plans for you, Lauri, and we've spent much of the day talking about it. Freda was quite envious, and if she wasn't too old to travel, I'm sure she would have wanted to come with us.'

'Thank God she didn't,' Vernon commented darkly. 'I can cope with two ladies, but not three.'

They drank their coffee in the drawing-room, and Lauri learned about the hotel on the banks of the River Thames where they were to stay, and her uncle showed her his book of some of the city's best-known landmarks, the Houses of Parliament and Big Ben, and the beautiful parks and Buckingham Palace, and St Paul's and the Tower…and although Lauri had heard of all these things from her father, she felt a surge of pleasure at knowing she was going to see them all for herself. It was more than she had ex-pected, and her eyes shone with a wild excitement.

Voyaging across the Atlantic had been no less thrilling than this.

Before she went to bed that night, having begged to borrow the book to study it more closely in her room, she gave her aunt and uncle a quick and uninhibited hug.

'You're darlings, both of you, and I can't thank you enough for being so nice to me. I just wish Daddy were here to know it.'

'I'm sure he does know it,' Helen said softly.

Lauri left them quickly before she betrayed how emotional those words made her feel. However practical Helen seemed, Lauri sensed that she still believed in the supernatural order of things, and Lauri couldn't *quite* forget the impact of Alice Day's avowed sighting of the Connors ghost and its reputed implications…

But she tried to ignore it as she undressed and slid into her comfortable bed, and spent more than an hour browsing through her uncle's book on the pleasures and treasures of England's capital city. The book was highly illustrated, and full of the history Lauri had so avidly wanted to learn as a child, when she had first heard about her father's homeland. The thought that she was to see more of it after all, was one of sheer delight.

But she didn't lose sight of the fact that no matter how he worded it, she was sure her uncle's main reason for the trip to London was to get Aunt Helen to Harley Street, to see a top man about her persistent cough.

Next morning, she wandered out to the outhouses where he was tinkering with his beloved engines, and

asked him outright. Vernon stood up from the gleaming yellow Wolseley that was his pride and joy, and
wiped his hands on a rag that looked as pristine as
the cherished engine of the motor.

'You're very perceptive, Lauri,' he said with a rueful smile. 'I'd hoped you might just see our proposed
visit as something to amuse you, and nothing more.'

'I could hardly think that, with the doctor's frequent calls here, and my own knowledge of illness.
It's perfectly obvious that Aunt Helen is not a well
woman, Uncle. But you don't think it's anything *really* serious, do you?'

It was suddenly terribly important to her to have
his reassurance, to hear his bluff laughter as he pooh-
poohed the very idea, and her heart jolted as she saw
the seriousness in his jovial face. It made him look
suddenly old, and vulnerable…as they all were…

'I won't pretend with you, Lauri. You're not a
child.'

*But, oh, how she wished that she was at that mo-
ment…so that she could be fobbed off with pretence,
and never have to deal with things that she was adult
enough to know…*

'Doctor Vine has begun to suspect that there's a
spot on her lung, so it's imperative that we get a
second opinion from a specialist.'

'You mean tuberculosis, don't you?' Lauri said
flatly.

She felt a sudden fear, and not only for her aunt.
Wasn't it contagious, or infectious…? And then the
instinctive fear for self-preservation was replaced by
a swift shame as her uncle went on speaking in that
controlled voice that told her he was afraid too.

'Perhaps. But it's not the only possible diagnosis,

and until we know for sure, I don't want to worry your aunt by showing her long faces. Your visit here is the best thing that's happened to her in months, Lauri, and you do more for her by being here with your bright personality than all the doctor's medicines.'

They both knew that it took more than a bright companion to cure a serious illness. But she nodded slowly.

'If that's what you want, then of course I'll be as cheerful as ever,' she said. At least for the next month, until it was time for her to leave for home…

Robert Connors came riding up to the house later that day while she and her aunt were sitting in the garden. He was very elegant on a horse, Lauri conceded again, dashing and forceful, and she had the feeling that he preferred it to the more mundane position behind the wheel of a motor-car. There was something primitive and fundamental in the relationship between a man and a horse…

'How are you today, ladies?' he greeted them both.

'We're both well, thank you, Robert,' Helen said at once. 'But what of Freda? There are no ill effects after her unpleasant experience, I hope? And is there any further news?'

'Freda's fine,' he said easily, 'and already in her element in relating the tale to her circle of old biddies—begging your pardon, Mrs Hartman, I don't mean to include your good self in that description, naturally.'

'Naturally,' Helen said drily, and Lauri could see that she understood this young man very well indeed. 'So what is the purpose of this unexpected visit,

Robert? You don't normally waste time on *old biddies*, so one must assume that it's the young one amongst us who is the main attraction.'

'I'm quite sure Robert has plenty of lady friends of his own, without bothering about me,' Lauri said.

'Ah, but that's where you're wrong, Lauri,' he replied in mock sorrow. 'I spend so much time abroad that each time I come back, any young lady who had previously caught my eye has already turned to someone else. You should take pity on me!'

'I doubt that anyone needs to pity you!' Lauri said smartly. 'I'd say you could have your pick of young ladies—'

She bit her lip, not having intended the words as a compliment, but obviously Robert would see them that way. The minute he spoke, it confirmed her opinion that he really was a very arrogant and self-opinionated young man.

'What a very forward and agreeable thing to say, my dear Miss Hartman. But one must expect such remarks from our colonial cousins, or so I'm told.'

'Is that a criticism?' she asked.

Robert pretended to be horrified at the suggestion.

'Never let it be said that I would ever criticise a lady. Especially when I've come all this way to ask you to accompany me to the country fête in Kingscombe on Saturday afternoon. I promise you'll enjoy it.'

Helen spoke at once. 'Oh, do go, Lauri. It will be a real chance for you to see an English country fête, and the way the village folk dress up in old costumes and enact some of the old customs for the visitors.'

'What sort of old customs?'

Robert went on boldly. 'Oh, as well as sack races

and three-legged races, and dunking for apples, they'll have some poor willing volunteer in the stocks and invite people to throw wet cloths at him for a penny a time. The older ladies will be selling their home-made jams and cakes and garden produce, and some of the prettier village girls will be selling kisses.'

'And I wonder which you'll be buying!' Lauri said.

'*Touché*, Miss Hartman! So will you come?'

'All right, and thank you,' she said. 'Will Steven be there too?'

She said it without thinking, but surely if the so-sophisticated Robert deigned to spend an afternoon at a village fête, then Steven would revel in it too. To her surprise, Robert shook his head.

'I'm sorry to disappoint you, but no. He's taking Aunt Freda to our lawyer's office in Exeter, to sort out the insurance claim from the recent theft.'

It sobered them all at once, and then Robert informed them that Alice Day had seemingly disappeared, with the constables now declaring that it was doubtful that Miss Connors would ever see her property again.

And for someone who was supposedly attracted to the missing Alice, Robert Connors didn't seem in the least concerned about her disappearance. Feckless, Lauri decided. That was the word for him.

Chapter Six

So there were two things to look forward to now. Saturday afternoon promised to be a delightful affair, and just the kind of thing Lauri's father had often spoken about nostalgically. And at the end of next week, there was the trip to London that she had so dearly wanted to take…she had instinctively wanted to tell Steven the news, and she felt an acute disappointment that he wouldn't be at the country fête.

Lauri told herself it was no more than a natural interest, because he had predicted it all, and because she felt she already knew and liked him better than his brother. It was nothing more than that, and she wasn't going to let it be. The fact that she had thought of him so quickly when Robert had invited her was simply coincidental.

'I'd like to send a letter to Sir Gerald Hawkes and his wife, Uncle Vernon,' she said to him later. 'They invited me to call on them if I was ever in London, and it would be only polite to do so, wouldn't it?'

'Of course. But why not telephone them when we arrive at our hotel, and arrange to see them on the afternoon that your aunt and I have the appointment at Harley Street?'

'So the appointment is all arranged then, is it?' Lauri said, remembering at once the main reason for going to London. It wasn't just for her benefit.

'For the Monday afternoon, so we shall have the whole of the weekend beforehand to settle in and see some of the sights,' Helen said.

'Are you nervous, Aunt Helen?'

She didn't mean to blurt out the question, but having seen illness at close quarters on two other occasions, she couldn't help it. Her aunt smiled faintly.

'I've always had a simple philosophy, Lauri. What is destined to be, will be, and providing you do all you can to help yourself, there's no use worrying needlessly about anything. So I refuse to be unduly nervous.'

'Then you're far braver than I would be,' Lauri said.

'No, my love. Just older.'

On Saturday, Robert Connors roared up to the house at the wheel of a fast sports car, belying the fact that he was merely a first-class horseman with no other skills.

'You be sure and take care of our girl, Robert, and no excessive speeding,' Vernon warned him, once he had admired the aggressive lines of the motor, and the satisfying snarl of the engine.

Robert laughed, throwing back his head in the unconcerned way he had, and Lauri could see at once how he would have charmed those Spanish señoritas, with his handsome tanned skin coupled with that educated English voice.

'I've never lost a girl yet, sir, unless it was my intention, of course,' he said with an arrogant smile.

Except for Alice Day, Lauri couldn't help thinking. She had clearly been a match for him, and for any man. But if she had meant anything at all to Robert, he certainly didn't appear to be bereft at her disappearance.

Lauri concluded that he was either extremely shallow, or adept at hiding his feelings. Either way, she wasn't going to let it worry her. She was just going to enjoy this glorious spring day, and the delights of the village fête.

She saw Robert glance at her as they sped away from Hartman House, his eyes challenging.

'Are you afraid of speed, Lauri? You don't strike me as a girl who's afraid of anything.'

'I wouldn't say that. It's a foolish person who goes headlong into things,' she prevaricated, trusting he would know exactly what she meant.

For a second, he put his hand on her knee. She was well covered from neck to ankle in an elegant lime-green linen suit, but even so, she disliked the familiarity, and removed his hand without a word. She wasn't a prude, but nor did she want him to think she was easy.

It was strange how people from different cultures so often thought as much about each other. They might speak the same language—almost—but there were still differences that would excite a man like Robert Connors. She could almost hear herself analysing him in her mind as she stared directly ahead at the changing scenery.

'So, what do you think of my brother?' she heard Robert say coolly. 'I presume he's to your taste?'

'I like everyone I've met in this country so far,' she said, just as coolly. 'People are people wherever you go, aren't they? And as my father never lost his British accent, I was perfectly familiar with it.'

'That's not what I asked. What do you think of Steven?'

Lauri didn't answer immediately. She didn't care to be put on the spot like this, and she didn't particularly like Robert's directness. Steven could be probing too, but in a very different way. Steven was caring, while Robert...she had the certain feeling that Robert could be callous and ruthless if necessary.

'I like him very much,' she said deliberately. 'He's keenly interested in people, and he's a shrewd businessman who obviously loves his work.'

Robert burst out laughing. 'God, how utterly boring that sounds! Lord preserve me from ever having such a reputation with the ladies!'

Lauri was angry. 'That wasn't what I meant. I don't find Steven in the least boring, and I'm sure he wouldn't *want* the kind of reputation with the ladies that you imply!'

'Well, he's certainly found a champion in you, hasn't he?' Robert said drily.

'Look, can we please talk about something else? I don't want to spend the day soul-searching.' She took a deep breath, trying to think of a different topic and coming back to one that was still on her mind. 'I hope your Aunt Freda is fully recovered after her unpleasant experience.'

'Oh, completely. She never dwells on things that can't be changed, and it makes a good talking point among her cronies. For the present, she's the star attraction.'

He was careless in his dismissal of something that must have shaken the old lady considerably. Lauri remained silent as they neared the village of Kingscombe, but the thought that was uppermost in her head now was that, for all his physical charisma, she wouldn't have to try very hard to really dislike Robert Connors.

Kingscombe was *en fête* in the truest sense of the words. There were streamers and bunting criss-crossing the village street and a great banner proclaiming the annual celebrations. The place was too small to have more than a miniscule village green, but even so, there was a group of Morris dancers performing as Robert stopped the car.

'Do you want to watch this?' he asked boredly.

'Yes, please! It's wonderful!' Lauri exclaimed, uncaring whether or not Robert thought it rather a tame occupation for grown men to dress up and prance about, with bells jingling on their stockinged legs, and waving coloured handkerchiefs about in time to the music. Their movements were as intricate as any dancers', and a considerable crowd was watching them.

'Pardon me, ma'am, but is there any meaning to the dances?' Lauri asked a woman nearby, since Robert seemed disinclined to tell her anything, and simply lounged against his car until she had had her fill.

'Oh, all the different dances tell a story, me dear, and some of 'em have to do with fertility rites, I'm told, though I don't know the whys and wherefores of it meself,' the woman answered, then looked at

Lauri curiously. 'You'll not be from around these parts, I take it?'

'No. I'm from Boston.'

The woman looked blank. 'Is that in the north somewhere?'

Lauri smiled. 'No. It's in America.'

The woman lost interest as the applause rang out for the dancers, and Robert's voice was in Lauri's ear.

'You might as well have said you came from another planet for all she'll know of America. Have you had enough? The main events are held a short distance away from the village.'

'I'm ready,' Lauri said.

By now she had begun to wonder why he had suggested bringing her here at all. Unless it was simply to score over his brother…or perhaps Aunt Freda had insisted that he did his neighbourly duty. The thought annoyed Lauri, because she certainly didn't want to be beholden to anyone in that way.

'If you've got anything else you'd rather do, I'd be perfectly happy wandering around the fête by myself, Robert,' she told him, once they were seated in the car again. 'You can always come and collect me later.'

'Now, why on earth would you think I'd rather be anywhere else than with the prettiest girl in the county?'

She wished he wouldn't make these compliments that slid so easily off his tongue, and meant nothing at all. When she didn't answer, he gave a heavy sigh.

'I suppose if Steven had said that, you'd have taken him seriously, wouldn't you?'

She looked at him, startled. Just for a moment, he

had sounded almost jealous…almost *human*, rather than sending out the suave, sophisticated image he obviously preferred. But even as she thought it, he gave an amused laugh.

'It's all right, most people see him the way you do. He's the conscientious one in the family,' he taunted her, 'while I'm seen as the big bad wolf.'

'Robert, if you want me to enjoy this day, let's just leave it, can't we?' she said crossly.

She was thankful when they reached the field where she could see the marquees, and the tinny sounds of hurdy-gurdy music filled the air. Lauri felt her heartbeats quicken. Her father had told her of these village fêtes, and she had loved to hear of their homely atmosphere.

It might all be commonplace to a man like Robert, but to her it was new and interesting, and she wanted to absorb everything, so that when she went back home, she would be sharing the same nostalgic memories as her father's.

She watched the comical three-legged races and the sack races, and declined to dunk for apples, but she threw the wet cloths at the victim in the stocks who took it all in good part to the cheers and jeers of the onlookers. She couldn't resist buying jams and fruit pies from the various stalls, and hesitated outside the fortune-teller's tent.

'It's just one of the farmer's wives dressed up,' Robert told her. 'She's not a genuine clairvoyant, if such things exist at all, which I doubt, and she'll just tell you what she thinks you want to hear.'

'Well, that's what everybody wants, isn't it?' Lauri said, and swept past him to enter the gloomy tent.

It took a few moments to adjust her eyes. And of

course she knew it was a local woman dressed up in gypsy garb—she wasn't born yesterday. And seeing the woman hastily dropping her knitting out of sight would have confirmed it anyway.

'So what can I do for you today, my pretty one?' the woman said in a husky voice. 'Are you seeking to know the future?'

'Well, I suppose I am,' Lauri said with a smile. 'Do I cross your palm with silver?'

'That you do, my dear. A silver threepenny bit, for the church funds,' she added. She took it from Lauri's hand and gazed into the crystal ball in front of her.

'Oh, I see you've travelled a long, long way,' she droned. 'Across the sea, I'd say. I see water, lots of water.'

Well, that wasn't hard to work out, thought Lauri. Probably everyone in the neighbourhood knew who she was by now, and that she'd come from America.

'The crystal's growing murky, but I do see a man. No, wait. There are two men, and you'll have to choose.'

Lauri began to smile. It was the usual stuff…and although the woman spoke in a stage performer's pseudo-mysterious voice, it didn't quite come across with her homely image. And Lauri couldn't quite forget that knitting…

'And will I choose to go home, or will I stay?' she heard herself ask. She had never meant to say the words, they had just seemed to come out of her subconscious.

'Ah, now, that could be another choice you'll be needing to make, dearie,' the woman prevaricated.

'Let's just say you'll be mighty thankful you made the right decision when the time comes.'

For some reason, Lauri felt suddenly angry. Her head swam with the cloying atmosphere inside the small tent, and the herbal scents the woman had obviously brought in to add to it. There was a tightness in her chest, almost as if she was drowning, and she felt a great desire to get out.

'Well thank you, ma'am, that's all very interesting,' she almost croaked, and quickly pulled aside the curtain across the tent's opening, breathing in great gulps of the afternoon air. She had felt decidedly odd, almost fey, for a few moments, and it wasn't the way the practically minded Lauri Hartman cared to feel.

As she noticed Robert laughing with a local girl, Lauri's heartbeats slowly calmed down again, without her ever being aware that she had panicked. It was absurd. It was all nonsense, for the amusement of the locals…but just for one awful moment, Lauri had felt a deep sense of foreboding, as if she had somehow glimpsed something terrible.

But out here in the open, everything was the same as before. The fête was still continuing, and people were having a good time and enjoying the spring sunshine, and she was being extremely foolish and gullible…

Robert caught sight of her at that moment. He said goodbye to his companion, and walked quickly towards Lauri, a quizzical look in his eyes.

'Are you all right? You look pale. Did our fortune-teller have some momentous news to tell you?'

'Not really. Nothing that I didn't already know.'

What *had* the woman said? When she stopped to

think about it, it had been nothing but harmless trivia. It was Lauri's own intuition and imagination that had done the rest.

'What? She didn't tell you that you were going to marry a rich and handsome gentleman and live happily ever after? That's what you ladies like to hear, isn't it?'

'Not all of us,' Lauri said smartly. 'We're not all out looking for husbands, believe it or not.'

'And what a terrible waste, for a girl like you to prefer remaining a spinster than sharing your life with a husband.'

'I didn't *say* that—'

But his interest was already taken by the stall where several girls were selling kisses for a penny a time, well chaperoned by their fathers. Lauri was happy to excuse him as he went to do his duty on behalf of the church funds, as he glibly called it, and she wandered around the fête by herself, glad of a breathing space, and wishing that Steven was here to enjoy the day with her.

His image came into her mind so suddenly that she almost stumbled. No matter how charming Robert could be when he chose, she felt far more at ease with Steven. He might be the less outwardly aggressive of the brothers, but he had a quick brain, and she had already sensed that if he chose to do so, he would always better his brother. And just why she should think that, she had no idea.

'Would you care to come back to the house for afternoon tea?' Robert said, when they finally decided they had had enough. 'Aunt Freda will expect me to ask you.'

And that was another reason why he would never

come up to Steven's standards. He had no finesse, Lauri thought, as she accepted the casual invitation.

The minute they entered Connors Court, Lauri revised all thoughts of Steven being calmer than his brother. His face was dark with anger, and he leapt up from his chair as soon as they entered the drawing-room, his hands clenched.

'What's happened?' Robert said at once. 'You look as though you've dropped sixpence and found a penny.'

The trite words did nothing to alleviate Steven's mood.

'You may well think so when you hear what's to happen. My visit to Slater's Chambers with Aunt Freda was very convenient, apparently, as he was shortly coming to see us. But since I was already there, and once Aunt's business was settled as far as it could be—'

'Good God, get on with it, man!' Robert said irritably. 'I can't make head nor tail of what you're saying.'

'I think perhaps I should leave you two to discuss your family business...' Lauri began.

Neither of them took the slightest notice of her and, since she remembered she was obliged to wait for one of them to take her back, she sat down abruptly on one of the silk-covered sofas while the two of them continued to glare at one another. The phrase 'like two peas in the pod' didn't escape her thoughts at that moment. And right now they were definitely two very *snappy* peas, if there were such things...

'It's to do with Father's Will,' Steven stated.

Robert's eyes narrowed. 'How can it be? Everything was legally settled at the time of his death. What further news could there be about it at this late stage? If Slater knew something that we didn't, it should have been told to us long before now.'

'There's apparently a codicil on Father's Will that was not to be disclosed until our birthdays in May, and Slater says that it's watertight.'

'Well, go on. What is this so-called codicil?' Robert said angrily, and Lauri could see he was clearly anticipating unpleasant news.

'The old devil wouldn't tell me. But he felt it was his moral duty to forewarn us that not everything is as cut and dried as we think it is now.'

'*What?* And you left it there?'

'I could hardly wring it out of him if he was legally bound not to tell me any more—'

'Then I'll go to Exeter myself and force the bastard to explain,' Robert bellowed.

At Lauri's involuntary gasp, both brothers glanced her way for a moment, and Steven spoke quickly.

'You must forgive my brother's lapse of manners, Lauri, but in the circumstances—'

'In the circumstances, I consider it a word well used to describe the buffoon, and I can apologise perfectly well for myself,' Robert snapped.

Lauri stood up, smoothing down her skirt and feeling her face burn. All she wanted was to be away from these two now.

'Excuse me, but shall I go and ask for some tea to be brought in for us all? Or am I taking too many liberties?'

They both looked at her now, and she felt as intrusive as if she were a irritating insect that needed swatting at the first opportunity. It was a far from comfortable feeling.

'Please do, Lauri,' Steven said now, still seemingly unable to control his tension. 'It might be best if we continue this discussion in private.'

Well, wasn't that what she had suggested when they first came into the drawing-room…? She might as well have been talking to wallpaper for all the notice they had taken of her.

She shrugged, leaving them to their squabbles and finding her way to the kitchen, asking a maid to serve tea for three in the drawing-room in about ten minutes. Whether or not it was her place to do so, Lauri guessed that if she didn't take the initiative, there would be no refreshment in the foreseeable future, and by now, she was parched.

She wandered out into the gardens, basking in the spring sunshine, and wondered what it was that could put two brothers out so swiftly and with so little reason. Why should it be bad news in their father's codicil, anyway, and not good?

Maybe Father Connors had invested a hefty sum of money for them to acquire on their special birthday—though why the lawyer should think it necessary to forewarn them of that eventuality was another matter.

Lauri's head suddenly ached. It was none of her business, and she would be long gone before this birthday that had apparently assumed extra significance. But she couldn't help remembering that Steven had been less than charitable about his father's love for his sons. Robert had been his firstborn, if only by minutes, and had clearly turned out less than he had expected, resulting in the way the ship-building business was run now. And Lauri's uncle had also told her of Father Connors's unpredictability, so who knew what might be ahead of them…?

She stayed outside until she was sure the afternoon tea would have been delivered to the drawing-room, and went back reluctantly to the house. What had begun as a lovely outing had turned into an awkward embarrassment.

As she had surmised, the maid was now pouring out the tea and the brothers were looking less tense than before.

'I'm sorry you had to witness all that, Lauri,' Steven said shortly. 'I had barely got home with Aunt Freda when you and Robert arrived, and it was still foremost in my mind.'

'Please don't concern yourself on my account,' she murmured. 'And rest assured that anything I heard will go no further.'

'Thank you,' Robert said, his demeanor predictably slower to calm down than Steven.

But in any case, Steven had had longer to digest the lawyer's words, and worry over them.

'If you don't mind, I'd like to go home when I've had my tea,' she said to no one in particular.

'Of course,' Robert said. 'You'll have had enough excitement for one day.'

She looked at him in annoyance, unsure if he was being sarcastic, or if his words were just sharp for being on the tail-end of his brush with Steven. And if he thought that attending a village fête and listening to a stupid argument between brothers was the total sum of excitement she could deal with, he didn't know her at all, Lauri thought keenly.

She was glad to leave Connors Court, even though she would far rather it had been Steven who drove her home. Robert was still short-tempered at what he clearly saw as his father's words reaching out to them from beyond the grave.

Lauri shivered, wishing the thought hadn't entered her head quite so graphically. And it was just as likely to be some generous and belated bequest as any other kind…

'You mustn't take too much notice of any family wrangling you hear between Steven and me,' he said abruptly, when they were nearing Hartman House after a considerable silence. 'I'm told that you had no brothers or sisters, but it's often the way siblings behave, especially when they're close in age. And none could be closer than twins, of course.'

And none more inclined to a certain rivalry, Lauri supposed. But her silent disapproval had obviously irritated him, and she strove not to show it.

'I'm not unfamiliar with family disputes or any other kind,' she said coolly. 'There were many heated debates in my hearing among my father's friends and colleagues, both political and social, and I was allowed to participate whenever I felt I had something to offer.'

'Ah, yes,' Robert drawled. 'I had forgotten how progressive you Americans were compared with the rest of us. It's a trait we have not yet learned to appreciate.'

And if he was implying that English ladies didn't indulge in heated debates, Lauri decided to ignore it. They were nearly home, and, yes, she admitted, she had had enough excitement for one day. Or at least, enough to think about, and not least was a definite feeling of curiosity about Steven's unexpected outburst. It was Connors business, but she had been inadvertently involved.

She felt a small thrill run through her, remembering Steven's flashing eyes and the sinewy veins in his throat. His work was physical, and he had the powerful physique that reflected it, since she knew instinctively that he wouldn't be a man to sit on the sidelines while others did the work. And although some might call him less adventurous than his world-wandering brother, there was nothing less manly about him. Far from it.

'You know, you really should stay on to join in the birthday celebrations,' Robert continued, changing tactics as if realising he had gone too far in his criticism. 'It's a pity you've already booked your passage home. Have you ever been to a masquerade ball?'

'Actually, no,' Lauri said. 'And I admit that it does sound intriguing.'

'It is. And it's going to be a lavish affair. Your aunt and uncle have already been invited, of course, and if you decide to stay, I promise you'll be at the top of the guest list. Whatever costume you chose to wear, you'd outshine all the local girls.'

'Well, thank you, kind sir, though I'm not sure that's a very gallant thing to say, considering the pretty girls I've seen you with today!' Lauri said, starting to laugh now, and thankful that his black mood seemed to be over.

'But I mean it!' Robert said. 'I really want you to stay. We all do.'

She could hardly disbelieve that by now, and it was nothing short of emotional blackmail, even if it was of the very nicest kind, Lauri thought again, as she bade him goodbye at the house. As she heard the rasping roar of his engine as the car sped off again, she was still smiling to herself as she went indoors.

Helen was browsing through a magazine in the drawing-room, and she looked up as her niece joined her.

'Have you had a lovely day, Lauri? Your cheeks are so pink that I think you must have, unless Robert has been saying things to you that he shouldn't. He's a charming rogue, my love, but I'm sure you're wise enough not to take too much heed of his nonsense.'

'Oh, I'm not likely to take any of it seriously, Aunt,' she answered. 'So what are you studying so intently?'

Helen showed her the pages of medieval dresses.

'I've decided to go to the Connors masquerade ball as a lady of the medieval court. We have some old costumes in the attic, so I'm sure something can be adapted. What do you think?'

The birthday ball was more than a month away, so it was reasonable that plans for the ball itself, and for the guests' costumes and the like, must be under way. It just seemed to Lauri that the more she thought it had nothing to do with her, the more she was being drawn into it in some way or another.

She looked at the pages of pictures her aunt was showing her, taken from one of the London museums.

'They're beautiful,' she agreed, reading the text about the rich velvets and brocades, and seeing the illustrations of the elaborate headdresses.

'So they are,' Helen sighed, 'and you would do

them far more justice than I, but perhaps you'd like to see what we have in the old trunks and help me see if there's anything my dressmaker could make use of.'

If her eyes were innocent enough, the implication was quite transparent, Lauri thought, but when the maids brought down the trunk from the attic and the clothes were spread out on Helen's bed, she simply refused to imagine any possible adaptations for herself. That wasn't part of the plan.

But she couldn't deny the sensuality of the lovely fabrics in the old-fashioned gowns and accessories her aunt had obviously treasured. The lovely bronze velvets and kingfisher brocades just cried out to be used...

'I wonder what you would choose to wear, supposing that you were going to the masked ball, Lauri,' Helen mused.

'Now, Aunt, you know that's not a likelihood—'

'But you can dream about it, can't you? I thought all young girls dreamed,' Helen persisted.

'Well, then,' Lauri was suddenly reckless. 'Since I'm an American, and perceived as being more modern than most, for some reason, I'd wear scarlet silk and feathers, and go as a Western saloon girl. That would be guaranteed to shock the whole county, wouldn't it?' she finished, laughing at the imagery it evoked.

'On the contrary, I should think it would have all the young mens' blood racing with delight,' Helen said drily. 'We'll keep it in mind.'

Lauri laughed again. 'Please don't bother, Aunt, because it's not going to happen.'

* * *

Over dinner that evening, she couldn't resist mentioning the sudden outburst between the Connors brothers and the reason for it. Vernon Hartman nodded sagely.

'Old Connors was a hard taskmaster and father. He wouldn't allow his sons to think everything came easily to them. Robert constantly infuriated him with his wild ways, but he always wanted the boy to be involved in his shipyard. It was something he yearned for until the day he died.'

'But he wouldn't have left something really hurtful in his Will to emerge at this late stage, surely?' Lauri said. Seeing things from the safety of her own secure and loving childhood, she simply couldn't imagine anything so vindictive.

'I didn't say he wasn't a fair man,' her uncle pointed out. 'But he'd built up the shipyard to the prosperous business it is today, and he had no intention of letting Robert dispose of it to go on some wild goose-chase or other.'

'How could he, if it was left to both of them—which I assume it was—and Steven's obviously made such a success of it?' Lauri said, remembering the hum of activity when she had visited it, and the prestigious order for Sir Gerald Hawkes's boat. She knew she was prying into other peoples' business, but she was unable to quell her curiosity now.

Her uncle went on patiently. 'Because Robert's the older brother by ten minutes, and on his thirtieth birthday the business becomes legally his. When old Connors became too ill to manage the shipyard any longer, it was left in the hands of a consortium to be managed by Steven, since Robert had little interest in it and had been spending so much time in Spain.'

Lauri could hear the slight contempt in her uncle's voice for Robert, but she didn't see how anyone could force an enthusiasm in a business that held no interest for them. She didn't comment, and he went on speaking.

'Connors could see the way things were going, and he made sure his shipyard was in safe hands by decreeing that it was to continue that way after his death. There was a great deal of bitterness on all sides after his wishes became known, as you can imagine.'

'And this situation was destined to remain until this year,' Lauri finished for him, and starting to see so much now that hadn't been clear to her before.

'Exactly. Robert has always resented the indignity of it all, and knowing him as well as I do, he'll be hellbent on claiming his birthright, no matter what he intends to do with it. And Steven will be just as determined to stop him—though there's really nothing he can do about it. If Robert wants to sell up, that will be the end of it.'

Helen spoke from the far end of the dining-table. 'Don't you wish you could be here to see the fireworks, Lauri? And I don't just mean the birthday celebrations!'

She certainly wouldn't deny it would be interesting to observe, but she wasn't going to defer her own plans for the sake of finding out just what Father Connors's codicil meant for Robert and Steven.

Whatever it was, she considered him a mean old man, and she had every sympathy for the two of them. And anyway, even if Robert did want to sell, what was to stop Steven from putting in a bid for it? Surely that would solve everything.

Chapter Seven

The Hartmans were en route for London. Lauri's excitement mounted with every mile they covered in her uncle's motor, though Helen complained mildly from time to time that it might have been easier and quicker to take the train.

'Nonsense, my dear,' Vernon said stoutly. 'This is the only way to travel, in the comfort of our own vehicle.'

Lauri and her aunt exchanged glances. Luxurious though the yellow Wolseley might be by many standards, it was still a very long drive to London, and the jolting became wearisome, even though several welcome overnight hotel rests were necessary.

'You'll never dissuade your uncle from this mode of travel,' Helen sighed to her niece on the second night when they had been shown to their respective rooms. 'He can't resist showing off his precious motor to the world. I've no doubt Sir Gerald Hawkes will be treated to all the mechanical details. You must telephone him as soon as we reach the Park Hotel, Lauri, and make your arrangements.'

As if to underline the main reason for their trip, a sudden spasm of coughing racked her, and she sat down, pale and gasping, on the chaise-longue in her room, while Lauri pressed a glass of water to her shaking lips.

'I'm all right now,' she said faintly. 'Go and get some rest before the morning, dear. We're due to leave early.'

'Well, if you're sure,' Lauri said uneasily. 'I don't like to leave you like this.'

Heaven knew what Uncle Vernon was doing right now. Usually solicitous, he was probably showing off the Wolseley to an admiring audience in the courtyard of the old coaching inn where they were currently staying, thought Lauri. Helen hated him to be constantly fussing her, as she called it, and at the gleam in her aunt's eyes now, Lauri knew she was in danger of doing the same. She moved swiftly to the door.

'I'll see you in the morning, then. Sleep well.'

But it had reminded her again that the reason for this trip was not merely to indulge Lauri Hartman, but to see a Harley Street specialist who would give an expert opinion on what really ailed her sweet-faced aunt.

They reached London in record time, Vernon announced expansively, as if personally responsible for the Wolseley's performance. Which he probably was, considering the loving care he lavished on it, thought Lauri in amusement. The Park Hotel was luxurious, and Lauri revelled in the sights of the capital city that she had only ever heard about and never expected to see.

Her aunt's appointment was for the following day, and knowing better now than to hover about anxiously, she telephoned the Hawkes residence as soon as she had settled in to her hotel room. A maid answered, and moments later Lauri heard Lady Hawkes's voice.

'Miss Hartman, how pleasant to hear you. My husband will be so pleased that you remembered to contact us. Now, when can you come and see us?'

'I wondered if tomorrow would be convenient? I'm only here for a very short time with my aunt and uncle, you see. And they have some private business of their own tomorrow.'

Despite the effusive welcome, Lauri suddenly realised what an important person Sir Gerald Hawkes was. Why on earth would a Member of Parliament take the time to escort a visiting American college student about the town!

'Then you're in luck, my dear. We're in recess at the moment, and we can be at your disposal for the whole day. I suggest that you take a taxi, and come to the house around eleven o'clock in the morning. We'll take a boat ride on the river, have lunch at an old inn and show you the sights. How does that suit you?'

'It sounds marvellous! Thank you so much, Lady Hawkes.'

'Then I'll mark it in the diary at once, and we'll look forward to seeing you tomorrow.'

Her casual comment reminded Lauri again that Sir Gerald was an important man, and even days out during his recess had to be marked in the diary and kept to a schedule. But it didn't dim her excitement as she relayed her news to her relatives.

From Vernon's relieved look, she sensed that he was glad tomorrow was theirs alone, that even a loved niece's presence would be superfluous. It told Lauri, more than anything else, how anxious he was about the outcome of this visit.

But there was no point in anticipating the worst, and no reason to suppose that this specialist was anything short of a miracle worker. And if that was clutching at straws, then she was clutching them firmly now.

The Hawkeses' house was a splendidly appointed place, as befitted a wealthy man, and when the taxi had deposited her there, the couple greeted her warmly.

'It's good to see you again, my dear, and looking such a picture,' Sir Gerald said. 'And how is that clever young man of yours?'

'If you mean Steven Connors, he was very well when I last saw him, but he's not my young man, Sir Gerald,' she began with a laugh.

'Nonsense. Any young man who looked at you the way he did is more than halfway in love with you. And I can't say I blame him. A gel could do far worse—'

'Gerald, don't tease the poor girl,' his wife put in, turning to Lauri. 'I'm sorry the children aren't here today, my dear, but we'll ensure that you enjoy yourself.'

'You'll like a trip on the river, I daresay, with your special interest in boats, Miss Hartman?' he continued with a wicked smile.

'I'd love it. And my name's Lauri.' She couldn't

remember if she had asked them to address her so
before, but it seemed too stuffy not to do so.

'You're travelling home on the *Titanic*, aren't
you? That must be a great thrill for you, Lauri,' Lady
Hawkes commented when they had been served coffee in the thinnest bone-china cups Lauri had ever
seen.

'I am, and it is,' she said with a smile. 'Though I
shall be really sorry to say goodbye to my relatives
and the friends I've made here. I'm enjoying every
minute.'

She prayed that Sir Gerald wouldn't make more
coy remarks about certain friends probably being
rather more important than others, but she couldn't
deny that she had been thinking about Steven at that
moment.

But she pushed them out of her mind now. Today
was for seeing London in all its glory, and everywhere they went, they were chauffeur-driven in Sir
Gerald's motor. London was a wonderful sight in the
spring sunshine, with the parks glowing with flowers,
and the ancient buildings more majestic than anything Lauri had ever seen in her life before.

'I can see exactly why people fall in love with
London,' she said later, gazing at the vast expanse
of the Parliament buildings and the tall tower of Big
Ben from the vantage point of a river-boat. 'Even
though he was a countryman at heart, my father
loved to come here, and he always wanted me to see
it for myself.'

'It's such a pity you only have a few days here,'
Lady Hawkes said. 'You can't possibly see everything in so short a time, and you can only get the
flavour of it all.'

'I know,' she said sorrowfully. 'But something else my father said was that you should always leave something to see for next time, then you'd be sure to come back.'

Now why on earth had she said that, when it was so unlikely she would ever be able to visit these shores again? Once she was immersed in her old life and her work, such indulgences and such expenses would be beyond her reach.

'He was a very discerning man, and you obviously loved him very much,' Lady Hawkes observed.

'Very much, yes.'

By the time Sir Gerald insisted on his chauffeur taking her back to the Park Hotel late that afternoon, she was feeling exhilarated, but quite exhausted, and thankful that the chauffeur was disinclined to talk. In fact, he was far snootier than his delightful employers, Lauri thought, in the same way that servants of royalty were reputed to be.

But she quickly forgot him as she went up to her room and removed her hat and gloves and then the rest of her clothes, thankful to slip into a hot bath in her splendid adjoining bathroom, needing to feel relaxed and human again before seeking out her aunt and uncle.

A little later, she knocked on the door of their suite, and was admitted into their sitting-room. And the moment she saw her aunt's pale face and her uncle's grim one, she knew it wasn't going to be good news. Quickly, she went to sit beside her aunt on the sofa, and took hold of her cold hands.

'Has it been a bad day for you?' she asked quietly, not knowing how else to put it.

'Somewhat,' Helen said with a faint smile. 'But hardly unexpected, even though Mr Jellyman couldn't give us any conclusive answers to his various tests immediately.'

When they had first heard his name, they had all thought it so incongruous, if not downright hilarious, for a specialist who was in the business of frequently giving people bad news, but it was obvious that none of them felt like laughing now.

'We have to return to Harley Street the day after tomorrow for a detailed assessment,' Vernon said. 'And hopefully, Dr Vine will be able to continue with whatever treatment is necessary.'

And if he couldn't...

'But this is not going to stop our plans, Lauri,' Helen said, in a surprisingly firm voice. 'I'm sure you've had a lovely day today with your friends, and you must tell us all about it. Then, tomorrow, we shall visit some of the places you would still like to see. It's years since your uncle and I have been to London, and we don't intend to waste a moment.'

She was a marvel, Lauri thought with real admiration. And a darling too. She gave her a swift hug.

'I'm so glad I came to England, Aunt Helen,' she said in a rush. 'You've made me feel so welcome, and I do admire your spirit so much.'

'No more than I admire yours, my love, but since we don't want to start getting maudlin over each other, let's talk about your day, and what we're going to do tomorrow.'

Lauri glanced at her uncle and saw his small nod. It was the way they were, she realised. They were so stoical, and she was enormously fond of them. Quickly, she related all that she had seen that day,

and saw the colour begin to return to Helen's face
as she took a vicarious pleasure in her niece's activities.

'I'd really like to see St Paul's. My father once
told me about the Whispering Gallery, and it sounded
so spooky that I could never quite believe in it,'
Lauri told them. 'And Westminster Abbey, too—is
that possible?'

'Of course, though I dare say your aunt will de-
cline to climb the spiral stairs to the Whispering
Gallery in St Paul's,' Vernon replied.

'Oh, I didn't think—'

Helen brushed her embarrassed words aside. 'It
will suit me very well to sit in the body of the ca-
thedral and contemplate while you two make the
climb,' she assured Lauri. 'I did it once in my youth,
and it needs more stamina than I possess now to get
to the gallery. Besides which, I'm not overfond of
spiral staircases,' she added.

'Then that's settled,' Vernon said. 'And if there's
time when we've done all the sightseeing we can
cope with, we'll take a drive into the country hereabouts.'

In other words, thought Lauri, when Helen began
showing signs of fatigue, enough would be enough.

It all went according to plan, and even though
Helen was pale, she was clearly determined to enjoy
her visit to London, and the ride into the country in
the later part of the following afternoon was just what
was needed to restore her strength after the morning
walks.

But dinner that evening was more subdued, and
Lauri knew they were all thinking about the next

day's visit to Harley Street, and the specialist's assessment. Not wanting to intrude on their privacy, or to let them think she felt she should accompany them, she remarked that she might visit Madame Tussaud's Waxworks exhibition.

'An excellent suggestion, my dear,' Vernon said, poker-faced. 'Just be sure to keep moving.'

She looked at him blankly for a moment and then saw the familiar twinkling in his eyes.

'You mean in case I'm mistaken for a waxwork model, I presume!'

'Don't tease her so, Vernon,' Helen chastised him. 'No one could mistake you for anything but the lovely young lady that you are, Lauri.'

There was such affection in the smile she gave her niece that Lauri felt the first real stab of remorse that she wasn't going to stay with them longer. Or even to make her home here in England in the lovely Devonshire county she had already come to love. But it was a reckless thought, and she didn't want to dwell on it. As she kept telling herself, it wasn't part of her life's plan.

And how dull that sounded, for pity's sake! She was twenty years old, and hardly ready to settle into a life's plan! She was as free as the wind, which was how she came to be here in England in the first place.

But she kept her uncle's teasing advice in mind while she toured around the famous London waxworks the following day, and kept moving among the exhibits that were so extraordinarily lifelike. She saw a child touch one of the exhibits, only to leap back with a squeal of excited alarm as it turned out to be one of the assistants.

All the same, she realised she was really just marking time, and all her thoughts were concentrated on what was happening in the Harley Street consulting room right now. When she returned to the hotel, her aunt and uncle were already sitting quietly in their suite drinking afternoon tea, and Lauri couldn't miss the pallor in her aunt's cheeks.

She felt suddenly awkward, not wanting to rush over to Helen and demand to know what had been said. It was too intrusive, and she didn't want to make it seem as if she had every expectation of hearing the worst, either.

Thankfully, Vernon took the initiative from her, smiling at her cheerfully. She took heart from that.

'Come and join us, my love. We thought you'd be back soon, so there's an extra cup for you. You'll be glad of some tea, I daresay, and you can tell us how you enjoyed Madame Tussaud's.'

'It was fascinating,' Lauri said. 'I had a lovely day, Uncle. And how was yours?'

The words had to be said, and once she had said them, they wouldn't go away. Her hands shook a little as she poured her own tea, knowing she was remembering her father's demise, which was still all too real to her, and applying her desolate feelings then to her aunt's situation now.

It was foolish, but she couldn't help it. Then, to her astonishment, she heard Helen give a short laugh that was quickly stemmed by a burst of coughing.

'Don't look so concerned, Lauri dear,' she said, albeit breathlessly. 'I assure you I'm not about to expire at any minute, and Mr Jellyman has assured me that I'm not suffering from any terminal illness...'

She paused for breath, and Vernon took up the telling.

'Thankfully we may dismiss any of Dr Vine's dire predictions, but we should not dismiss the warnings that Mr Jellyman gave you, my dear.'

Lauri could hear the rare seriousness in his voice, and knew that she hadn't been told everything yet. Her first brief sense of relief faded.

'So what did he tell you both?'

She looked from one to the other, not sure whom to address. Helen looked exhausted, and these extra days in London had clearly taxed her, making Lauri feel guilty for wanting to come here at all. But presumably she would have had to come here in the end, since an eminent London consultant would hardly have travelled to Devon to visit a patient.

It would be so nice to be back in the comparative calm of the countryside right now. To be walking along the springy cliffs and watching the ever-changing sea; to be laughing with Steven Connors over some silly shared joke in the intimacy of a Plymouth restaurant; or even racing around in Robert's sports car and feeling a vicarious sense of the adventurous life he so enjoyed. Or to be scrambling over rocks and looking for sea shells and fossils on the sands near the shipyard, and having Steven explaining what the fossilised remains were...

She blinked, realising her thoughts were going off at a tangent, when she should be concentrating on what her uncle was about to tell her.

It didn't mean she had lost interest...it was more a way of delaying any unpleasant news she was about to hear... It was a trick she had sometimes employed in the past...

'Your aunt has a serious condition, Lauri,' Vernon said, 'but chronic bronchitis is something that can be treated, and in many cases the worst effects can be eased. Jellyman has given us a letter for Dr Vine, recommending a course of medicines and steam inhalations that will alleviate the condition as much as possible.'

'I see.' The thankful thought swept through Lauri's mind that bronchitis was not the ogre illness she had expected to hear about. But her uncle was still looking grave, and she guessed she hadn't heard everything yet.

'And will these treatments bring about a vast improvement?' she asked, willing him to agree.

Helen smiled faintly. 'I think not. Oh, they'll help, I've no doubt, and one must trust in the consultant's judgement, but they won't cure it. And then there's the other nuisance, of course.'

'What other nuisance is that?'

'Your aunt also suffers from an asthmatic condition which causes her much distress, though she does her best to hide it from everyone, and usually takes herself off to her room when the attacks occur,' Vernon said, almost accusingly. 'But she couldn't hide it from Jellyman, and the combination of the two conditions is not to be taken lightly. Asthma is a strange condition, as likely to be brought on by emotional stress as by an allergy to certain things. Summer pollen is always particularly distressful to her, and she must take things easily, which is something she does not take kindly to.'

Helen spoke more firmly now. 'I would be obliged if you would stop talking about me as if I'm not here, Vernon, and I don't care to be discussed as if I'm a specimen under a microscope. In any case, Lauri's heard quite enough of it by now, and there's nothing more to tell. I would dearly like to hear more about Madame Tussaud's. It's a place I've never visited, and am not sure if I would care for it.'

'You certainly wouldn't have cared for the Chamber of Horrors, Aunt Helen,' Lauri said quickly, seeing that she was determined to talk about something other than illness, and glad to oblige. 'It was really gruesome to see those waxwork figures of murderers and the like. They looked far too real for comfort.'

'Then I'm glad I didn't go with you. Now, if you don't mind, I think I'll postpone any more discussion after all, and take a nap before dinner.'

'That's a good idea. Lauri and I will leave you in peace and take a stroll around the gardens,' Vernon said at once.

But, as she suspected, it wasn't merely to take the air that her uncle invited her to inspect the fragrant and well-planned hotel gardens.

'How serious is it, Uncle?' she asked quietly, when they were strolling arm-in-arm in the shrubbery.

'It's not good,' he admitted. 'The medication will help to control the condition, but part of the trouble lies with Helen herself. She *must* take things easily and not overdo things, and that's simply not her way. She was always such a vibrant woman, and any hint of inactivity appals her.'

Lauri wished he hadn't used the past tense, but she knew he didn't mean anything by it, even if he noticed it.

'While I'm here, I'll do my best to see that she

doesn't overdo things,' she said. 'And it's time she stopped trying to arrange all these visits with her friends on my account. I'm perfectly capable of finding my own way around, Uncle, and she's already been so sweet in introducing me to so many people. You both have—and now you must think I'm sounding terribly ungrateful.'

He patted her hand. 'Not at all, my love, and nobody would want to keep you fettered in any way. But Helen wanted to do so much for you while you were here. I think she imagined she could fit in a lifetime of experience in a few short weeks, and it just can't be done.'

'Uncle Vernon—would it really mean so much to her if I was to stay longer than my planned visit?' Lauri heard herself say slowly.

She hadn't meant to say the words, but they had emerged before she could stop to think.

She felt Vernon squeeze her arm. 'It would mean a great deal, but I wouldn't dream of asking you to do such a thing, Lauri. I know how much this voyage back home on the *Titanic* means to you.'

'It's just a ship, isn't it?' Lauri murmured, with the greatest of understatements.

But when you boiled it all down, that was exactly what it was, and *all* that it was…

'And Helen would never forgive herself if she thought she was depriving you of something you've looked forward to so much,' he added. 'No, my dear, you mustn't dream of doing this, especially now that we have a second opinion about her illness. Your aunt is very sensitive and self-defensive about it all, and she'll be doing her utmost to hide the seriousness of it, even from close friends like Freda Connors.'

'Then no one will hear it from me, Uncle. But would it distress her so much to think I was staying a little longer, if it was on her account? She's suggested it herself.'

'But she was able to say it—and mean it, of course—because we're both so very fond of you, and she didn't think it remotely likely. No, much as we would dearly love you to stay longer, and even to live with us permanently, I'm afraid you would get a very different reaction if Helen thought your decision was because you began to see her as invalid.'

'But what if she thought it wasn't on her account that I decided to delay my return? What if I was so excited by the thought of—of—' she sought in her mind for a feasible reason '—well, of the Connors's masquerade ball, for instance. Aunt Helen herself is looking forward to it enormously, I know, and I've never been to one before, and both Steven and Robert have tried to persuade me to attend it.'

She felt herself blush as she said it, and she hardly knew why she was searching so hard for logical reasons why she should stay. She saw her uncle look at her more quizzically.

'Well, of course, if we planted a little seed in her mind that it was one or other of the Connors boys who was the instrumental reason for your staying on, I'm sure she would accept that. Do you have a favourite?'

'It certainly wouldn't be on Robert's account that I stayed!' she said, so vehemently that she felt her colour deepen even more.

'On Steven's, then?' her uncle queried.

Lauri drew a deep breath. 'I'm—fond of Steven, Uncle, but knowing that my time here was limited, we had a rather frank discussion on not allowing our relationship to go beyond friendship. And now I suppose you'll think that was terribly forward of us to discuss something so intimate.'

'Not at all. But if you're saying what I think you are, I beg you to think seriously about what you might be giving up before you cancel your passage, Lauri,' he said.

She flinched, feeling her heart jump. Until now, even until this very moment, it had been no more than idle musing about cancelling her passage home—or rather, to postpone the date. In either event, it entailed missing out on the greatest voyage of her life, and she couldn't deny the acute disappointment of that fact.

When the April day of departure came, she couldn't imagine what her feelings would be, not to be taking the great adventure alongside all those other privileged passengers on the maiden voyage. And then she remembered her aunt's pale face, and she swallowed the lump in her throat.

'I think I would very much like to attend the Connors's masquerade ball,' she said carefully. 'And perhaps we could invite the family to dinner one evening and enter into another small deception. They will certainly be discussing the ball, and with Steven and Robert's persistence, I could allow myself to be persuaded to stay on for it. Aunt Helen has such a romantic heart that she'll be sure it's because of one of them that I'm staying. What do you think?'

Vernon gave her a warm kiss on her cheek. 'I think you're the best tonic your aunt could ever have, and I'll see that you don't regret this, darling girl. Just be careful not to let the Connors boys think you're too enamoured with either one of them, though, or you could be getting yourself into hot water,' he added with a small warning.

'Then maybe it would be wiser to let them believe I'm unable to choose between them, wouldn't it?' Lauri said, not sure whether to laugh or cry at the irrevocable decision she had just made.

'And for the present, we'll say nothing to your aunt,' Vernon went on. 'It will be easy enough to suggest a small dinner party for the Connors, since the last thing she'll want is to treated like porcelain and lose contact with all her friends. They'll want to hear about our trip to London, and I'm sure Steven will be interested in your day with Sir Gerald Hawkes.'

It already seemed a long time ago, Lauri thought with amazement, and yet it was only a couple of days. But she felt as though she had gone through a whole range of emotions in those few days.

And now she had to alter her whole concept of what she was doing here. Not least was the thought that she no longer had to try to fit everything into a few hectic weeks. She could relax more, and enjoy fitting into her father's more leisurely way of life. She would look ahead, possibly to the end of May, for arranging a passage home.

Meantime, she could pretend that *this* was home— as long as she didn't let her aunt suspect her plans just yet. They had to get a dinner party arranged quickly, so that Aunt Helen knew, or thought she knew, why her ticket was going to be cancelled. She was under no illusions that her place on the ship would be quickly filled.

'I've never considered myself a particularly devious person, Uncle Vernon,' she said, as they went back into the hotel. 'But I must confess it's quite intriguing to indulge in a little cloak-and-dagger stuff.'

'And when it's all in a good cause, a little deception never hurt anyone, did it?' he agreed.

The weather turned chilly, and it was a more tiresome journey back to Devon than the journey to London, and they were all a mite scratchy with one another by the time Hartman House came into view. Lauri welcomed the sight with relief, having seen her aunt shrink down in the car seat during the last miles, and knowing that she was feeling the bite of the March wind more acutely than Lauri and her uncle.

'Thank goodness we're home,' she said fervently. 'I wouldn't want to make such journeys too frequently, much as I loved it all, and I do thank you both for taking me.'

'It was our pleasure as much as yours, Lauri,' Helen murmured. 'But I must confess, I've a longing to sleep in my own bed tonight. I'm sure we'll all be revived by tomorrow, though, and filled with happy memories.'

'And wanting to share them with folk, I daresay,' Vernon said. 'Your aunt can never keep things to herself, Lauri, and she'll be wanting to chew over the fat with Freda Connors as soon as possible.'

'How inelegant you are, Vernon,' his wife chided him. 'But of course I'll want to see Freda.'

'Well, perhaps we should invite them all to dinner one evening soon, and do the telling in one fell swoop. And Lauri will want to see Steven—or is it

Robert who's caught her fancy, I wonder?' Vernon said, with a teasing chuckle.

'I certainly hope not,' Helen began with alarm.

In Lauri's opinion, he was rushing in far too soon with the idea, before Helen had not got even half of her normal breath back. But she didn't know them as well as she thought, and she had reckoned without Helen's determination not to let any hint of illness deter her from her social activities.

'I think she has a sensible head on her shoulders, my dear, so perhaps we could ask Lauri to drive over there tomorrow to issue the invitation.'

He was being transparently obvious now, Lauri thought with a rueful smile, and how artlessly he had planted the idea in his wife's mind that she might be interested in one or other of the Connors boys. But, heck, in for a penny, in for a pound, she thought, just as inelegant as her uncle.

'I'd like that,' she said. 'I'm longing to tell Steven all about the trip.'

She saw her aunt and uncle exchanged meaningful looks, and she knew Vernon was going to further the illusion of a blossoming romance between her and—well, either one of them, she supposed, in some confusion. She only hoped neither brother would get the wrong idea.

Especially Robert, since the woman to win his heart would of necessity always be looking over her shoulder to see what he was up to, she thought shrewdly. She had no wish to be that woman. And she wished now that she had made it clear that it was Steven she preferred. Steven, whom she no longer bothered to deny could mean a great deal to her—if she let him.

Chapter Eight

Helen was nothing if not resilient, Lauri thought admiringly. The day after their return to Devon, Dr Vine was summoned and given the consultant's letter and directions, and the new medicines were dispensed and delivered with smooth efficiency. And since the lady was determined to be seen to be at least as hale and hearty as before, the question of the small dinner party for the Connors came up almost immediately.

Apart from the frequent sojourns to her room, where she could take her asthma inhalations in private, Helen's chalky pallor was the only indication that anything was seriously wrong, and the subtly applied rouge on her cheeks effectively disguised it from all except those who knew her best.

'I've written a note to Freda,' she informed Lauri two mornings later. 'So, if you wish, you may take it to Connors Court this afternoon. I'm sure you'll be wanting to see the boys again.'

'Oh, yes, of course,' Lauri said, knowing she must further the illusion of her interest. 'I can't wait to tell Steven about my trip on the river with Sir Gerald and his wife. And I suspect Robert will be more than interested in the gory details of the Chamber of Horrors,' she added.

Her aunt looked well satisfied with her reply, and a little later Lauri walked out into the sunlight with a smile on her face. How easy it was to deceive someone when they wanted to be deceived, even if they weren't aware of it.

But Helen wasn't unintelligent and, by now, she might even be toying with the idea that one of the Connors boys might be the catalyst to persuade Lauri to stay in England after all.

Lauri tried not to feel uneasy about the deception as she reached the outhouses, where her uncle was already beneath the hood of one of his cars. When she called out to him, he straightened at once, his rugged face streaked with oil.

'You look a picture,' he said approvingly, eyeing her citrus yellow jacket and high-necked blouse, and the long beige skirt that revealed the hint of an ankle above her high-buttoned boots.

'It's not too bright, is it?' she asked. 'I haven't worn this jacket here before, but I thought if I'm to play the vamp, it might be the thing.'

She laughed as she spoke, feeling her heart give a sudden leap. She would be deceiving Steven and Robert, too, in letting them think it was on their account that she intended staying here long after her allotted vacation should have been over. It was necessary, but for the first time she hoped uneasily that neither of them was going to get the wrong idea.

Robert would soon get over any idea that she was attracted to him, and turn to other diversions when he knew it was all for nothing. But Steven…she certainly didn't care for the thought of deceiving Steven.

But she wouldn't go back on the plans now, and playing the vamp was going to be a challenge, if nothing else. It was the only way she felt able to view it, and she became aware that Vernon was laughing at her now.

'What have I said that amuses you?' she asked.

'It's just that I hardly think anyone would think you needed to act the vamp in order to attract a young man, Lauri. The wonder is that we haven't had half the young bucks in the county inviting you out by now.'

She laughed back. He was a dear, and she was enormously fond of him, but she couldn't resist teasing him.

'That's because you and Aunt Helen have effectively guided me in certain directions, but once this masquerade ball is over, be warned that I may strike out on my own, Uncle, and find my own beau!'

'So you might, but you could do no better than the one you already know best, and I'm saying no more than that,' he agreed. 'But don't let me detain you, love. Your chariot awaits you, and from now on it belongs to you. And for the time being, that's also our little secret. We'll make the gift public once your aunt knows you're staying.'

She looked at him, not understanding for a moment. It almost sounded like a bribe, but the very sweetest kind of bribe she could imagine, since she had already given her word on her future, and she gasped.

'You can't mean you're *giving* me the Model-T, Uncle?'

'Of course I can, and it's my pleasure to do so. So go along now, and enjoy your toy as much as I enjoy mine.'

Lauri was so taken aback at what she was hearing that she couldn't speak properly, so after stammering a few inadequate words of thanks she merely gave him a fierce hug. Then she went quickly to the car that was now her own, and ran her hands lovingly over the grey leather upholstery as she had done before, before driving away with a wave of her hand.

She had never been particularly covetous, but the unexpected gift was so exciting that she wanted to shout it to the sky. And she had to remind herself that, as yet, the new ownership was a secret known only to herself and her uncle.

But she felt suddenly reckless, and it was tempting to drive very fast to Connors Court. Instead, she restrained herself, and took the lanes carefully, remembering the first time she had almost run into Robert's horse on this very journey. Not that it had been totally her fault, but she didn't want to risk a similar encounter.

Once at the house, she announced herself to the stiff-necked butler, and was ushered at once into Freda's sitting-room, where the old lady was sitting by the window, reading. She closed her book at once and looked up with pleasure as Lauri entered the room.

'Well, this is a lovely surprise, my dear. Though you've not come to tell me any unpleasant news, I hope?' she added, knowing that the Hartmans' trip to London was not entirely for Lauri's pleasure.

'Not at all, ma'am,' Lauri said, thinking, too, how easy it was to tell little white lies when it was for the benefit of all. 'Aunt Helen is fairly well, and has been given some new medicine, and I'm sent here with a note for you.'

'Thank you,' the lady said, taking the envelope. 'And did you enjoy your visit to London with your aunt and uncle?'

'I did, very much, thank you,' Lauri said. 'And you'll see from your note that I'm here to invite you and your nephews to dinner on Saturday evening, so that we can tell you all about it together. I'm longing to see Steven in particular, and I had so hoped he would be here,' she said, leaving the sentence in the air for Freda to inwardly supply her own answer to Lauri's eagerness.

'Oh, you'll find him at the shipyard as usual today. And for once, Robert's there too, I believe. But do stay and have some refreshment first, my dear.'

Lauri spoke hurriedly, sensing that some pertinent questions might well be in the offing about her apparent rush to see Steven.

'Would you mind if I don't? I'm simply longing to take the air on this lovely day. And I know Steven will be interested to learn that I've seen Sir Gerald Hawkes and his wife again.'

And if the slightly raised eyebrows of the older lady meant that she began thinking the Hartman girl was more than just interested in her great-nephew, it was all to the good, thought Lauri, almost gleefully. It all added to the mischievous game she and her uncle were playing…

Then she realised that she might be offending the lady at her obvious impatience to be gone, but it seemed that Freda had cottoned on very quickly to the nuances in Lauri's voice, and was giving her smiling approval.

'Go along, then. I know how you young people always like to get your heads together and gossip away like young magpies. But you may tell your aunt and uncle we shall be delighted to come to dinner on Saturday evening, Lauri. I know I can speak for the boys as well.'

Lauri escaped, hiding her surprise at hearing that the boys were both at the shipyard. But she supposed she shouldn't be surprised if it was due to come under Robert's control in a few weeks' time.

For the first time, Lauri wondered just how that felt to Steven. She could tell that he cared for the business as lovingly as if he cherished a woman, while Robert was apparently content to step in when the time was right, and reap all the profits and prestige that Steven had built up.

If ever she had thought them similar in any way, that fact alone emphasised the vast difference between them. But it was really no concern of hers, and she had a mission of her own to undertake that day.

And knowing that she had now burned her own boats, in a manner of speaking, she was aware of a growing excitement that she would be here for the Connors masquerade ball, which promised to be such a lavish affair.

It would help, in a small way, to allay the undoubted disappointment of not travelling on the *Titanic*'s maiden voyage. But she also had to keep reminding herself that, as yet, no one but her uncle and herself knew of her plans.

* * *

When Lauri arrived at the shipyard, she parked the Model-T alongside the car she recognised as Robert's. She breathed in the usual scents of wood and sawdust that mingled with the tang of the sea, and one and another of the carpenters and painters nodded as they recognised her.

She was told that Steven was in the office, and she picked her way carefully towards it. If he and Robert were both there, it meant she could kill two birds with one stone.

She heard their raised voices before she reached the small wooden structure, and her heart sank. It didn't bode well for anyone to arrive with a frivolous invitation, if the two of them were deadlocked in some kind of business argument. She already had some experience of how they could effectively shut out anyone but themselves.

After hesitating for a moment, Lauri raised her chin. It was nothing to do with her, and if they were so ill-mannered as to be rude to a lady, that was also to their discredit. But she smiled inwardly, knowing that in having such a thought she was unconsciously playing the part of the English lady.

Her smile faded as she caught the gist of the argument before she even reached the office door. Steven's voice was vitriolic with rage.

'If you think you're going to walk in here and dispose of everything I've built up in the past few years, Robert, you're very much mistaken.'

Robert's response was insultingly crass. 'You won't have any say in it, brother, because once the shipyard belongs to me, I can do with it whatever I choose. The legacy is watertight—and whatever that buffoon Slater has to say about some confounded codicil, I'll fight tooth and nail to keep what's rightfully mine.'

'But you don't want to keep it, do you? That's my whole point. You want to sell it to the highest bidder and take your profits off to Spain to set yourself up as some ne'er-do-well vintner—'

'And why should you assume that I'll be a ne'er-do-well, you jackass? You know nothing about viticulture, so don't demean it. Anyway, if you're so damn keen to keep the shipyard, I'll be quite agreeable to you buying me out.'

Lauri heard Steven's furious reply. 'Father always knew it meant nothing to you, which is why he insisted that you didn't get control of it until you were mature enough to handle it, though God knows when that will ever happen. He had some twisted ideas, but he still had to do things right by his elder son, more's the pity. And you don't have the decency to sign the shipyard over to me without getting your pound of flesh, which is typical of you, you bastard—'

'Careful, brother. If I'm one, then so are you, remember? But I take it from your response that you won't have the funds to buy me out.'

'Of course I won't, and you know it—'

Lauri was too embarrassed to be an unwilling eavesdropper a moment longer. Besides, curiosity aside, at any minute one of the workmen might approach, and wonder why she had been standing there so long already. She rapped on the door, and had to repeat it several times before it was wrenched open.

'Yes?' Steven snapped, before registering who the intruder was. His eyes widened at the sight of Lauri in her spring-like outfit, and as he muttered an apology for his sharp tone, she heard Robert's drawling voice.

'Well, well, like the cavalry coming over the hill, Miss Hartman has arrived to put an end to our wrangling.'

'Oh, were you wrangling? Surely not, Robert!' she said innocently. 'But it's fortuitous to catch you both together, and I've already been to see your Aunt Freda and got her approval of my mission.'

She paused, hoping her breathlessness would be seen as youthful exuberance, and not the reaction to overhearing things that she shouldn't. She tried not to glare at Robert, while having overwhelming sympathy for Steven if his brother meant to go ahead with his plan to sell the shipyard.

'You'd better slow down, Lauri, and tell us what it is that Aunt Freda has approved,' Steven said shortly, not yet prepared to change his mood as quickly as Robert.

And why would he, when he had everything to lose? Lauri thought. She pretended to ignore their respective bad tempers.

'You're all invited to dinner to hear about our trip to London, and while you're there, *I'*d like to hear more about your masquerade ball. Aunt Helen has been telling me what she intends to wear, and it makes me really envious, and wishing I was able to come as well.'

And, dear Lord, but if this wasn't acting the coquette, she didn't know what was, Lauri thought again. She only had to flutter her eyelashes like some Victorian maiden, and the whole thing would be so blatantly obvious that she was setting her cap at one or other of the Connors boys.

And it wasn't intended to be like that at all...but at least she had somehow managed to put a temporary stop to the bitterness between them. Robert responded to her archness at once, just as expected.

'Just say the word that you'll stay a little longer, Lauri, and I promise I'll make your visit the best ever.'

'Steven's already promised me that,' she said quickly, knowing she was playing one off against the other, and womanly enough to relish the feeling. It meant nothing, and they would soon realise that it didn't, since she knew she could never fall in love with Robert... But just for the moment, it made her blood race to know she was stirring up a different kind of rivalry between them.

'But Steven's always busy, while I prefer to spend my time escorting a lovely lady around,' Robert said.

'You'll discover it's the kind of life a playboy leads, Lauri, at least until he returns to Spain, or wherever else his fancy takes him,' Steven snapped.

Lauri could sense the dangerous undercurrents beginning to rise again, and she backed towards the door.

'Well, for now, since I have my own transport and don't have to choose an escort to take me home, I'll say good day and see you both on Saturday evening.'

Daringly, she blew them a collective kiss as she swept out of the door, and found herself almost running to get away from the awkward scene. All she wanted was to be out of here, and breathing in the clean air of the moors.

Before she could open the car door, she felt someone's hand over her own gloved one, and she spun around at once.

'I'm sorry if you overheard any of our family squabbles, Lauri,' Steven said shortly.

'I'm sorry, too. I don't like being involved in matters that don't concern me.'

She was conscious that his hand still covered hers, and she made no attempt to pull it away. Her heart was beating faster than usual, and she began to realise she had been more upset by the scene she had witnessed than she had believed. She hated Robert for his insensitivity, and she admired Steven for his passion in continuing the shipyard in the way his father had wished, while it seemed that Robert only wanted to sell up and get out. What kind of loyalty to a family heritage was that!

'How much *did* you hear?' Steven asked abruptly.

She felt her face redden. 'Most of it,' she admitted. 'I'm afraid I was just too embarrassed to move at first, but I knew I had to make my presence known, before it looked as though I was snooping.'

'And were you?'

'No! Not intentionally, anyway—' But as she floundered she realised his face had relaxed, and he was teasing her.

Thank goodness, she thought fervently. For a moment, she had really thought he was accusing her, and she didn't want him to think badly of her in any way.

Before she could think what he was going to do, he had suddenly lifted her gloved hand to his lips and kissed her open palm.

'Don't you know by now I'd be more than happy to involve you in every part of my life, sweet Lauri? But a short-term relationship is as much of a pointless condition to me as it is to you, as you've made perfectly clear.'

'Well, I don't really recall actually saying such a thing,' she murmured. 'And although we haven't known one another very long, I am as fond of you, Steven, as I am of any of my friends.'

The words came out clumsily, almost against her will, for if she wasn't careful she knew she was in danger of saying far more in her outspoken way. And it wasn't done for a young lady to admit to feeling warmth for a young man until he declared himself first.

She realised, too, how very incongruous it was to be standing here, thankfully out of sight of his business world, and discussing such personal matters. With a shaky laugh, she pulled her hand away from his.

'Goodness, how serious we've become.'

'And how very tame it sounds to have you confess a fondness for me, when what I feel for you is a far deeper regard.' He spoke almost angrily, and continued with a shrug, 'But of course, we must abide by our unspoken rules. A temporary attachment is worse than no attachment at all. You'll be leaving these shores soon, and I must learn to forget you.'

'Steven, please...' Lauri said, filled with mixed emotions now. If she wasn't headlong in love with him already, she knew she could very soon learn to be, she thought faintly. And where would that leave her, returning to Boston in due course with a broken heart?

But she had planted the seeds in the older generation for an apparent attraction between them, and she wondered now just whom she would be deceiving.

'All right, I won't make you any more distressed than I can help,' he went on, softening at the stricken look on her face. 'But despite my love of boats and shipping, it's hardly flattering to know that any woman would prefer sailing on the *Titanic* to the love of a good and honest man. I'm speaking objectively, of course,' he finished mockingly.

'Of course. And I think it's high time I left,' she said swiftly, wrenching open the car door and almost desperate to get away from him now.

Once up on the moors, she stopped the motor and applied the brake to give herself time to think. It had been an extraordinary afternoon, and one that she hadn't anticipated. In the silence, she let out her breath in a great sigh, hardly realising how tightly she had been holding herself in check until she released all the air in her lungs.

She forced herself to ignore the personal meeting with Steven, and concentrate on what she had overheard between the brothers. If she had ever thought about it seriously, she would have believed in the unbreakable bond between twins that was part-telepathy, part-sharing of a life before birth.

But these two seemed intent on tearing each other apart, and she would have thought it sensible and desirable for them to live as separately as possible. The idea of Robert taking control of the shipyard and for Steven to continue working under him was clearly unthinkable.

She leaned her arms on the steering-wheel, wondering how it was that the Connors father had never seen the rivalry between his sons—unless this was his clumsy way of trying to restore something that simply didn't exist. She shuddered, thinking it a shocking, if not an evil, thing to do, to leave the codicil in his Will so late.

It was like reaching out from the grave to further his wishes, like the dictator she suspected he had been, still adhering to strict Victorian control over his family. She also began to suspect something else about him, from her various sources of information about the man. He had also been completely mad.

And how could he have thought Steven and Robert were so fundamentally alike, that they would share their lives in harmony once his requests were known? Lauri wondered if he had really known his sons at all. Not even twins could share every thought and idea, for all that they were supposed to have such a bond...but in this case, the bond seemed to be forcing them farther and farther apart.

She tried to forget them as she drove back to Hartman House and parked the motor in one of the outhouses. Her uncle was nowhere to be seen, and she was about to go towards the house when a small sound from the rear of the building made her heart jump. It was so quiet in here, and every sound seemed to be magnified, especially when it was the sound of someone or something in pain.

'Uncle Vernon?' she called cautiously.

'I'm back here, Lauri,' she heard his tortured voice. 'I thought you were never coming. I need your help.'

Her heart in her mouth now, Lauri followed the sound of the voice. She knew she should rush to his aid, and in essence she was doing so, but she realised she hadn't yet overcome her fear of illness. All she could think about now was her own father, and her feet seemed to move forward in leaden steps until she reached the collapsed figure of Vernon Hartman.

'What on earth's happened, Uncle?' she quavered, hating her spinelessness, but still wishing she could get as far away as possible from his ashen face.

She despised herself and was ashamed of the feeling, but it simply refused to go away. If this was a heart attack similar to her father's, then she didn't know how she—or Aunt Helen—would cope.

Thinking of her frail aunt, she pulled herself together with a great effort, and knelt down beside her uncle, as he leaned against the back wall of the outhouse.

'Tell me exactly where the pain is, Uncle,' she said, remembering what a doctor would require to know.

'It's my blasted ankle, girl. I think it may be broken, which is why I daren't move it. Couldn't, anyway, without shouting the place down. But you've taken such an age to get back from the Connors's place. Lord knows where Helen is now, and it seems as if everybody has deserted me today.'

Because of his pain, his voice was accusative and petulant, but in her relief, Lauri felt the most ludicrous and appalling urge to laugh out loud. It was no more than a broken ankle, when she had feared the very worst!

She smothered her feelings quickly, because he did look so white and ill.

'I'll go to the house at once and send for Dr Vine,' she said quickly. 'One of the servants will come and make you comfortable until he gets here.'

'And send me out some brandy. If I've got to suffer the indignity of lying here, I may as well make the best of it,' he said feelingly.

Lauri eyed his twisted foot. 'Should I try to remove your boot?' she asked dubiously.

'If you do, I'll probably kill you. I'm not as intellectual as your father was, Lauri, but I do know that you should leave an injury well alone until a doctor takes a look at it. Now go about your errands, girl, and don't forget the brandy. At least it will help to dull the pain—and the indignity,' he added.

She fled up to the house, thankful beyond belief that it wasn't anything more serious than a suspected broken ankle. It might not even be that, but no more than a severe sprain. Whatever it was, it would certainly curtail his driving for a while, and that would hurt as much as the pain of the injury.

Helen was cutting flowers in the garden when Lauri came rushing towards her, holding her skirt out of the way in order to gain extra speed.

'Good heavens, is there a fire?' Helen began, and then her expression changed as she saw the girl's face. Sensing at once that something was wrong, she dropped the wicker trug she was carrying, and the spring flowers spilled unheeded to the ground. 'What is it? Is it Vernon?'

Even as she spoke, Lauri could hear the hoarseness in her voice, and knew that this incident was going to bring on an asthma attack. She tried to keep her own voice perfectly calm.

'He's hurt his ankle, and it's nothing more serious than that, Aunt. But since he's worried that it's broken, he shouldn't be moved, and we must telephone the doctor right away. He's asking for brandy, but I suspect it's not so much to alleviate the pain as to hide his fury at having to stop driving for a few weeks.'

She made light of it as far as possible, while knowing that it wouldn't do to appear too frivolous. After all, Vernon *was* in pain, but her aunt was clearly thankful to hear it was nothing more serious.

'I'm sure you're right about the brandy, love,' she said. 'I'll telephone Dr Vine at once, if you will see to his other needs, and I'll come down to the outhouses directly.'

By the time Dr Vine arrived, the servants had made Vernon more comfortable with several cushions behind his head and a blanket over his legs. He was also well fortified with brandy, and the company of his womenfolk.

'You're fortunate that it's not broken, but it's a severe sprain that will need binding tightly,' the doctor pronounced, after Vernon's boot had been cut away from his foot and the whole area examined minutely. It was done to the accompaniment of barely suppressed oaths from the patient that the ladies chose to ignore.

'You call these manipulations fortunate, man?' Vernon growled. 'You all but pulled my foot off.'

'It was necessary, my dear sir, to ensure that you had done no serious damage in your fall. Is there any other injury that you wish me to examine?'

'There is not!' Vernon roared. 'Just give me some medication to deaden the pain and let me get back to the house.'

'It may not be wise to give you further medication

if you've drunk a considerable quantity of brandy,'
Dr Vine said accusingly.

The oaths were not so subdued this time, and
Helen and Lauri hastily left the outhouse while
Vernon ranted at the doctor until he got his required
medication. The servants were helping their employer carefully to a vertical position by the time the
doctor joined the ladies outside, considerably redder
in the face than when he had arrived.

'Mr Hartman is a gentleman of great character and
determination,' he said, with admirable understatement. 'He'll doubtless have troubled nights until the
swelling in his ankle subsides, but I'll leave you
some powerful sedative powders that will give him
some rest. And you as well, ma'am,' he added mean-
ingly.

'He'll not be a good patient,' Helen said with a
wry smile. 'Inactivity doesn't suit him.'

'I'm afraid he has little choice for the next few
weeks,' the doctor retorted, handing her the sachets
of powders. 'I'll bid you good day now, but don't
hesitate to call me again if you feel the need.'

Lauri looked at her aunt. 'Oh, dear. Does this
mean we're in for a sensitive time, Aunt?'

'It does, dear, and how delicately you phrase it!
Your uncle is normally a placid man, as you know,
and he has infinite patience with my illness. But
when it comes to his own, it's a different matter, and
he can be as tetchy as a flea. Perhaps we should
cancel Saturday's dinner party—'

'You'll do no such thing!' Vernon said, emerging
from the outhouse at that moment with his arms
around the shoulders of two male servants as they
supported him in a human chair. 'I shall be perfectly

recovered by then, and weary with looking at four walls. There's no need to cancel anything on my account, and Lauri will be disappointed not to see Steven, and tell him of her meeting with Lord Hawkes. But this damnable injury is an unholy inconvenience when I was preparing to try out the new braking adjustments to the Wolseley.'

'When you feel well enough to sit in a car, perhaps you'd allow me to drive it, Uncle, and you can sit beside me and observe,' Lauri said as the small procession made its way back to the house, registering the sharp look Helen had given him after his reference to Steven, and guessing that she would be quizzed on it later.

But he was right, for all that. She would have been bitterly disappointed if the dinner party had had to be cancelled, and not simply for the joy of relating their experiences in London, either.

She knew she was being drawn more and more into the pleasure of knowing Steven, and the life here. If she ever dared to let herself fantasise a little further, she wondered what the outcome of their association might be if she remained in England even longer than she had already decided.

Or had fate already decided that for her…?

Chapter Nine

By the time Saturday came, the three of them were becoming exhausted and exasperated with each other's company, and thankful to have some diversion ahead of them.

Lauri had telephoned Connors Court and told the family what had happened, insisting that none of them wanted to cancel the dinner arrangements. Steven had answered, and the timbre of his voice was strong and vibrant over the wire.

'I'm very sorry to hear of the accident, of course, but I suppose it could have been far worse. And dare I ask if the patient is an easy one?' he said, and she could hear the smile in his voice.

She laughed back. 'You may ask, but I suspect you already know the answer. Uncle Vernon's not the easiest of patients, and there's also a limit to how long he can remain still. He's not supposed to hobble about on the foot any more than necessary, but you can't stop him.'

'Then don't try. He'll not thank you for it,' Steven said. 'Incidentally, do you know how attractive your laughter is? The telephone seems to accentuate it, somehow.'

How odd, when she was thinking something of the same about the sound of his voice...

'Thank you, kind sir,' she said, with a touch of embarrassment. 'So we'll see you as arranged this evening. My aunt and uncle were very insistent that we shouldn't cancel it on his account.'

'And what about on your account?' he said.

'Oh, I'm always happy to meet any of their friends,' she said sweetly, and then dissolved into laughter. 'Stop fishing for compliments, Steven!'

'Why not? I've never understood why such a thing should be solely a ladies' prerogative.'

'I suppose there's no reason why it should be. Well, then, of course I'm looking forward to seeing you. And Robert. And your aunt,' she added for good measure.

'Then I'll take that as enough for now, though I'd prefer to think it wasn't all of us *en masse* that attracts you.'

It certainly wasn't, she thought, and even though this was all getting a mite personal, she remembered the plan that she and her uncle intended putting into operation, and she laughed again.

'Maybe it's not, but you have to allow a lady some secrets, don't you? And now goodbye!'

She put the receiver back on the hook, but she was still smiling as she turned away from the instrument, and she started as she saw her aunt hovering nearby.

'Goodness, you startled me. I didn't hear you coming.'

'It's never been in question that when a young lady is enamoured of a young man, she's oblivious to anything else. So was that Steven or Robert you were talking to?'

'Oh, Aunt Helen, you'd be a wicked matchmaker, given the chance, wouldn't you?'

'It's one of the pleasures in a dowager's life, my dear, and since I have no daughters of my own, I'm naturally concerned that when you marry, you make the right choice.'

'And what if I choose not to marry at all?' Lauri asked facetiously. 'I may decide to devote my life to good causes.'

Helen's lips pursed. 'Well, noble as it all sounds, I sincerely hope you won't do any such thing! It would be a terrible waste of womanhood—'

Lauri's laughter effectively stopped her.

'For pity's sake, Aunt, you make me feel like a commodity, just waiting for the right man to come along and sweep me off my feet.'

'There are worse fates,' Helen said, unabashed. 'So which of our Connors boys has caught your eye?'

Lauri pretended to consider. 'How can I decide such a thing when they're both such delightful company? If I were staying here longer, it might be easier to do so.'

She felt guilty then, knowing she was provoking her aunt into the predictable comment that she only had to say the word, and this house would be her home for as long as she chose. And seeing the sparkle in Helen's eyes, she accepted it would be the best tonic she could give her. But it would be foolish to rush any suggestion of romantic attachment when she had already shown herself to be an independent young woman.

Falling in love might sometimes be a lightning affair, but Lauri Hartman preferred to take such things slowly. And if that showed a rather more analytical approach to love than that of some frivolous young thing, then it merely went to prove to her that she hadn't yet fallen in love.

Or was she simply fooling herself?

'Your uncle has been asking for you, Lauri,' Helen said next. 'If you could bear to do so, he'd like you to join him in the library where he's poring over his wretched motoring manuals. Meanwhile, I shall take my afternoon nap.'

Lauri hid a small groan as Helen went away with an obvious sigh of relief that she wasn't the one who was required to entertain her husband for the next couple of hours.

Much as Lauri loved her uncle Vernon, he had become the proverbial bear with a sore head ever since his enforced rest, just as everyone had predicted. But she had reckoned his agile mind, at least, hadn't been forced to abandon normal activities. He looked decidedly perkier when she found him sitting by the window in the library, with his injured ankle resting on a footstool. As soon as he saw her, he put his books on a side table and smiled.

'Ah, Lauri, send for some lemonade and then come and sit by me and we'll have a talk,' he said, and she guessed at once that he had one of his devious plans in mind.

He was the type of man who would never really grow up, and she felt a surge of real affection for him, knowing that everyone who knew him was uplifted by vicariously sharing in his enthusiasms. No wonder this injury irritated him so much, and not just physically, she thought sympathetically.

When a maid had brought them their refreshments, she poured them each a glass of lemonade, and looked at him enquiringly.

'What are we going to talk about? Is it to be about life in general, or something more specific?' she asked.

He gave a deep chuckle. 'You know me too well already, my girl,' he said. 'Of course it's something specific, and I've had a new and better idea than the one we first discussed.'

She pretended to look dismayed. 'You mean I'm not to pretend a sudden attachment to Steven or Robert Connors that will keep me here after all!'

She laughed as she said it, but at the same instant she was aware of a surprising pang in her heart. Yet it was absurd to be averse to abandoning it. The whole scheme was playing with fire. Someone could easily get hurt in the process. Hearts could be broken...

She blinked, realising how her thoughts were running away with her now. She should be glad if her uncle had thought of some other way...but that depended on what he had in mind.

'This wretched ankle of mine could be a godsend,' he announced. 'I shan't be able to drive for weeks, and I shall need a chauffeuse, so I'm appointing you for the job. What do you say to that, Lauri?'

She didn't take him seriously. 'You don't mean you'll be trusting me to drive your precious Wolseley, do you? Still, I'm sorry the Model-T is hardly big enough for you to stretch out your leg in any comfort—'

'Of course I mean the Wolseley, girl! And once your aunt sees how indispensable you've become to us all, and how pathetic I'm becoming, she'll be even keener to get you to stay. You'll not need much persuasion, will you?'

'Well, I don't think you'd better put on too pathetic an act, Uncle, for nobody will believe in it for a moment,' Lauri said drily. But she couldn't deny how her heart beat faster at the thought of driving her relatives about whenever it was necessary to do so. The Wolseley was such a beautiful motor, smooth and sleek and efficient…

'So do we have an agreement then?' Vernon said, seeing the gleam in her eyes.

She bent down to give him an impulsive hug. 'If you really mean it, then of course we do!'

'And when the time comes, how would you feel at taking us all to Southampton to see the departure of the *Titanic*?' he added, his gaze never leaving her face. 'Would it upset you so much, knowing you weren't going to be sailing on it? Your aunt and I were both looking forward to the festivities.'

Lauri spoke evenly, ignoring the lurch in her heart. 'I'm sure I'll manage to conceal my disappointment, Uncle. At least, I'll try.'

He gave her a smile of true affection. 'You have your father's spirit, Lauri.'

It was the best compliment he could have given her.

They told Helen about the chauffeuring arrangements, but as yet, there was no talk about Lauri staying indefinitely. It didn't do to make her suspicious that it was mainly on her account…and Lauri still didn't admit to herself that there were other, more personal reasons, why she wanted to stay.

By the time the Connors family arrived for dinner that Saturday evening, the Hartmans were full of remembered anecdotes to tell them of their trip to London. By then, Helen had already assured Freda that she was not about to expire at any minute, but that she was simply to take things easier. As if Freda knew exactly the right words to say, she glanced at Lauri, seated beside Robert at the candle-lit dining-table, while Steven sat beside his aunt on the far side.

'Has all this excitement made you decide to extend your visit to us, Lauri? I understand that you're going to drive your uncle's splendid motor whenever he and Helen want to go anywhere. They must be even more glad that you're here at such a time. When one doesn't have children of one's own, it's one of life's bonuses to be able to borrow someone else's.'

Coming from a spinster lady, this could be construed as an arch remark, but the fond glances she gave her nephews confirmed that she had her own reasons for saying as much. Where would she be without the companionship of her boys, as she called them?

'I've tried hard enough to get her to stay, Aunt Freda, but she has a cruel heart,' Steven said with mock sadness.

Lauri responded teasingly, feeling her heartbeats quicken as she saw the gleam in his handsome eyes.

'Oh, I could be tempted,' she said lightly. 'Especially as we don't know how long Uncle Vernon's ankle will incapacitate him. At his age, things take longer to heal, don't they?'

She knew this would provoke him, and his mischievous laugh told her he knew exactly what she was playing at.

'My love, if it will keep your delightful presence with us longer, then I might take to my bed for ever.'

'You had better do no such thing,' Helen replied smartly, but she looked at Lauri with hopeful eyes now. 'But have you really had second thoughts, Lauri? I know how much you were looking forward to that voyage home.'

'But if she does that, she won't be able to attend our masked ball, and I've promised her an occasion not to be missed,' Robert said, leaning towards her so that she breathed in the scent of the male toiletries he used. They were not cloying, but somewhat over-done, and she shifted her position slightly and looked directly at Steven.

'I begin to feel there are more reasons for me to stay than there are for me to go. And with my father no longer there, and my only family on this side of the Atlantic now…'

'And it would be different if you had a young man waiting for you,' Vernon agreed, a world of inno-cence in his voice. 'What has America got that we haven't got right here?'

Lauri forced herself to look away from Steven then, knowing her face was flushed. She was a worldly American girl, but right now her heart was doing all kinds of topsy-turvy things. The next mo-ment she felt Robert's hand close over hers, and she moved away in annoyance as he spoke archly.

'That's what I've been trying to tell her all this time.'

To Lauri's relief, Freda gave a snorting laugh, her

eyes keen as she looked across the table at her great-nephew.

'I would hope Lauri had more sense than to take *you* seriously, my boy. You're as likely to flit off to foreign parts the minute the inclination takes you.'

Robert grinned at her. 'Perhaps. But presumably there will come a day when I'll want to settle down to a more domestic life, however dull that sounds.'

'How condescending of you,' Steven said drily. 'But since millions of people find it a happy state, there must be something to be said for it.'

'Ah well, you're far more cut out for it than I am, bruth,' Robert told him, the familiar edge to his voice.

Lauri took a deep breath, glancing at her uncle, and noting the slightest inclination of his head, just as if he knew what she was about to say.

'Since you're all so interested in my future, it seems a good time to tell you all that I have definitely been toying with the thought of staying in England a while longer, if my aunt and uncle will have me.'

'My dear girl!' Helen exclaimed. 'You know it's our dearest wish. But this is not on my account, I hope?'

Even as she spoke, Lauri could see she was trying to suppress a cough, and she shook her head quickly.

'Well, obviously, you are a great part of my wish to stay, but only because I've grown so fond of you, Aunt Helen. But Uncle Vernon and I have already discussed the matter, and—well, now I've decided, and there's no turning back.'

She hoped that such a grand statement didn't sound as though it was some great sacrifice. Truly, it had never felt that way to Lauri. Not now, when she had examined all the options for leaving, and all the reasons for staying. There was nothing to go home to, and everything to stay for.

Steven spoke crisply. 'That's the best news any of us could have heard. And we'll all do our best to compensate for your disappointment in not travelling on the *Titanic*.'

'But, Lauri, I know that was one of your dreams,' Helen said.

'Uncle Vernon and I have tentatively discussed that too,' she said swiftly, hoping it didn't sound as if it had already been arranged before this apparently sudden decision. 'He will arrange for my ticket to be cancelled, and now I'll be looking forward to the masked ball I've heard so much about.'

She spoke brightly, unable to completely ignore her sickening feeling of disappointment, however well she managed to hide it from the others. That great ship's maiden voyage was such a tremendous occasion, and she would miss it…

'Anyway, I have one huge compensation. Since my uncle's ankle is troubling him so much, I've been appointed official chauffeuse for the Wolseley whenever it's needed.'

'Good God, we'd better keep off the roads then,' Robert retorted. 'The first time I met this madcap young lady, she came careering around the country lanes in her car and nearly scalped me and my horse.'

Freda chided him. 'Don't exaggerate, Robert. I'm sure Lauri is an excellent driver.'

'So I am, ma'am, but Robert and I did almost have a head-to-head collision, though I'm far too ladylike to say who was travelling the fastest, the rider or the driver.'

She was teasing him, but she caught her breath uneasily as she saw the glint of something that could almost be construed as lustful in his eyes at that moment.

She caught sight of Steven watching her, and knew another kind of thrill, as the blood ran hot in her veins. She had never courted any kind of rivalry between young men. She had never expected to find it here, and certainly not between brothers who were so similar in looks, and yet so different.

Or so she had thought. But remembering the clashes she had witnessed between them, she knew there was a strong bond of family temperament. And she knew at once that they both wanted her, for different reasons.

She was under no illusion as to Robert's womanising and fickle ways. Robert's reason would be only because he saw her as a challenge—or maybe to thwart his brother. As for Steven—they had made it plain to each other that a short-term relationship wasn't to be encouraged. But now she was intending to stay, at least for a while longer...

Her mouth dried a little. There had been tussles with some of the more ardent college beaux back home, and she knew only too well how easily a young man's passion could turn a girl's head. But she certainly didn't want to be any kind of a pawn between brothers.

'I think we should tell them our other news now, Lauri,' she heard Vernon say, and she dragged her mind back with some difficulty from the wanton thoughts searing through her head.

'What other news?' she said huskily, still caught up in the dreams that were still only in her own imagination, and best kept there if she didn't want to appear fast. At the dinner table, it was hardly the thing to appear so distracted.

'I've told Lauri that the Model-T now belongs to her—and before you all think this was a sneaky kind of bribe to make her stay with us, you're wrong. We had discussed it thoroughly, and she had already made it plain to me that she was definitely considering staying on.'

He lifted his glass to her as he spoke, and took a deep draught of his favourite red wine. Lauri felt her face flush almost as deeply, as Robert drawled beside her, 'You two seem to have got it all sewn up between you, sir, but as the end result is what everybody wanted, I'm sure we're not complaining.'

'It's really none of your business, anyway,' Lauri retorted without thinking, and immediately felt embarrassed at speaking to a dinner guest in that way. 'I'm sorry, that was very rude of me—'

'No, you're quite right, Lauri,' Steven put in. 'It *is* none of our business, but obviously we're pleased things have turned out the way they have.'

She warmed to him as always. Of the two of them, he was clearly destined to be more of a peace-maker than Robert, but it made him no less a man for all that. And clearing up a brother's provocative remarks could be a tedious business. She wondered just how often he had had to do it in the past.

'But can you really bear to watch the *Titanic*'s departure?' he said next. 'We were already planning to drive to Southampton to see you off, but perhaps it would be too disappointing for you—'

'Not at all,' Lauri said quickly, knowing it would be an even bigger disappointment for her aunt and uncle not to witness the departure of the ship on her maiden voyage. 'My uncle and I have wondered whether or not we might make a small vacation out of it, as a matter of fact.'

'Well!' Helen said. 'You two really have been making plans, haven't you?'

'I hope you don't think we were excluding you, Aunt,' Lauri said. 'It was all going to be a surprise, but a welcome one, I hope.'

Her aunt suppressed another threatening cough with an effort. 'You don't need to ask that, dear.'

The English Hartmans were nothing if not resilient, she thought again, and it was part of her nature as well. When one plan ended, another should be brought into play as quickly as possible...it wasn't a bad philosophy.

'Anyway, it's a spiffing idea,' Robert said. 'And perhaps we should join you in this venture. What do you say, Aunt Freda? Are you game for a little trip?'

By the time they all gathered in the drawing-room after dinner, Lauri gave up thinking of any disappointment about the sailing, and enjoyed the rest of the evening's conversation and the turn in their small vacation plans that would now include the Connors family.

They would stop at an inn en route to Southampton, and again on the way back. That way, the older ladies, in particular, wouldn't be too tired by the long drive. Though, remembering Helen's stoicism on the drive to London, Lauri knew she wouldn't complain, however bumpy the country roads.

It was an added pleasure to know the Connors

family would be accompanying them, and by the time April 10th drew near, Lauri was amazed to find how stoically she herself could put aside the fact that she wouldn't be taking up her allotted place on the ship itself. As she was now constantly reminding herself—what was there to go back to Boston for?

'You know the real reason I'm so glad you're staying, don't you?' Steven asked her, the week before they left for Southampton. He was taking her for an evening drive along the Devonshire coast. He had parked the car on a headland, and the sea glittered far below them, calm and beautiful in the last dying rays of the sun.

'I don't know. Do I?' she said, suddenly husky.

As his arm slid around her shoulders, she made no move to push him away.

'I think you do. I've loved you from the day I saw you, and you only have to say the word—'

'But you and I both know we've both resisted saying anything as definite,' she said carefully. 'I'm still not here permanently, so nothing has really changed, has it?'

'Hasn't it? I think we both know that it has. But if you're still determined to go back to Boston…'

She could hear the frustration in his voice, tinged with anger. 'I still haven't made my mind up about my future, Steven,' she said. 'Please don't rush me. I'm here for a while, so why don't we just take the time to get to know one another properly?'

She was impatient with herself. She was supposedly a confident, sophisticated American girl, but the proximity of this charismatic man made her as nervous as the proverbial kitten. And she knew she sounded more feeble and indecisive than she ever had before.

'I know all I need to know about you, Lauri,' he retorted. 'As for me—I'm pretty uncomplicated—'

'Oh, come on, stop being so modest! You're a darling man, and any girl would be a fool—' She stopped abruptly, knowing she was about to say *any girl would be a fool not to fall in love with you.*

'Yes?' he said, his face very close to hers now.

She knew he was about to kiss her, and she wanted it to happen. Without any warning, she knew just how badly she did want it. And why not? They were both adult and unattached, and there was no one else in the vicinity... With a small sigh, she seemed to merge into his arms, and she felt the firmness of his mouth on hers. She was pressed close to his chest, and she could feel the unevenness of his heartbeats.

And she loved him.

'All right, since you insist on it, I'll try not to go too fast, but it'll be the devil's own job not to, when I want you so much.'

He murmured the words against her mouth. It was erotically intimate and sensual. Her lips parted slightly, and she could taste him, and the rush of adrenaline in her veins was intoxicating her senses. She was drowning in pleasure at his merest touch.

'I just want to be sure my attentions are not unwelcome, dearest girl,' he went on, and from the thickness in his voice she knew how he was restraining himself. She could see it in the darkening of his eyes, and she respected his restraint, but her every nerve-end was responding to his touch by now, and her breathing had quickened.

'They are not unwelcome, Steven,' she whispered.

'But for now, can we keep our feelings to ourselves? Other people would think it was far too soon for us to become too openly attached to one another.'

'Do other people matter?' he asked, in a way that was reminiscent of Robert's arrogant tones. But since the words had such lovely, possessive connotations for them both, it thrilled, rather than alarmed her.

But she laughed ruefully. 'You know they do. We both have families to consider. Besides, as I said, there's no rush. You and Robert have a big birthday celebration coming up, and we have the whole summer ahead of us.'

And maybe the rest of our lives, she thought, catching her breath. It was a wonderful, delicious thought, but one that she was keeping to herself for now. She had to be quite sure that staying in England was the right thing for her to do. There was no family back home, but there would be friends there who would think she was completely mad to change an entire way of life...

They drove back to Hartman House slowly, and she was beginning to feel euphoric, wishing these moments could go on for ever, and that they never had to face anyone else. But it couldn't be so, and by then he had agreed to her wish to keep their feelings private for the time being.

It was better so, because Lauri suspected that however much her aunt might desire a connection between her niece and one of the Connors boys, she would think it had all happened with indecent haste. There was still a latent sense of Victorian prudery in Helen Hartman that Lauri had no wish to upset. Besides, there was added excitement in knowing that for the present, nobody knew of their attachment but themselves.

She should have known it was not so easy to fool her uncle. Her aunt was resting when they returned, and Steven didn't come into the house. But Vernon looked at her searchingly, seeing her flushed face, and the mouth that looked as though it had been thoroughly kissed.

'You and Steven have been getting along all right, I take it?' he asked with a meaningful smile.

'Of course. You and Aunt Helen wanted me to like all your friends, didn't you?' She gave him a wide-eyed look.

He laughed outright now. 'All right, I won't pry. All I'll say is that it would please us both greatly if you came to an understanding—'

'Then don't say any more, Uncle,' Lauri said quickly, not wanting to be pushed too quickly, nor wanting him to think that they were already more than mere friends. 'Steven and I find pleasure in one another's company, but don't read anything more into it than that.'

'Then if that's the way you want it, I'll keep my opinions to myself. But you had better allow your cheeks to cool down after one of your assignations, if you don't want the whole world to suspect that my girl's in love!'

She felt herself go even hotter, and then she gave him a hug. 'Stop fishing, Uncle! And it wasn't an assignation. It was just a little drive along the coast.'

And one that had probably sealed her fate, she thought, knowing her words were the greatest understatement of all.

'I think I'll have an early night,' she went on airily, considering the way her heart was drumming now. 'I need to let people know I'm staying in England for a while longer.'

She left her uncle in the library, needing to be alone in her room with her thoughts. She caught sight of herself in the mirror, touching her fingers to her mouth where Steven had kissed her, and wanted him with a fierce and primitive desire that took her breath away.

They were both strong-minded people, capable of passionate feelings and emotions, and if things developed further between them, she wondered how they would keep up the pretence of being no more than friends for the time being.

But they must. Aunt Helen, in particular, would still expect her niece to observe the correct courting rituals, however much she approved of the outcome. And as yet, the outcome was far from certain.

Lauri turned away from her tell-tale reflection. She felt as though she had known him always, and also that such a feeling was one of the dangers of instant attraction. Because she didn't know him in the way that people who had grown up together in the same environment did. In that respect they were still strangers. She just knew the heart and soul of him…and that was a dangerously romantic way to feel.

But she had letters to write, and explanations to give. Her father's colleagues who had wished her well on this trip would think she had taken leave of her senses to remain in England. And her own friends would think her completely mad to give up the chance of voyaging home on the *Titanic*.

She used her aunt's poor health as the main reason for her decision and invented the fact that she had discovered on the voyage across the Atlantic that she wasn't a good sailor, and didn't relish any more sea voyages just yet.

But she felt a tug at her heart as she re-read her words knowing she was also deceiving these good friends. It would have been wonderful to be rubbing shoulders with dukes and duchesses on that grand ship, and to envy the women with their lovely jewels and Paris gowns, many of whom would be rich Americans travelling home.

Whenever there was a suitable occasion, she too would be exotic, she resolved, wearing the new evening wrap of coral velvet with the gold fringing. She would wear the delicate crêpe de Chine gown in eau de nil that was split up the front to show a creamy silk underskirt…and the long-waisted, sequined chiffon gowns that were so feminine…

She laughed inwardly at her own racing thoughts. But they cheered her, and she knew now that however exciting the prospect of the voyage had been, it didn't compare with the knowledge that Steven Connors was falling in love with her.

Chapter Ten

The day before the *Titanic* was due to leave for America, the Hartman and Connors families planned to set out early for the drive to Southampton. By then, the newspapers had been full of the voyage, and now that the time was so near, Lauri frequently had to smother her acute disappointment at not being a part of it. But she daren't let her aunt and uncle know her feelings as they settled themselves in the Wolseley that she was now adept at driving.

Her uncle's ankle was so much better that he might well have managed some of the driving himself by now, but he seemed perfectly content to let Lauri continue. And besides, it aided the illusion that she was staying on as his chauffeuse, and not because her aunt was ill.

They had arranged to meet Steven and Freda Connors at a designated point. Robert had already gone ahead on some business matter of his own, and would meet them on the morning of April 10th in Southampton.

It was a relief to Lauri that Robert wouldn't be joining them at the intimate little inn en route where her uncle had booked rooms for them all. Robert irritated her, and sometimes she found it hard to be civil to him. He was what her father would have called a man always looking out for the main chance—whatever that was.

She promptly forgot him as Steven's car came into view, and they exchanged a brief, private smile as the senior members called out greetings to one another, before they set off in convoy, with Steven leading the way. But they were all relieved to reach the inn where they were to stay that evening. Since the weather was reasonably fair, they had picnicked on the way, but they were all weary by the time they reached their halfway destination.

The rooms were comfortable, and they were given a hearty supper in the dining-room, and the two older ladies went to bed straight afterwards. Vernon chatted for a while, and then said that his ankle was starting to throb, so he thought he would retire as well.

'You don't mind, do you, Lauri? I'm sure Steven will keep you company, if you're not ready for bed yet.'

'I need to sit for a while, Uncle, so don't worry about me,' she said, giving him a warm smile.

He kissed her cheek, and she watched him walk heavily towards the stairs, using the stick he was obliged to now.

'I'm not sure about that last remark of his,' Steven commented. 'I'm more than ready for bed.'

He took her hand and raised it to his lips as he spoke, and Lauri's heart leapt. She would have been blind not to recognise the desire in his eyes, and the meaning in his words. And they echoed a rising tide of passion in herself that she had never known until now.

'Steven, remember where we are,' she said in a low voice, suddenly nervous.

'I do remember, and an intimate little roadside inn seems a most delightful place to be for two people who want each other so badly.'

She caught her breath and looked at him mutely. He had never been so frank before, and even if his words echoed her own feelings, they scared her too.

'Steven, you know how dangerous it would be to let our feelings run away with us. My time here is still limited.'

'Why do you persist in saying such things?'

'Because they're true! After your birthday ball, I shall be thinking about going home—'

She stopped, knowing how bleak that prospect felt to her now, but anxious that he should understand.

'You needn't be alarmed, my love,' he said, more distantly than before. 'I'm not made of wood, but I'll always honour you. That's one promise you can be sure about.'

'Then I think perhaps we should go to bed as well. To our separate rooms, I mean,' she added nervously, in case he thought she was covertly issuing an invitation.

At his wry smile, she knew he guessed exactly what she was thinking, but he made no provocative remark. They left the room together, and parted company at their separate doors. And Lauri found herself unexpectedly bemoaning the fact that lovers were required to restrict themselves from all but the most benign of physical contacts before marriage.

She must be quite wicked at heart, she thought,

undressing quickly in the cold bedroom, and sliding into the narrow bed. It wasn't done for a woman to dream about a man with such yearning, even in the enlightened years since Queen Victoria had died and they had entered the Edwardian Age. There were still the strictures of protocol and accepted good behaviour, and she supposed there always would be. But none of it took account of feelings and emotions, and the frustrating knowledge that the man she loved was no more than the width of a wall away. And he was probably sleepless, too...

There was still a considerable distance to drive to Southampton in the morning. The ship sailed at noon, and there were all kinds of festivities to watch before she left the port, sailing first to Cherbourg to pick up passengers before heading for New York.

'I hope you have no deep regrets about today, Lauri,' Freda commented as the travellers prepared to leave the comfortable inn the following morning.

'I do not, ma'am,' Lauri assured her, hiding her true feelings. And wondering what the lady might think, to know she had construed her question rather differently.

For of course she had regrets, but of a rather different kind. She had regrets that she wasn't one of those fast and loose women who could have knocked boldly on Steven's door last night, and spent the hours in his arms... She felt her face flush as she caught Steven watching her, and from his small smile she had the certain feeling that he knew what she was thinking. But of course he did, since he would have been feeling the same way too...

Her heart lifted because, whatever else she was

losing in not going home on the great ship, she would be in close proximity to the man she loved, even if it was no more than a temporary love affair.

And a ship was only a ship, after all, however majestic and unsinkable she was…

Lauri revised all such thoughts the minute they approached Southampton. The whole town seemed to be *en fête*, with flags and bunting everywhere, bands playing, and people swarming like bees to get the best vantage point.

It was impossible not to be caught up in the excitement, and impossible not to be completely awed at the sight of the enormous vessel, unparalleled in size and luxury anywhere in the world, and the source of such national pride.

Lauri instantly recalled everything she had read about the ship, avid to know everything about it. Until this moment, she had pushed the memories out of her mind, but now they wouldn't be denied. She knew there was a swimming pool installed for those daring enough to use it; a skating rink and gymnasium where the more daring still could even take a mechanical camel ride; there were grand pianos and orchestras and libraries; a complete hospital for those unfortunate enough to be ill; even glorious rosebeds on deck, tended by a full-time gardener, to bring a continuing breath of home for British passengers.

The sketches of the interior that had been issued to the press had left Lauri gasping, and she had visualised it all so many times, glorying in the fact that she was going to know all those wonderful scenes…not least were the number of splendid dining-rooms and intimate cafés and restaurants, and the reported range of food to be taken on board sounded simply fabulous. Her mouth watered, just at the memory.

The images were still whirling around in her head when she felt the squeeze of Steven's hand on hers, under cover of the crush of people.

'There will be compensations, I assure you,' he said.

'I know,' she murmured, knowing how well he understood her feelings in these first moments. And how could she doubt what he said, when her visit promised so much more than an inanimate ocean crossing, however glittering and glamorous? She returned the brief clasp of his hand before they were temporarily separated by the crowd.

'Well, well, that was a pretty little scene,' she heard a mocking voice say. 'And how long has this been going on!'

She turned with a sigh, recognising the voice at once. How could anyone ever think it was identical to Steven's...? She was prepared to give Robert a scathing reply, when she saw the young woman hanging on his arm. Robert was an out-and-out ladies' man, though Lauri wasn't too sure that this one merited the title, and she wasn't above giving back as good as she got, verbally at least.

'I could say the same for you. Won't you introduce me to your companion? I'm sure your aunt would like to meet her.'

It was perfectly obvious that this didn't suit Robert or the girl. She tugged at Robert's arm, and he scowled at Lauri for her artless suggestion.

'Rose and I are meeting friends so we're not joining the party for the present. Perhaps you'd be good enough to pass the message on to my aunt. I doubt that she'll miss my company.'

Lauri watched as he and Rose moved away from her and melted into the crowd. There always seemed to be an undercurrent of anger in Robert, she realised. It could have come from the way his father never had much trust in him, and had always favoured Steven, she suspected. But all that was surely history now, and Robert was no longer a child. Then she remembered the late codicil on his father's Will, which was to be revealed on their birthdays. She shivered, thankful that such complications had never arisen in her own life. Wealth and position had its problems...

'So here you are,' she heard her uncle say. 'We were beginning to think we might have to send out search parties for you. We're going back to the cars for some refreshment.'

Lauri saw at once how heavily he leaned on his stick. It was a good thing his ankle was virtually better, or he might have been howling with pain whenever anyone came too close to it. But the stick was a useful tool to keep a clear passage for them all, and Vernon's persona was always impressive enough to make his presence known.

'I'll be glad of something to drink too,' she told him.

Steven and the older ladies joined them at that moment, and they headed back to the cars, where the picnic baskets were stowed. There were little snacks and champagne, as befitted such a celebratory occasion, and Lauri felt her head spin as she drank, realising how dry her throat had become in all the excitement.

But time was passing, and once it neared noon, they would want to be at a good vantage point— although, since the ship was so large, anywhere was a good vantage point. They were at as good a point as any, and they would be ready for their own departure once the ship had headed out through Southampton Water to the English Channel.

'Have you seen Robert?' Freda asked suddenly. 'He really is a bad boy, and never appears when he says he will.'

'I saw him briefly,' Lauri said, hiding her amusement at the description of Robert being 'a bad boy'. A boy he certainly was not, although she thought the rest of his aunt's comment was undoubtedly correct. It didn't endear him to her. If anything, it seemed to emphasise his immaturity.

Before anyone could question her further about Robert, they were hailed by Sir Gerald Hawkes and his family. The MP shook Steven's hand, then greeted the rest of the group.

'We knew we'd find you all here to bid *bon voyage* to this little lady, and it seemed a good opportunity to take a few days' holiday and call at the shipyard to see how the work is progressing on my yacht.'

He turned to Lauri. 'I'm happy we caught you before you embarked, my dear, but shouldn't you have done so already?'

Lauri stared at him, realising that of course he couldn't know of her decision not to travel today.

'I—I—' but somehow she couldn't get the words out, and she looked dumbly at her uncle. He supplied the information for her while she recovered herself.

'Lauri has decided not to leave us after all. The

darling girl is acting as my chauffeuse, since I foolishly sprained my ankle rather badly. So we're able to treat her as our daughter for a few weeks longer, at least.'

'How generous of you, Lauri,' Sir Gerald's wife exclaimed. 'But it must have been an enormous decision to give up such a voyage.'

'It surely was, of course,' Lauri said, not denying it as she tucked her hand inside her uncle's arm. 'But now the decision has been made, I'm looking forward to being a real Devonshire girl, and getting to know the county even better. And I know my father would be pleased I'd made this choice.'

'Well, as long as you're happy,' the lady said, shaking her head slightly, as if she couldn't understand anyone who would deny themselves such a great adventure.

'I am,' Lauri said, hoping that no one would interpret the warm, swift smile she gave to Steven Connors at that moment. Being on the brink of love was the happiest, most glorious feeling in the world...

But when the sirens began to blare out, accompanied by wild cheers as the departure time became imminent, she could no longer ignore the sick feeling in her stomach. It truly was one of the world's greatest adventures, she thought dramatically, and she had denied herself any part of it.

She felt Steven's hands on her shoulders as he stood behind her, and the small pressure of his fingers told her that he understood her feelings. Sunlight glinted on the bright gold band encircling the ship's hull as she edged away from the quayside, the out-

ward promise of all the gilded splendour inside. It
would all have been so magical...

'I can't promise you anything to match up to that,
but I'll try to make every day we're together equally
memorable, if you'll let me,' he said quietly.

She caught her breath. Until this moment the question of marriage had never come up, and she certainly shouldn't read any such hint into his words. It
was far too soon, and she was feminine enough to
want the luxury of an old-fashioned courtship. It
seemed as if the cautious Britishness she had inherited from her father was tempering the so-called
brashness of the American in her after all, she
thought.

But she leaned back against Steven for a moment,
not prepared to make any answer in this crowded
atmosphere. Besides, it hadn't been a question, and
maybe it had just been said to see how she would
respond. And her reply was not to respond at all.

By the time the ship had left Southampton and the
crowds had finally dispersed, people were hot and
exhausted, and beginning to be irritable. It was time
to drive back to the halfway inn for another night's
rest before returning home. Sir Gerald's family
would be in Kingscombe in two days' time, and
quickly accepted the dinner invitation at Connors
Court.

Lauri steered the yellow Wolseley carefully
through the crowded Southampton streets and out towards the open road west, feeling oddly disorientated
now, and trying not to imagine what the passengers
were doing on the ship at this minute; and trying
even more to forget what Steven had whispered to

her. She should have been thrilled, and so she was; but there was still that strange feeling of not wanting things to go too fast. She had had plenty of that from some of the college boys back home, who had looked for nothing more than a torrid affair, and she didn't want that sense of rushing things from Steven.

She was becoming alarmed at her own disturbing feelings, and in a moment of scary self-examination, she asked herself if she could actually be turning frigid. She would never have thought so. Her passionate nature in all things had always had to be curbed, and she was passionate about Steven. Or could be, given half the chance.

And maybe that was where the trouble lay, because she had never felt so deeply for anyone before, and she was afraid of just how far her own desire might lead her. Coupled with Steven's, it could prove a mighty and unstoppable force...and she was also aware of the shame and stigma on a young woman who let her passions run away with her.

It had happened to a well-connected young woman in Boston, ending in disgrace for her and the family, and ruining the girl's life.

No, it was far better to keep things on an even keel, even to act more coolly than she wished, and to make it clear that she had no intentions of getting amorously entangled with anyone for the present. She was only twenty years old, and there was all of life ahead of her.

She deliberately pushed Steven's image out of her thinking, knowing that she was denying herself something wonderful, but not yet prepared to fall headlong into a relationship from which there was no turning back. Even if she knew how far she had already fallen...

'Are you quite well, Lauri? You've become very quiet,' her uncle said, when she had driven in silence for some miles. 'Has today been too much for you after all?'

'I dare say it was more of a shock to my system than I realised it would be,' she answered, glad of the lifeline he had unwittingly thrown her. For what would her darling uncle think of her, to know she was contemplating whether or not she was frigid, and deciding to act like a nun in order to ward off her own desires for a man she hardly knew? Worse still, what would her more puritan-minded aunt think?

'We'll do all we can to make your stay a happy one, Lauri, dear,' Helen said from the back seat. 'We won't forget the sacrifice you've made on your uncle's account, although I begin to wonder if we should have allowed it, since he seems perfectly well now, and quite capable of driving himself.'

None of them could miss the suspicion in her voice, and Lauri knew she must bring Steven's name into it, despite her own convictions. But how bizarre it was, to pretend to her aunt that there was an affection between them, while deciding that nothing untoward must happen between them.

'My uncle wasn't the only reason I wanted to stay, Aunt Helen. You must have seen how I've grown to love everything here, and since Steven is such a gallant escort right on my doorstep, I'm having a wonderful time. In fact, I may never want to go home at all,' she added airily.

In her heart, she knew she had already decided on

that too, but she could hear the surprise and pleasure in Helen's voice now.

'I couldn't be more pleased if that was the case, and Steven is such a dear boy. Nothing would please me more.'

Lauri's laugh was a little strained. 'Now, don't go reading too much into what I said, Aunt. He's a gallant escort, not a prospective suitor!'

Why on earth was she feeling like this? she thought in some dismay. Recalling the ardent young Boston fellows who had tried to press their kisses on her, she knew it had all meant so little, and she had easily been able to laugh them off. However, Steven's kisses disturbed her so much because she was experiencing the first and only real love of her life, and it scared her. Lauri Hartman, smart and sophisticated as she was, could be as vulnerable as a country hick when it came to romance. It was some eye-opener, she admitted.

'Just be happy, Lauri. That's all I ask,' Helen was continuing seriously. 'Whatever you decide to do in life, you'll always have our wholehearted support.'

She was such a darling, thought Lauri.

'I know it, and I thank you for that. My father would thank you too, if he could.'

But if her father were still alive, she wouldn't even be here, since it was his legacy that had made the trip possible. It was strange how fate played its own game with people…and she must be getting touched in the head to be harbouring such dippy thoughts.

She changed the conversation as they travelled along the quieter roads with Southampton well behind them, saying the first thing that came into her head.

'Did you see Robert and his lady companion among the crowd? She looked very smart.'

Vernon snorted. 'She looked just the type of flighty young filly that Robert seems to favour these days. He has extraordinarily bad judgement of women, if you ask me, if the disappearing Alice Day was anything to go by.'

'Good heavens, I had forgotten all about her,' Lauri said, remembering the companion who had filched Freda Connors's belongings. '*She* certainly didn't look flighty—'

'But you can't judge a book by its cover, can you, dear?' Helen put in. 'Isn't that the way the saying goes?'

'That's right.' And if Robert and Alice had really had something of a fling, then you certainly couldn't judge a passionate woman by her appearance. Lauri was perfectly sure Robert wouldn't pursue anything less.

So was that how he saw *her*? As someone fast and flighty and ready for any kind of sport...? She flinched, knowing she was letting her imagination run riot, and that it must be the tension of this day that was filling her mind with such unwanted thoughts and images. This day, which should have been the culmination of such dreams...

'I shan't be sorry to reach the inn,' she said. 'And I'm sure you'll be glad of a rest when we arrive, Aunt Helen.'

'We both will,' Vernon put in. 'You and the boys can amuse yourselves until it's time for supper, I'm sure. I presume Robert will deign to join his family, since there's a room booked for him.'

The thought gave Lauri a decidedly shivery feeling. Steven was too gentlemanly to knock at her door during the night. But Robert...? And now she really *was* seeing things that weren't there, she thought, angry with herself.

Ahead of them she could see Steven's car, leading the way back to the inn. Where Robert was now, was anybody's guess, and it wouldn't worry her if he didn't turn up at all.

He did, of course. And he was alone, although Lauri was sure she could smell Rose's cheap perfume on his clothes. Either that, or he was purchasing some very effeminate toiletries for himself, and she didn't think that of him.

'Well, this is a cosy get-together, isn't it, bruth?' he said arrogantly, when the three of them were seated in the comfortable visitors' room, and the older members of the party had retired for an hour or so.

'I'm surprised you bothered to join us in this humble establishment,' Steven commented. 'I would have thought you had other fish to fry, as usual.'

Robert laughed. 'What, and miss the chance of seeing the delectable Miss Hartman?' He raised his glass of wine to her as he spoke, and Lauri felt her face flush.

'Robert...' Steven said warningly, and his brother's eyes widened in mock innocence.

'What have I said? I'm sure Lauri isn't averse to a few well-deserved compliments, are you, dear girl?'

'It depends on whether they're sincere or not,' she retorted. 'And it depends on who is making them.'

He laughed, and she thought there was no shaming him. He was so sure of his own masculinity he simply brushed aside the thought of any woman resisting him.

'If that's meant to put me in my place, sweetness, it only makes me more eager for the chase,' he said insultingly.

'For God's sake, Robert, if you can't be more subtle than that, then keep your thoughts to yourself,' Steven snapped, his eyes furious, and his hands clenched.

Before he could reply, Lauri spoke up for herself.

'I don't need to listen to any of this nonsense. You might just remember that I've had quite a day, one way and another, and I'm tired from driving. If you don't mind—and even if you do—I'm going to take a bath, and I hope you'll have calmed down by supper-time, otherwise we're all in for a disagreeable evening.'

And if you dare to offer to scrub my back, Robert, I shall slap you.

But not even Robert would be so crass, she thought savagely, as she stalked out of the visitors' room, wishing the thought had never entered her mind at all. His bedroom was in another part of the inn, and she was thankful for that too. Though just why she was getting into such an almighty tizz about him, she couldn't think. He meant nothing to her— and any woman who fell for Robert's straying eyes would need her wits about her for the rest of her life, Lauri thought keenly.

But when he and Steven became heated with one another it was sometimes hard to separate them. It was only when she and Steven were alone that it was all so different…

She collected her things from her room and sped

along the corridor to the bathroom. She wallowed in the bathwater for as long as she dared, dreamy-eyed, and wondering if she was being a fool in not agreeing to let the world know of their growing feelings for one another. But she still preferred to hold back for a while.

Lauri shivered slightly, realising the bathwater had gone a little cold. She stepped out of it swiftly, swathing herself in towels and then donning her nightgown and a heavy dressing-gown before speeding back along the corridor to her bedroom. But not quickly enough.

'This is a sight a gentleman doesn't often get the chance to see,' Robert's sardonic voice accosted her. She put her hand on her door handle, and his hand covered hers at once.

'A gentleman would have lingered at the end of the corridor until the lady had got inside her room, rather than embarrass her,' Lauri retorted.

He laughed. 'This is the twentieth century, sweetness, not the Dark Ages. I'd have thought you were new-worldly enough not to be embarrassed at such a minor indiscretion.'

Lauri's face flamed. 'I think you have a very poor opinion of women, Robert.'

'On the contrary, my pet, I think very highly of women, especially those who allow me a little favour...'

He leaned towards her, and his fingers were still firmly fastened over hers so that she couldn't open her bedroom door. She knew he was about to kiss her, and she didn't want it. His other arm was tight around her waist now, and she wrestled silently with him, not wanting to rouse the entire inn and cause a scandal.

And then he was wrenched away from her.

'You just don't know when to stop, do you?' Steven snapped at his brother, his eyes as cold as steel. 'Can't you see that Lauri is disgusted with you?'

'And your attentions are so welcome, are they, bruth?' Robert sneered, and when they both said nothing, his eyes narrowed, and he looked from one to the other. 'Or have I been missing something while I've been away from home?'

Before Steven could say anything to confirm or deny it, Lauri had opened her door and burst inside, slamming it shut behind her. And if that hadn't wakened the entire place, she didn't know what would!

She could still hear raised voices outside her door, and she prayed that they would move away to settle their differences. But then a few words caught her attention, and she pressed her ear to the door, unable to resist listening.

'Once the bloody shipyard belongs to me, I'll have my say in a lot of things, and you can go to hell,' Robert was taunting now.

'And I'll have plenty to say about that—'

'You'll be helpless to do anything. Whatever the lawyer's got to tell us, it'll be watertight, and not even Father would deny his son his birthright, however mad he became.'

'You're not his only son—'

'But I'm the eldest, and don't you forget it.'

'I'm never likely to,' Lauri heard Steven say bitterly, 'since you're forever reminding me.'

As the voices faded, Lauri realised they had

moved away from her door. She was sick and trembling at overhearing the squabble, and even more so at knowing she hadn't *had* to listen, if she hadn't been so darned curious.

But as she dressed quickly for the evening, she realised that at least the little scene had managed to divert her thoughts from the disappointment of this day. She had stopped imagining where the *Titanic* was steaming to now, and what the most fortunate passengers in the world were doing at this moment. She had stopped thinking of anything except that she had no wish to be a point of dispute between two brothers.

Supper that evening might have been difficult and strained, had it not been for her uncle's determination to make it a jolly occasion with champagne, evidently suspecting that Lauri was hiding her natural feelings at the outcome of this day.

In any case, it served to supply the reason for her shadowed eyes, and the fact that she was quieter than usual. And the two older ladies were full of the sight of the great ship, and could talk about nothing else. Steven was attentive to them both, but to Lauri's relief Robert hadn't joined them for supper.

'I trust you'll forgive his lack of manners, Lauri, my dear,' Freda said. 'Robert has always followed his own pursuits, and his absence doesn't mean any slight to you.'

'I assure you I never thought anything of the kind,' Lauri told her, thinking that the company was considerably more relaxed without Robert's presence, anyway.

All the same, she was glad when the ladies retired,

and Vernon stayed down jawing with some of the regulars at the inn. She said goodnight to him, and Steven escorted her upstairs, and paused at her door.

'Look, you know I'm sorry about what happened earlier,' he said abruptly.

'Why should you be? It wasn't your fault,' she said, suddenly awkward. Part of her wanted desperately to invite him inside, to feel his arms around her and to make her forget everything but the fact that they loved one another. And another part of her rejected the very idea, knowing that if they were once alone together in such compromising circumstances, there would be no turning back...

He spoke slowly. 'You don't understand, do you? What affects Robert, affects me. The bond between twins is powerful and unique. It can draw them close or tear them apart. But they can never deny it, however much they hate being two sides of the same coin, so to speak.'

'But you're not!' Lauri said, finding it strange that he should speak of themselves as if they were two other people. 'In outlook and temperament you're so very different—'

'Are we?' His voice was bitter. 'Sometimes I wonder, especially when it's obvious we want the same thing, and will fight tooth and nail to get it.'

For a moment, Lauri thought he was referring to herself, and her face paled. Because she didn't want Robert wanting her...and then she realised Steven was thinking of something quite different.

'But if he means to sell the shipyard and destroy everything my father and I have built up, then I'll go to every court in the land to keep him from getting his greedy hands on it.'

Lauri said nothing. In any case it was going to be his father's words in the codicil that would put the final seal on what was to become of the shipyard. And none of them really knew what that codicil was as yet. But this wasn't the time to speak of it, and it wasn't her place…

'Steven, why don't you sleep on it?' she said quietly, putting her hand on his arm. 'Things always look better in the daylight.'

It was an aimless thing to say, and she knew it certainly didn't happen that way, but right now she couldn't think of anything better. And after a swift glance along the corridor, he took her in his arms and kissed her waiting lips. It held none of the passion of previous times, but to Lauri it was as emotional a kiss as any other.

'Goodnight,' she whispered, before she went into her room, and wishing, rightly or wrongly, that she had had the courage to ask him to stay with her tonight.

Chapter Eleven

The next few days consisted of a round of engagements for the Connors and the Hartmans. Sir Gerald Hawkes and his family were staying in the area for two more days, and were invited to each house for dinner, where both families converged. It seemed as if they were all destined to live in one another's pockets for the time being, thought Lauri, but by now her uncle had tried out his ankle in his beloved Wolseley and declared himself fit enough to drive again.

'So you're relieved of the task for the moment, Lauri, though there will still be times when I'll be glad of my chauffeuse,' he announced.

'And you know I'll always be happy to oblige, Uncle,' she said, though secretly it was a relief not to be always on call, and to be able to go off by herself in her own small car. There were times when she was simply glad to be alone.

She glanced at her aunt. Helen had kept tolerably well during the hectic days that had just passed, but she was looking paler right now, and Lauri thought it would be good when these London folk departed, and they could all relax a little more.

Almost to her own surprise, Lauri realised how she was putting herself in the role of countrywoman, and she knew how very tempting it was becoming to settle for good in her father's native county. Even if it was merely as a surrogate daughter, and nothing more…

Lauri didn't overlook the fact that it was mainly because of her aunt's health that she had really decided to remain here, even if the lady wasn't aware of it yet. Soon she would tell her, she decided. Soon, she would say that she wanted to stay in Devonshire, at least for the foreseeable future… Now that the Hawkes family had gone, she spent hours walking in the lanes and breathing in the scent of the hedgerows and wild spring flowers, glorying in the pleasures of the county.

And trying to put out of her mind the disturbing thought that she hadn't had a proper conversation with Steven in days. He was perceptive enough to know that something was amiss, and might well be simply giving her time to get over the hectic days that had just passed. But a vivacious young woman of twenty years shouldn't need time for such things… She commented on his absence to her uncle, hoping she didn't sound resentful.

'I know Steven had some business dealings to conduct recently,' her uncle told her. 'I gather this big project he's been doing for Sir Gerald is almost completed, and there are some legalities to sort out.'

And it would be a good chance to try to get the lawyer to divulge something of what lay ahead, Lauri surmised. But since she knew that lawyers were usually as closed as clams, she doubted that he would get anything out of him.

She saw the sudden twinkle in her uncle's eyes.

'I wouldn't let it worry you, love,' he said with a grin. 'If I'm anything of an observer, I would say the boy's head over heels about a certain young lady. He's certainly not his brother, with a girl in every port of call.'

'Do you really believe that about Robert?' she asked, turning the conversation away from herself.

Vernon shrugged. 'I'm surprised he hasn't had plenty of irate papas in England chasing after him. But so far he's always managed to keep the hounds at bay.'

'What a rogue you make him out to be, Uncle!' Lauri said with a laugh, knowing how irresistibly dangerous such a charmer could be to the female sex, and glad that she hadn't been one of them.

'So he is, and we've always known it. I'm just very thankful you didn't fall for him yourself.'

But she might have done so, she mused honestly, if Steven hadn't been the yardstick to measure him by…and if she'd been born yesterday.

Steven's motor came roaring up to the house at high speed the following morning, while Lauri and her aunt and uncle were still having a late breakfast. It was so unusual to see him at such an hour and in such obvious disarray that they knew at once that something must be wrong. But surely it wouldn't be anything to do with Freda, or he would have telephoned.

Therefore, it must be something that concerned the

Hartman family more personally… Lauri's logical mind spun through the alternatives as if her life depended on it, just as if she wanted to stave off the inevitable moment when she sensed she was going to be told something terrible… She didn't like premonitions, but there were times when even the sanest of people admitted them, and she was no exception.

'Well, you're an early visitor, my boy,' Vernon said at once, not having the same intuitive sense of disaster.

'Can I talk to you all privately, sir? It's a matter of great importance,' he said in a clipped voice. The maids were still clearing the dining-table, and Vernon nodded at once, and led his family to the drawing-room.

The ladies sat down, while Vernon stood expectantly, and Steven's face was a mask of anxiety, as if he would give anything not to share this moment.

'Are you going to tell us why you're here, Steven?' Lauri said nervously, knowing that somebody had to break the sudden deadlock of silence that seemed to have engulfed them all.

'Yes, my boy, I think you'd better tell us at once,' her uncle said sharply, as if suddenly aware that this was certainly no normal early-morning visit.

Steven nodded. 'Very well. Sir Gerald Hawkes telephoned me early this morning. He thought it best to speak to me first, rather than come directly to you, but there's no way I can stop you knowing, Lauri, and everybody will know soon—'

'Dear God, what's happened?' she whispered through dry lips. By now she had risen to her feet, and moved to his side without knowing how she reached him. She clung to his arm, seeing his dark, haunted eyes, and knew that whatever her presentiment of disaster was, it was about to be realised.

'There's no easy way for me to tell you, so I'll come straight out with it. It's the *Titanic*. She's gone down. Struck an iceberg and gone down with the loss of so many lives, and—oh God, it's just terrible—'

Helen gave a muffled cry, and Vernon swore loudly and expressively without bothering to excuse himself. And Lauri heard her own incredulous, high-pitched laughter.

'Don't be *stupid*, Steven. How can she go down? She's unsinkable. Everybody knows that.'

The laughter died as quickly as it had burst out, and she felt as though her limbs were turning to water as she clung to Steven. The unwelcome analogy didn't escape her.

'What did Sir Gerald say, Steven?' Vernon snapped. 'Tell us exactly, boy, and don't mince words.'

'God knows how it happened. They say the night was clear and icy cold, but the sea was as calm as a sheet of glass. The passengers were at dinner, when the look-out spotted an iceberg shortly before midnight. The ship turned hard to port, but it was too late. Once the damage was confirmed, it was estimated that there were around two hours before she sank, and all the passengers were called to the lifeboats.'

He ignored Helen's gasp, and went on, too enmeshed in the grim detail of his tale to pause now.

'They don't know the extent of it all yet, but there may have been about fifteen hundred still on board when she finally went down. Some of the rescued have described how they watched the bow going down with the stern rising higher all the time. All the lights were still blazing on the eight decks as she disappeared. It must have been a horrific sight.'

He went on relentlessly, as if wound up by a spring, and needing to tumble everything out at once while the others listened in silent horror.

'Distress rockets were fired, of course, but passing ships probably assumed it was nothing more than fireworks. The survivors are saying that even more than an hour later, while the ship was up-ending so ominously, they could still hear the band on the boat deck playing ragtime, and for some inexplicable reason any ships in the vicinity were not responding to any wireless messages. Of the people still stranded on deck, Sir Gerald reports that there were many steerage deck families, as well as the Captain and senior officers—'

'Stop it!' Helen suddenly gasped out. 'That's enough! I can't bear to hear any more of this—'

Lauri realised how ragged her aunt's breathing was becoming, and she saw her fumble in a pocket for the ever-present bottle of smelling salts. Her own breath was tight in her chest as she grasped the enormity of all that Steven told them in that flat, dead voice, as if he dreaded showing too much emotion for fear of breaking down.

'We *must* hear it, my dear,' Vernon rapped out. 'It will be in every newspaper in the country later on today, and it's every Englishman's duty to mourn the poor souls who didn't survive such an ordeal.'

'But *Lauri* would have been among them. Don't you have any imagination, Vernon?' his wife almost screamed now.

'I'm trying not to have,' he said grimly, seeing exactly where his wife's thoughts were leading her.

Lauri's mind was going in the same direction. But for her decision to remain behind in England, she, too, might have been one of those poor, wretched survivors...or maybe not. The terrifying image of floundering in that icy-cold water and being sucked beneath it to her death was the only thing in her head at that moment, and her blood felt as if it had turned as cold as that evil, treacherously beautiful water.

She hardly realised how badly she was shaking until Steven grasped her arms, uncaring that it was hardly his place to do so. But by then, out of the corner of her eyes, she could see that her uncle was more concerned with attending to Helen, who seemed to have slipped into a dead faint.

'I would have given anything not to have brought you such news,' Steven said harshly against her cheek as he held her close. In the circumstances, it was no more than a friend would do, and it should have been an enormous comfort to have him near.

But, perversely, she almost hated him for having to tell her at all. She struggled to get out of his embrace, but he still held her fast.

'I must go to my aunt,' she gasped. 'She's unwell, and all this will have been a great shock to her—'

'Your uncle is taking care of her. And what about the shock to you, my love?' he said in a low voice. 'You'll be feeling an even greater shock than any of us about all this, and it will take you a while to recover. Don't try to be all things to all people.'

She finally extricated herself from his arms, and where she had felt so icy cold just minutes before, now she felt as though her blood was on fire. *But for the grace of God*…and the persuasiveness of this loving family… She could think of nothing else. She rushed to her aunt's side, seeing the pallor in her face. Her eyes were closed, and Vernon was doing his best to revive her, but the smelling salts were having no effect at all.

It would be the worst of ironies, Lauri thought in agony, if her aunt suffered a stroke at hearing of the appalling tragedy from which her niece had been mercifully spared.

'We should send for Dr Vine at once, Uncle,' she stuttered. 'She needs proper medical help.'

'If you'll allow me, sir, I'll telephone him for you and explain the circumstances,' Steven said at once.

'Please do. I don't think I can bear to repeat it.'

The starkness of his words told Lauri more than anything how much he was fearing for her aunt's health. He was normally so garrulous, but the news, and the effect it had had on his wife, were clearly taking a terrible toll on him too. He looked old, and ill… She straightened up.

'The telephone is in the library,' she said to Steven, and without asking, she went with him to the wood-panelled room, guiltily thankful for the chance to leave the other two alone for a few moments.

'Lauri, darling—' Steven began at once, and she backed away from him.

'No, please don't,' she said in a brittle voice. 'I've no emotions left in me but anxiety for my aunt right now. I don't want to think of anything else.'

Not even him. And she knew that the time for her vivid imagination to hold her in thrall again would come later. She had been spared the actuality of the disaster, but she knew herself too well. All the images of what might have been would be like moving pictures in her mind, as keen as memories. She would have to face them eventually, but not yet.

She heard Steven asking for the doctor's number, and then he rapidly explained why he was calling. Lauri closed her mind, not wanting to hear about the *Titanic*'s fate all over again. She just prayed that the doctor would hurry, and tell them all that Aunt Helen was going to be all right.

'He'll be here directly,' Steven told her when he put down the receiver. 'If you want to go back to your aunt and uncle, I'll find Cook and organise some brandy.'

'Yes. Thank you,' Lauri said woodenly. She felt as lifeless as a leaf in the wind now, unable to think for herself, and ready to be directed wherever anyone decreed.

She saw Steven look at her warily, before he took her arm to lead her out of the library and back to the others. This time, she didn't resist. If she had done so, she thought the effort would probably have used up what little strength she had left. She had never felt so disorientated, or so afraid. She swallowed hard, realising that fear was one of the major feelings inside her now. She had so nearly lost her life…

Her aunt had still not recovered consciousness when Steven left her in the drawing-room to fetch some brandy. She didn't know if it was a good idea to give it to Helen in the circumstances, but she couldn't think sensibly, and she left it to the others to decide.

'The doctor will be here soon,' she told Vernon. 'Should we move her, do you think?'

He shook his head. 'I think not. The less exertion she has, the better. But I'm afraid this news has had a traumatic effect on her.'

'Yes,' Lauri said.

Her uncle looked at her sharply, seeing how large her eyes looked now in her pinched, white face. The blue eyes seemed to burn with a strange fire, and he felt a stab of alarm. Until now, all his thoughts had been with his wife.

'And what of you, my love?'

'What of me? I'm still here, and I thank God that I am, but it fills me with a terrible sense of guilt to know that I survived, when someone else must have been so thrilled to take my ticket and my passage.'

She hadn't really formed the thought in her head before, but now that it was there, she knew it would be difficult to be rid of it. Because of her, someone else had probably perished in the icy waters of the Atlantic, drowning in the dark, terrified and alone, the way that everyone was alone in their last moments. People would tell her it was needlessly irrational to think that she was responsible for someone else's death, but she knew it was true, and it was all she could think about at that moment.

'Drink this.'

She was hardly aware that Steven was thrusting a cold glass to her shaking lips now, or that she was trembling so much she knew she would spill most of the bitter liquid he tried to force down her. He held her head still, and pushed the glass between her teeth until it hurt, and the brandy trickled down her chin and stained her morning dress as she swallowed what she could with an almighty effort.

'That's better,' he spoke almost accusingly in her

ear. 'How do you think you're going to help your aunt if you fall apart now? They need you to be strong.'

She stared at him. Didn't he know that she *wasn't* strong? And she wanted to weep, and rail, and scream… She didn't want Steven Connors telling her what she should do, or how she should behave…she resented his very intrusion into her innermost feelings…

If it was contrary to everything that had passed between them to feel so, she was just sane enough to know it was because the first surge of impotent rage had to be concentrated on someone.

And he was the nearest, and the most obvious…and the anger inside her now was the only real emotion she had felt since he had arrived at the house. It was such a short while ago, and yet it had changed the tone of her life.

He didn't deserve her anger, but right now, she couldn't spare any more of her precious emotions to tell him so.

'Thank God, the doctor's here,' she heard him say a little later.

He went to greet him, taking charge, even though he was the stranger in the house. But he was more than that, Lauri reminded herself. He was a neighbour, and a friend, a very dear friend… She brushed the thought aside as Dr Vine entered the drawing-room and went straight to his patient, to take her pulse and sound her chest.

'This is a bad business, sir,' he said briefly to Vernon, 'but you can thank your stars that the little lady wasn't on the ship, or you'd be grieving for more than a recurrence of your good wife's troubles.'

Lauri gasped at the callousness of the man, but presumably a doctor was so hardened to the precarious nature of birth and death and everything in between, that he saw nothing untoward in his statement. She was just thankful that her aunt hadn't heard it, though to her great relief, she saw that Helen's eyelids were beginning to flicker.

'Good,' the doctor said. 'If she had been out of her senses for much longer, we might have had more troubles to deal with. As it is, she's suffering badly from shock. I recommend several weeks of complete rest, since this will have set her back considerably. The great consolation is that she has the young lady to attend her.'

Then I'm glad to be of use, and it's a jolly good thing I didn't go down with the ship, Lauri thought, and was immediately aghast to think she might have said it out loud. But she obviously hadn't, and she swallowed hard and nodded.

'I'll be here as long as my aunt needs me,' she murmured. 'In fact, I shall probably stay here indefinitely now. Certainly, the very last thing I could think about in the foreseeable future is taking a sea voyage.'

She shuddered, thinking how strangely fate was shaping her life. She had spoken quickly, but what she said was absolutely true. Setting foot on board a ship now would be as terrifying as stepping into a pit of vipers.

'They say the best way to overcome such a fear is to get right back onto it,' she heard Steven say. 'Even a trip around the bay would help to dispel your worries.'

'I don't think so,' she told him coldly, wondering

if the whole world was going to be so insensitive from now on. 'Anyway, I'll be needed here to care for Aunt Helen.'

'I'm not an invalid, dear,' Helen said in a thin voice, and saying the first words she had uttered since her faint. 'But if you really mean that you're not going to leave us, it will do my heart a power of good.'

'I'm not leaving you, Aunt Helen,' Lauri said in a choked voice, at her side once more, and squeezing her hand.

It wasn't solely on her aunt's account now, though, or even because she had found the love of her life. Here, she was safe. Because of being here, she had cheated death. She wouldn't think beyond that, even if it meant she was feeling more of a coward than in the whole of her life so far.

As expected, from then on the whole country was talking about nothing but the fate of the so-called unsinkable ship. Coming so soon after the massive displays of excitement as she left Southampton on her maiden voyage, the stark reality of the disaster was even more terrible.

The newspapers were full of reports, some garbled and wild, but making good newspaper copy; others supposedly straight from the mouths of the survivors; and yet more from the ships who might have been able to help, had they understood the significance of the *Titanic*'s flares and the inevitable end of the luxurious vessel.

Nothing could have saved her from the ripping terror of the iceberg or the swiftness with which the sea engulfed her. But so many more lives might have been saved had the distress signals been heeded, but in Lauri Hartman's head only one life had tragically ended, and that was the life of the person who had bought her ticket.

She knew it was crazy to try to surmise anything about him or her. The person might be alive and well, and one of the many survivors who had lived to tell the tale, and was relishing the fame, as some of them undoubtedly were. But then again, maybe not. It was something that continued to haunt her, no matter how much she tried not to let it.

Robert Connors was under no illusions about the way she should handle her problems. Back home from his few days away, and already satiated with the news, he called on the Hartmans for news of Helen's condition, and confronted a white-faced Lauri in the conservatory, looking far less than the vibrant girl he remembered, and more like a little waif. Once he discovered the reason for it, he was brusque to the point of rudeness.

'You've got to stop feeling guilty, Lauri. Just thank your lucky stars that you're still here. Or, if you believe in such things, then just accept that Somebody Up There was looking after you, and deciding that it wasn't your time to join Him in the Great Upstairs.'

'I don't like that kind of talk,' she snapped. She might not be a regular churchgoer, but she had prayed constantly since the disaster, asking for guidance and trying to come to terms with her own unnecessary guilt.

'Why not? Because you know how futile it is? You don't know who bought your ticket or what happened to him. It's history now, Lauri, and you can't change it.'

'I know that. But he must have a family who will be devastated, and how do you think that makes me feel?'

She was breathing shallowly now, the way her aunt did when an asthma attack was coming on. She felt faint, and the heady scent of the exotic flowers and the heat of the conservatory were making beads of perspiration stand out on her forehead. She didn't want to put a name or a face to her replacement, but she couldn't get him out of her mind, either.

And then someone's arms were around her, holding her close. Someone was speaking softly in her ear, and nuzzling his chin against her cheek. Someone who was taking every advantage of this moment when she felt so vulnerable…

'Thank you for your concern, Robert,' she said, struggling to get away from him. 'But I don't need mollycoddling, and I'm perfectly all right now.'

She wasn't, but she had no wish to be standing here with this man's arms around her, practically compromising herself in broad daylight. She eased herself away from him and they moved outside, but he kept her arm tucked in his as they found a bench seat in the grounds for her to recover herself.

'Just promise me one thing,' he said arrogantly.

'What's that?'

'That you'll make no attempt whatever to try to find out who it was who bought your ticket. Because if you do, it's a sure route to madness, Lauri.'

'I know you're right,' she said slowly, admitting that such a wild thought had entered her mind—and that he was more perceptive than she had believed to think of it too.

'Good,' he went on, immediately dashing the illusion of the good guy. 'Because I don't see you as Lady Bountiful, carrying goods and chattels to the poor and needy. And you can bet your bottom dollar, as you quaint colonials say, that once those people got wind of the fact that you were feeling guilty and desperate to help them any way you could, they'd play on your sympathies, and take you for every cent you've got.'

'My Lord, you're all heart, aren't you, Robert?'

'No. Just practical. I leave the dreaming to my brother.'

'Oh, really? I doubt that many folk would consider a practical businessman like Steven a dreamer!' she said, defending him, and seeing Robert's caustic smile.

'Well, it's easy to see he's found a champion in you. But he'll have to find some other business to occupy himself if he can't buy me out when the time comes.'

'You're not really serious about that, are you?' She was thankful to be talking about something other than the disaster, even though this was none of her business.

He shrugged. 'Why not? It means nothing to me—'

'But it means everything to Steven.'

Robert's eyes flashed with anger. 'And if we're going to continue getting biblical on this fine afternoon, then I might remind you that I'm not my brother's keeper.'

She extricated herself from his grip on her arm.

'I thank you for your company, but I'm going inside the house now,' she said deliberately. 'My aunt will be wondering where I am.'

He leaned towards her before she could stand up.

'How about one kiss, for friendship's sake?' he said mockingly, as if knowing full well it wouldn't be for any other reason.

She jerked back from him. 'And how about saving your kisses for ladies who appreciate them?' she snapped, and whirled away from him before he could reach out and pull her back. Her heart thudded. She didn't like him, but she couldn't deny the animal attraction of him. He would probably be a good lover, the wickedly sensual part of her told her...and a bad enemy. Not that there was ever a good one...

'Has Robert gone already?' her aunt said in surprise, as Lauri joined her in the drawing-room. 'Didn't you ask him to stay for afternoon tea?'

'He had business to attend to. You know Robert. Always flitting here, there and everywhere,' Lauri said glibly, and thinking she couldn't have borne sitting here listening to him making polite small talk with her aunt.

She didn't know how much of it she could bear herself, and she realised with some alarm that she was in danger of shutting herself off from the world with her thoughts. It would pass, she told herself wildly. It had to be no more than a natural reaction to the thought of all those people herded together in death...

She flinched, spilling her tea. At this rate, she would have no dress left in her closet that wasn't stained, she thought hysterically...

'It's time we thought about our costumes for the Connors masked ball,' Helen said.

Lauri looked at her stupidly, wondering if she could possibly have heard aright. She saw her aunt give a slight smile as she went on.

'I know what you're thinking, Lauri. How can you turn your mind to something so frivolous, when such a terrible event has just occurred? But when there's nothing you can do about it, it's the only way, my love. You can only grieve for so long for those poor souls, and then you have to let the memory go, or it will eat into your life like a cancer.'

'I'll never let the memory go—'

'Yes, you will, and you must. Your uncle and I will do all we can to help you. We all have to deal with things in our own way, but in the end we have to accept the things that can never be changed.'

'You don't understand, Aunt Helen—'

'I believe I do. If my guess is correct, you're putting yourself in the place of the poor unfortunate who took your place, is that it?'

Lauri shook her head slowly. 'I was, but now I'm thinking more about those he or she left behind.'

'Well, *don't*. All humanity will be sad for them and all the others like them, but they're no personal concern of yours. The sooner you get that into your head, the better.'

Lauri gave the ghost of a smile again. 'And I thought I was supposed to be cheering you up by being here! Instead of which, I seem to be dragging you down.'

'Nonsense, you could never do that,' Helen said briskly. 'But I insist that we start to cheer each other up by thinking about our masquerade costumes. If there's nothing suitable in the old trunks in the attic, then we must have something made, and that will take time.'

It still sounded callous to Lauri, but she knew that Helen too had her own way of getting over catastrophes. She too, would be imagining how different things might have been, and that this might well have been a house of mourning by now. But in a strange way, she seemed stronger than Lauri herself. Perhaps it was because, at her age, she had seen more people come and go, Lauri thought cynically...

'You're sure they'll still continue with the ball?' she asked quickly. 'In the circumstances, I wondered. This is a national disaster, after all.'

'Lauri, there are some things that you can't change. One is the moment you're born and the other is the moment you die. We all have to make the best of what comes in between, and to celebrate whatever milestones we're lucky enough to reach. Robert and Steven won't cancel their birthday ball, and besides, it's still a month away. The sadness and shock of the disaster will have faded by then. It's the way of things, my dear, and there's no altering it.'

She was a wise woman, thought Lauri, and in her own saner moments, she knew that she was right. Sorrow didn't last for ever, even when you almost hungered for the pain of it to keep the memories alive a little longer. Her lips trembled, knowing she was thinking of her father at that moment, but she took a deep breath, seeing the concern in her aunt's eyes.

'You're so right, Aunt Helen, and I'll try not to let it consume all my thinking. But just give me another day or so, and I'll try to think more positively about things.'

Though how she could project her thoughts into a night of frivolous dancing and harmless flirting and enjoying herself, was as alien to her right now as flying to the moon.

Then she paused, eyeing her aunt more keenly.

'But you're supposed to be having several weeks of complete rest on doctor's orders, Aunt Helen.'

'Piffle,' the lady said inelegantly. 'I'll rest when I need it. Right now I need to feel part of the world again—and so do you.'

Chapter Twelve

It was true, Lauri thought. There were days of intense newspaper attention about the fate of the *Titanic* and its passengers, and then it was overtaken by other events. If the world was fickle in the duration of its outward show of sympathy, it was also something of a relief, she thought. It helped to lessen her own sense of guilt, which she had finally accepted was useless.

A local fund was set up to help the relatives of those survivors who needed it, to which the Hartmans had given generously. Most of the passengers, though not all, had been wealthy, but certainly most of the crew were not, and it was hoped that their families wouldn't be too proud to accept charitable gifts. In that respect, the community felt that they were doing something, however little.

'My family have done the same,' Steven said, calling on them one fine morning in early May. 'But no one should dwell on it to the point of obsession, and that's why I'm proposing to take Lauri out in the bay today. The sea's as calm as a millpond—'

He saw her shudder, and knew at once that it had

been a bad and insensitive choice of words. The Atlantic had also been calm and beautiful on that April night...

'You know I can't do that,' she said flatly.

'You can, and I never thought you were a chicken. I thought that description was reserved for far lesser mortals than someone who had already crossed the Atlantic.'

This time he was deliberate, challenging her, and ignoring her stormy eyes as she glared back at him. He was hateful to do this, and the fact that her uncle was encouraging her to do exactly as Steven wished didn't make her feel any better.

'What harm can it do, my dear?' Vernon said. 'We can't show gloomy faces forever, and a day out in the sunshine will do you good, and bring back some colour to your cheeks.'

Thank God he omitted to mention the bracing sea air as well, she thought.

'Well?' Steven persisted. 'We don't have to be out for very long, and we could have a spot of lunch along the coast first, if you like. It's far too nice a day to be indoors—or to be working.'

Before she could reply, he reached out and drew her to her feet. 'You know you'll always be safe with me, Lauri.'

And if that was meant to be an enigmatic remark, everyone chose to ignore it.

Ten minutes later saw them driving away from Hartman House towards the coast, and with every mile they drove, and with the tang of the sea coming ever nearer, Lauri told herself that this was a big mistake, and if she had any sense, she would tell

Steven to stop the car right now. She felt his hand cover hers and hold it tightly for a moment.

'You know what they say, don't you? I'm sure I've told you before. Face your dragon.'

'Well, even if I've heard it before,' she said, prepared to be belligerent, 'I think it's just about the most idiotic saying I know. Who in their right minds would face a dragon!'

But she caught the smile in his eyes before she said what was becoming uppermost in her mind.

'We're not going out on Sir Gerald's boat, are we?'

'No,' Steven said. 'The privilege of taking her on her maiden voyage is reserved for the owner himself.'

He had said other words now that still made her flinch. *Maiden voyage*…it had been the *Titanic*'s maiden voyage too. But they were only words, nothing more, and she was being stupid to let them worry her.

They had lunch at a riverside inn, and when they reached the boatyard, Steven pointed out a much smaller sailing-boat than the gleaming vessel that was now adorned with bunting and awaiting its owner. Lauri's heart beat very fast as she stepped on board, but her hand was very firmly held in Steven's, and she couldn't let him down—or herself.

'I'm fine,' she lied, and quite suddenly she knew she must do this. It was right what people said. Facing your dragon was the only way to overcome your fear of it. Unless the dragon slayed you in the process, of course.

But in the end, the short cruise around the bay wasn't so bad, and she felt her jangled nerves slowly beginning to unwind. The breeze blew softly through the sails, and there was no other noise except the creak of the rudder and the swish of the water as the boat cut through it so effortlessly. It was another world…a world away from traumas, and she made herself believe it.

'Is the exorcism taking effect?' Steven spoke casually, when they were drifting slowly back to the boatyard on the swell of the tide.

'I think so,' Lauri said honestly. This small craft couldn't be compared with an ocean liner, but if she could feel safe and secure on the water now, then there must be something to be said for the power of its tranquillity.

'There's something I have to tell you, Lauri,' he said, his voice graver than before. 'And this might be the best time to say it.'

She looked at him sharply. She had been so wrapped up in her own fears that she hadn't been aware of any restraint in his voice. But she was aware of it now.

'What is it?'

He took a deep breath. 'I wish I didn't have to tell you at all, but when Robert got wind of it, he was obliged to tell Aunt Freda, since she'd have heard it soon enough from the police. And Freda will be sure to tell your aunt—'

'For pity's sake, Steven, don't keep me in suspense!'

She could see that he was dragging out the moment, and she couldn't think what it was that was so awful. Save for the deaths of her parents, nothing in her life so far could come remotely close to the awfulness of the disaster.

'Well then, it seems that Alice Day had booked a passage on the *Titanic*, and she couldn't resist sending a crowing farewell note to Robert to tell him so, although she declined to give him the assumed name she was travelling under. Presumably she left the note for someone else to post, since it has only recently been received.'

For a few seconds Lauri couldn't think who Alice Day was. She had become totally unimportant in her mind. And then she remembered. Alice Day had been Freda Connors's companion, the one who had robbed and betrayed her.

'But she was no more than a lady's companion! How could she possibly have afforded such a passage? Are you sure the note wasn't just a terrible prank on her part? Or that someone else wrote it?' Lauri said, unable to think of anything else for the moment.

'Robert took the note to the police, and it was confirmed that it was her handwriting. As to how she afforded it, they have been making further investigations in these past weeks, and it's been discovered that the lady was adept at using aliases and disguises. The proceeds of her robberies will have easily paid her passage money.'

'My God!' Lauri whispered, suddenly sick to her stomach. 'Steven, you don't think—'

'I do not, and neither must you,' he said brutally, knowing exactly where her thoughts were going. 'According to the note, her passage was booked long before you cancelled yours. She even had the gall to say she would look out for our new American friend, and be sure to avoid you.'

Lauri swallowed. For one awful moment, rather

than feeling guilt that Alice Day might have taken her own ticket, she had felt a tremendous sense of gladness that right had triumphed over wrong. Such thoughts were evil, and she was thankful Steven hadn't been aware of them.

'Do you have any more information?' she said carefully.

Such as…*did Alice drown*? Or was she, even now, telling some elaborate tale of survival to a sympathetic and gullible American audience?

'None,' Steven said, grim-faced. 'And I wish I hadn't had to tell you this much. But if you're thinking that whatever happened to Alice, might have happened to you, then forget it. She's not worth getting upset over—'

'How can you say that!' she said, appalled at such callousness. 'Whatever Alice did, she was a human being, and no one deserved the fate of those people—'

'I know, and I'm sorry. I phrased it badly.'

'Yes, you did. In fact, you sounded more like Robert at that moment. How is he taking this, anyway?'

Steven shrugged. 'Robert's attachments are generally short-lived, and although it came as a bit of a shock to get her note after the ship had gone down, he's taking it philosophically enough. What else can he do? He certainly wouldn't mourn her, and he doesn't want to trace her, although the police have already got the information in hand. She's still wanted for theft in several counties.'

'I hope they never do trace her,' Lauri said with a shiver. 'I don't think I want to know—'

'Nor do I. And from what we now know of Alice,

my guess is that, if she survived, she'll have gone to ground with another identity long before now. So let's try and forget her, and don't let the news spoil our day.'

It was easier to tell the sun not to rise each morning than to tell Lauri to forget it. But whatever had happened to Alice Day was no longer any concern of theirs. They might never know if she survived the disaster, but one thing was certain. She was out of their lives for ever.

'So, have you and your aunt decided what characters you're going to be for the ball?' Steven asked her, when she had said nothing for all of ten minutes.

It might be insensitive of him to mention such a comparatively frivolous event when they had just been discussing Alice Day's possible demise, but Lauri was thankful for the more normal turn of conversation.

She managed to make herself sound alert, even if her normal feminine enthusiasm in clothes was lacking.

'Of course, and the dressmaker has been on hand for days now, but you can hardly expect me to divulge what we're going to be wearing. Otherwise, there's no point in our turning up in masks, is there?'

He laughed. '*Touché!* But it would take more than a costume and a mask to disguise your lovely self from me, Lauri. I would only have to touch your hand and feel your fingers curl around mine. I would only have to see the curve of your mouth, even if I was unable to see those beautiful blue eyes behind the mask. None of it would matter, because I would know you anywhere.'

Lauri drew in her breath. It seemed so long since they had spoken endearments to one another, or kissed, or shown any signs of outward affection. She knew it was all due to her and her emotions that had kept him at bay all this time.

But she couldn't miss the longing in his eyes as he looked at her now, any more than she could deny the rapid quickening of her heartbeats, and the rush of answering desire that ran through her veins.

'I would know you too,' she whispered. 'Always, Steven.'

He gave a small smile, as if at some private thought. And then he was by her side, and she was in his arms, and his mouth was on hers in a long, sweet kiss.

They both felt the boat rock, and the moment passed as he regained control of it, and of himself, Lauri thought shakily. Because, had they been somewhere more stable than in a sailing-boat, she had no doubt that that kiss would have led to something more. Her own passions were aroused, and it hadn't taken a genius to know that their feelings were mutual. And something so normal, and so wanted, as being in love, was suddenly the most desirable thing in the world.

'But now I think we should be getting back,' she murmured regretfully. 'Aunt Helen will be anxious to know how I fared this afternoon.'

'And what will you tell her?'

She paused, and then said, 'I'll say I found myself again. I think she'll understand without my going into detail.'

And from Steven's smile, she knew he understood too.

She felt buoyant and alive at last as they returned to the boatyard and she stepped onto dry land again. It was probably crazy to feel so elated, merely because she had survived the short trip, and nothing untoward had happened. But she knew it was far more than that. Nothing had happened, except for a silent avowal of the love she knew existed between herself and Steven Connors, for however long it lasted. And that meant all the world to her.

Her aunt and uncle were looking serious when Steven left her at the house, deciding against coming inside. Vernon cleared his throat gruffly.

'We've had visitors,' he said cautiously. 'Robert brought his aunt to see us.'

'You needn't worry, Uncle. I know about Alice Day.'

'So Steven told you,' Helen said, as careful as Vernon as she tried to gauge her niece's reaction. 'It was a shock, wasn't it?'

'It was, but I'm not reading anything personal into it. Justice sometimes has its own peculiar way of dealing with things, and I prefer not to know anything more. So did the dressmaker come today for your fitting?'

Helen was clearly relieved at her reaction.

'She did, and she's left your costume for you to try for movement, as she called it, Lauri. She'll be back again tomorrow. I must confess I weary of all this constant climbing in and out of petticoats and frills.'

'But think how splendid you'll look when it's all finished. Good Queen Bess was never more regal than you'll look at the ball, Auntie, dear,' she grinned.

'And you will make a beautiful Western saloon girl,' her aunt returned the compliment.

'Well, I hope so, though I have begun to have second thoughts about it. Miss Brandon is making my costume *very* provocative,' Lauri said with a frown. 'I'm no prude, but I don't want to display myself unnecessarily!'

'You have to play the part, my love,' her uncle put in. 'And there's nothing wrong with the female form. Great artists through the ages have adored and revered it.'

'Besides,' her aunt added, 'you'll be wearing the elaborate mask Miss Brandon is creating, and providing the three of us don't stick together like glue, you can remain incognito for as long as you choose.'

Remembering Steven's recent avowal that he would know her anywhere, Lauri wasn't at all sure that would be the case. But she found herself hoping that Robert wouldn't be so cute in identifying her, and that the other young lady guests would be more than sufficient to keep him occupied.

'Oh—they've delayed the ball by a few days,' she remembered to tell her aunt. 'Steven says everyone will be getting official invitations very soon.'

'So you were right.'

'Yes, but this has nothing to do with the disaster. They've decided it will be best to hold it a week after their birthday, so they can get this Will-reading with the lawyer over and done with beforehand.'

Or, in Steven's words, *So that whatever Slater has to tell us, Robert can get over his bombastic mood well before we entertain our guests.*

And hers: *Are you so sure it will result in trouble between you?*

Totally.

'I wonder just what old Connors had up his sleeve,' Vernon Hartman mused thoughtfully. 'Whatever it was, I suspect it's going to upset one of them. Otherwise, why bother to instruct a codicil to be read after all this time?'

'Steven says it's because the business was due to become legally Robert's when he became thirty years old, and his father knew how uninterested Robert was in it and was probably making certain provisions. Steven knows how cantankerous his father was, and is preparing for whatever comes,' Lauri said. Her face felt hot as she realised that for a stranger, she seemed to know so much about their private affairs. And her aunt clearly thought so too.

'Steven seems to confide in you a great deal, Lauri.'

'Only when he needs someone to talk to, and I happen to be the handiest person around,' she said hastily. 'I don't invite confidences, Aunt Helen.'

But she avoided her uncle's glance, since he seemed more keenly aware of the attachment between herself and Steven Connors than her aunt. Which was odd. It was usually the woman who sensed the merest hint of a romance.

'I think I'll go to my room and try on my costume, now that it's finished,' Lauri told them. 'I'll send for Maisie to help me, since she's the most discreet maid here, and I don't want a whisper to get out about my disguise.'

Her heart gave a little leap as she said it. Dressing as a Western saloon girl had been a spur-of-the-moment choice, and although the dressmaker had enthused so much about it, Lauri had had many doubtful moments since. She just hoped she wasn't going to look *too* daring. Even for these enlightened days, there was a limit to how much of oneself it was decent to bare in the name of authentic costumery.

The illustrations, and even the fabric samples Miss Brandon had collected to get Lauri's approval, were all definitely on the daring side. But the costume was finished, and there was no time to change her mind and go for something less revealing. A Western saloon girl she would be.

She collected Maisie on the way to her room, and gave up worrying as the two of them gazed silently at the costume hanging up in Lauri's closet. The very short skirt was a rich scarlet silk, and the attached blouse top was a shimmery white silk, and very, very low in the neck. There was a scarlet silk bow tie to wear around the neck.

'You'll look a picture, miss,' Maisie told her admiringly. 'Miss Brandon found a wonderful colour for the skirt. It almost matches the wig Mrs Hartman found in the attic. And the feather boa will add the finishing touch.'

It will make me look the complete tart, you mean...

'At least the wig will disguise me a little more,' Lauri said quickly, knowing that her own silvery-blonde tresses would be tucked well inside the flamboyant wig. Even for a saloon girl, that flaming hair was a bit much, she thought...

'What worries me is how much of myself I'll be showing!'

Maisie laughed. 'You should be happy that you've

got something to show, if you'll pardon the liberty, Miss Lauri. Many a young lady would be pleased to have such assets.'

'Hmm, you may be right—'

'Anyway, you could hardly pretend to be a proper flashy piece without 'em, could you, miss?'

'All right, you win, Maisie,' Lauri said with a laugh, finding it a pretty backhanded compliment, but knowing the girl didn't even see it that way. 'Now, help me into it, and let's see if I'll do.'

'And then I'll tease out the wig still more to get the full effect, shall I?'

'If you like.'

Maisie was clearly entering into the spirit of the thing, Lauri thought. She wouldn't be on the guest list, but seeing her young lady done up to the nines, as she put it, was the next best thing. And once the outfit was fitted onto Lauri's shapely figure, Maisie teased out the wig hair to its fullest and wildest effect, and fitted it carefully over Lauri's head. She draped the pink feather boa around Lauri's shoulders, and only then did the saloon girl turn around to take in the finished effect.

'My Lord, I look like a street woman,' she gasped.

'Well, ain't that a bit how you're supposed to look?' Maisie said dubiously.

Lauri couldn't argue with that. But she simply didn't recognise herself, even without the silk and feathered mask that Miss Brandon had promised but hadn't yet been delivered to the house.

She let her gaze roam slowly over the reflection of herself in the long bedroom mirror. And what she saw was a voluptuous woman, with the upper swell of creamy white breasts provocatively displayed

above the far-too-low neckline. She was suddenly
nervous at how she was going to appear in public,
and the shiny silk bodice emphasised the sudden
peaking of her breasts, and she had to resist the urge
to put her hands over herself to hide them. The tiny
waist of the swirling scarlet skirt was nipped in to
emphasise the rounded hips that completed the effect
of the wanton, she couldn't help thinking. And showing her legs in this way, clad in silvery white stockings with impossibly high-heeled red shoes beneath,
was surely going way, way too far…

Even more than that…somehow the garish colour
of the wig seemed to illuminate her whole face, making her eyes sparkle more than usual, and her parted
mouth seem rosier and glossier and more pouting…
She *definitely* looked like a flashpot, and what was
more, the entire outfit made her feel like one…and
with the thought her pulses throbbed with a wild and
unexpected surge of excitement.

She lowered her eyes before Maisie could see the
sudden gleam in them, and understand what it meant.
For the only thing Lauri was seeing in her mind's
eye now was the moment Steven Connors would see
her, and know her, and *want* her…

'I think I've seen enough,' she murmured to the
maid. 'At least I won't need any more fittings, so
will you please help me off with it all, Maisie?'

'I'm sure your young man will love you in it,
miss,' the girl said, doing as she was told.

Lauri laughed. 'I don't have a young man,' she
said.

'Then you should have! A lovely young lady like
yourself!' Maisie said daringly. 'I'm surprised half
the county bucks ain't in love with you.'

'I'm rather glad they're not! What would I be doing with so many beaux?' she teased her.

Especially when she only wanted one...

But now she needed to calm down a little, and she spent a couple of hours writing to people back home, and writing up her diary. Thankfully, those who knew her had been informed beforehand that she had cancelled her ticket on the *Titanic*, or they would have been bombarding the shipping company for news of her. But now it was time to tell them she was staying in England indefinitely. Burning her boats, she thought, not missing the irony of the words...

She rejoined her aunt and uncle in time for dinner that evening, and told them that she had finally come to a decision about her future. Vernon already knew, of course, but Helen was overjoyed at the news, her eyes filling with tears as she hugged her niece. For her aunt's benefit, she accorded part of her decision to having cold feet over the prospect of a long sea voyage—but by now Lauri knew it was far from being the only reason for remaining here.

'I can't tell you how happy this makes me, my love. Now you'll truly be the daughter we never had.'

'And you know what it means, don't you?' Vernon added.

'That I can borrow the Wolseley on occasion?' she said mischievously, knowing it was his dearest possession.

'More than that, Lauri—' and she could see that he was being serious '—I'm altering my Will to ensure that after Helen and I have passed away, you will be our sole heir. Everything here will eventually belong to you, my dear. As my brother's daughter, it was always understood, of course, but I want to make it legal and official.'

Lauri knew it was meant to make her feel secure and loved, and so it did, but she wished he hadn't mentioned death and Wills, which had figured far too much in her thinking in recent times. He saw at once that it had disturbed her, and hastened to make amends.

'But now it's been said, and we need never refer to the matter again.'

'I should think not,' Helen said vigorously. 'We've had enough dismal talk for a while. For heaven's sake, let's talk of something more cheerful, Vernon. Tell Lauri what you've decided to wear to the Connors' ball.'

'Yes! You've never given me a hint so far!' Lauri said, glad of her aunt's intervention.

His face regained its normal jovial expression.

'Your aunt thinks we shouldn't appear as a matching set of characters, so I shall be Blackbeard the pirate. What do you think?'

Lauri giggled, picturing him. 'I think it's an excellent choice, and certainly no one will connect Blackbeard with Good Queen Bess and a saloon dolly!'

'I wonder what Steven and Robert will decide on,' Helen said. 'Has Steven said anything to you, Lauri?'

'Not a word. I think he has other things on his mind at the moment to be giving too much thought to it.'

By the time the birthday was imminent, they saw nothing of the Connors boys; knowing Steven as well as she thought she did now, Lauri guessed he would be immersing himself in work. The Hawkes family were due to take possession of their boat, and they made a brief courtesy call on the Hartmans before sailing around the British Isles on their own maiden voyage.

What Robert did with his time before and after the appointment with the lawyer, was something else. For all his professed interest in the Spanish viticulture and love of that country, Lauri thought he seemed less inclined to travel abroad at present than to play the gentleman of leisure that seemed to suit him far better.

Unless, of course, he was merely biding his time in waiting for the inheritance to be his, and to sell it off as he had warned Steven he intended. With all the assets at his disposal then, he could do anything, and go anywhere, and Lauri doubted that they would see hide or hair of him.

And it was none of her business to speculate about his movements, she thought crossly. Except that she couldn't bear to think of Steven's distress and anger if Robert did as he threatened, and which he would have every right to do once he attained his birthright.

She gave up thinking about it. By now, she had also decided it was no use worrying about her choice of costume, having been assured by her aunt that many people dressed daringly for a masquerade ball. It was tradition...but Lauri had never attended one before, and it wasn't traditional where she came from.

The day after the Connorses' appointment with their lawyer, the telephone rang early in the after-

noon, and Lauri was told it was for her. In some
surprise she took the instrument and said hello. And
then her heart jolted at the sound of the male voice.
He simply spoke her name, and he sounded so near,
as if he was standing right by her side.

'How nice to hear you, Steven,' she said formally,
despite the way her heart was jumping.

He gave a short laugh. 'Not Steven, dear girl! It's
Robert. Sorry to disappoint you.'

'You haven't,' she lied. 'But you sounded remark-
ably similar at that moment, and I didn't know you
were around—' she floundered.

'Well, I am, and I wondered if you'd care to come
for a ride, since we missed out on it once before. The
horses need exercise, and so do I. So what do you
say, Lauri?'

She still wasn't keen on horse-riding, but it was
too tempting to refuse, even though she was going
to make very sure it was just a ride, and nothing
more. She didn't trust Robert, but even if he was a
philanderer, her heart was already given elsewhere,
and he couldn't touch her.

And if any trouble had erupted between the brothers since their meeting with the lawyer, it wasn't evident in Robert's demeanour—and nor had Steven
reported anything to her. But why should he, when
it was family business?

Pushing aside all other thoughts, she told him
she'd agree to go riding with him, providing she was
given a gentle nag. She didn't want to be the one to
antagonise her uncle's neighbours by refusing, especially since they were now her neighbours too.

* * *

A little later, she drove to Connors Court, to find Robert waiting for her with the horses already saddled. It was a truly wonderful day, mellow and warm, and they cantered across the scrubland and down towards the cove where she had been before. He could be good company when he wasn't trying so hard to be the world's champion bucko, Lauri thought irreverently. No wonder women fell for him.

'Time for a rest, I think,' he said at last, when they had raced the horses along the sands, and all four of them were breathing heavily. He slid off his animal, and reached up to help Lauri down off hers. As she reached the ground, his arms went around her, and there was no escape.

'Robert, don't do this, please—'

'Why the devil not?' he said, amused at what he clearly saw as her token resistance. 'We're both young and single and healthy, and don't tell me you're totally naïve about life, sweetie. I know about you American girls—'

'Then you shouldn't believe all you hear,' she said, feeling foolish to be silently wrestling with him on this deserted stretch of beach. And not yet alarmed...

'Maybe it's not just what I hear, but what I know,' he said, oozing seduction. 'I'm a touch more worldly than my brother in that respect, I assure you.'

'Steven's a gentleman,' she couldn't help saying.

He laughed, bending his head towards her. She stood quite still, knowing he was going to kiss her, and that she could do little to stop it, short of bringing up her knee where it would hurt him most. And that seemed a particularly stupid thing to do if one kiss was all he had in mind. One kiss never hurt anybody, especially if she simply didn't respond...

Robert spoke with an edge to his voice when the kiss ended. 'You're not quite so immune as you pretend, are you? I could even think of settling down with a girl like you. What would you say to helping me end my wild ways, sweet Lauri?'

She stared at him. 'If you mean what I think you mean, then forget it! The woman who tames you would have to be very tolerant of your behaviour, past *and* future, I suspect—and I don't have that kind of tolerance!'

She couldn't believe she was answering him in this way. And he hadn't *really* intimated a more permanent and serious relationship, had he? Alarm bells were truly ringing in her head now, because she didn't want this conversation, nor to even consider marriage with Robert Connors, if that was what he *really* meant—any more than she believed he wanted to tie himself down in marriage. It wasn't his style—unless there was some very good reason for it...

He suddenly let her go, backing away from her, and giving her an elaborate bow.

'I apologise if I seemed to go too fast for you,' he said, impossibly humble now, she thought irritably. 'People always tell me I've been too used to getting what I want without any effort, but perhaps that's because I've always taken the dross instead of the gold. And you're pure gold, my dear American cuz.'

'Bosh!' Lauri said, unable to keep a straight face, or believe in this chameleon-like change of mood for one moment. 'Keep your smooth talk for those who appreciate it, Robert. And before you say anything more that you'll regret, I'm going for another canter before these animals get chilled. Are you with me?'

'Of course. Isn't that what I've been telling you all this time?' he said with a seductive smile.

Chapter Thirteen

Lauri saw Steven once more before the date of the masked ball, when she went on an errand for her aunt to Kingscombe village, and couldn't resist calling at the boatyard to say hello.

She was dying to know the outcome of the brothers' meeting with the lawyer, but she didn't dare to ask unless he volunteered the information. To her relief, he was quick to do so, and his news stunned her.

'My father had the last word after all, although I should probably have expected something to twist the knife a little more,' he said bitterly. 'And now it seems that Robert has turned turtle, and is toying with the idea of keeping the boatyard and moving into its management with me.'

'*And?*' Lauri said cautiously, not following his entire train of thought as yet, and loath to interrupt him.

He gave an explosive oath beneath his breath. '*And*, my dear, sweet innocent, it will mean the end of a beautiful relationship, if such a thing ever really existed between us. He'll want to run it his way, and he'll ruin everything I've built up all these years.'

'Are you so sure of that? It's his inheritance, after all, and surely he'll want the best for it—'

He turned on her, his eyes flashing angrily.

'Believe me, Lauri, I know Robert. He's got no real interest in the business, and never has had. For him, it will be a nine-day wonder. Or, I suppose I should refer to it as more of a six-month wonder.'

He stopped speaking so abruptly that Lauri knew there must be more to come. She sat down in the small office, folding her arms determinedly.

'I know it's none of my business, but are you going to explain that cryptic remark, or do I go away wondering what in thunder you were hinting at?'

He was brusque to the point of rudeness, but as she listened to his crisp voice, she could hardly blame him.

'My father's codicil stipulates that Robert marries within six months and settles down to a proper and decent way of life. Those are his exact words. If he does not, then the boatyard passes solely to me, and he also loses his inheritance of Connors Court. You can imagine the shock and fury that produced. So, after an hour's wrangling with Slater to try to prove that the old pater was out of his mind at the time, which did no earthly good at all, Robert stormed off in a black rage, declaring his intention of doing just as my father decreed. He would marry the first woman who took his fancy, and run the business himself in any way he saw fit. And then he'd do as he always intended, sell up everything, the house included, and clear out.'

'But won't that invalidate the terms of the Will?' Lauri exclaimed, shocked beyond belief at such ruthlessness, and such inconsideration for his brother's feelings.

'Not if the marriage lasts the six months, even if the ceremony only takes place a week or so beforehand. There were other legalities that I won't bore you with, but that's the gist of it. Whatever happens, it seems that I'm the loser.'

'Steven, I don't know what to say, except that of course I'll respect your confidence in telling me all this,' Lauri said weakly. Clearly, this wasn't the time to go to him and show any loving sympathy. He was a man whose pride had been deeply battered, and no woman could compensate for the jolt to the male ego until he was ready for it.

'Thank you, but I assure you I won't give in to it without a fight. Just be on your guard in the future.'

She looked at him blankly, not understanding what he meant. Then he gave a bitter laugh.

'My brother needs a wife, sweetheart, and who is the most convenient, and the most delightful candidate for the post?'

Lauri's face flooded with colour, and she felt both sick and angry as she registered what Steven meant. It was bad enough to realise what he was implying on Robert's behalf, but as for *her*...

'Do you think I would marry a man just for convenience and position? I thought you knew me better than that!'

And he *must* be wrong about Robert wanting her, when he had plenty of ladies to catch his eye, and appreciate his prospects! But her thoughts whirled, for hadn't she already had that ride with him along the sands, when he'd paid her more compliments than usual, and almost, *almost*, made what amounted to a clumsy proposal of marriage?

Her heart leapt sickly, because the last thing she wanted was to be was the object of rivalry between these brothers. And from the look in Steven's eyes right now when he didn't answer right away, she could guess what devils were in his mind. She put her hand on his arm, speaking urgently.

'Don't you *know* that I'm not interested in Robert, or material possessions? It's not the American way to be so covetous, in case you weren't aware of it,' she said.

She didn't dare to say more, because there were limits as to how frank she could be, even for a progressive American girl, until a man's intentions were definite.

And Steven hadn't yet formally proposed to her, nor had she known him long enough to expect it. The delightful rituals of courtship had to be observed, and rightly so, even though the unpredictable Father Connors would seem to have put an end to all that as far as his elder son was concerned.

Robert had to find a wife, and marry her within six months. And Lauri Hartman was here, and available.

Steven drew her to her feet, his fingers caressing her cheek for a moment. It wasn't the place, or the time, or the right mood, for intimacy, but the simple gesture moved her.

'I hope you'll always feel that way, Lauri,' he said roughly, 'if it ever came about that I could offer you nothing but myself.'

The reply choked in her throat, because she could see how serious he was being, and she didn't want to throw herself on him, nor to sound as though she was a gold-digger.

'I assure you that possessions are of little importance to me, Steven,' she said again. 'But for your own sake, and because it means so much to you, I hope you find a solution to it all.'

But she drove back to Hartman House, more disturbed than when she had left it. How any father could drive such a wedge between his sons in this way was beyond her.

And all because of a ten-minute difference in their births. It was cruelly unfair that one should have it all, and the other so little. If there had been a year or more between them it wouldn't have seemed so outrageous, but for Steven to be in danger of losing everything he loved because of ten precious minutes…

But it was pointless to speculate on what might have been. Instead, she was thankful that he had told her in confidence about the codicil, and that he had warned her to be on her guard against Robert.

Not that it did her feminine self-confidence a whole lot of good to know that he'd only be making up to her because he needed a wife—*any* wife, presumably.

What damn cheek, she thought now, bridling at the very thought of it. If she didn't think it would throw too many cats among the pigeons, she'd play right back up to him, and then drop him at the last minute.

But she knew that was a dangerous game to play. It would hurt Steven too much, and the thought of involving him in such a subterfuge was against her principles, just as she knew instinctively it would be against his.

No, the only thing to do was to rebuff Robert's advances—if he even made any. There was no reason to think she was the *only* one on his horizon—in fact, she took comfort in being perfectly sure she was not.

The flowers arrived the next day, a great sheaf of early yellow roses in an elaborate basket arrangement. A maid delivered them to Lauri while she and her aunt were enjoying the afternoon air in the garden. The scent of the full-blown blossoms was sensuous and fragrant.

'It seems you have an admirer,' Helen said with a smile. 'Which doesn't surprise me, of course.'

And why did it not surprise Lauri to guess at once who the flowers were from! Her heart jumped uneasily as she took the card out of its little envelope and read the words aloud without thinking.

'To a lovely lady, with my abject apologies for any misunderstandings between us. R.C.'

Lauri saw Helen raise her eyebrows. Naturally, she knew at once whose initials they were. 'Have you and Robert had words, dear? I know he can be abrasive at times—'

'It was nothing, and it certainly didn't warrant such an elaborate apology!' Lauri said, knowing full well that there was a deeper meaning behind the tribute.

And the thought of Robert being abject towards anyone was almost laughable.

'It shows he thinks highly of you, all the same,' Helen went on. 'I suppose he does have some good qualities…'

Lauri smiled, seeing the way the older woman's thoughts were turning. 'Aunt Helen, stop it! I didn't think you had such good feelings towards Robert! And I know you'd dearly like me to marry one of your favourite boys, but I really think you must leave my choice of husband to me. Not that I'm even thinking in that direction yet,' she added hastily.

'Then perhaps you should be. It would give me such pleasure to plan a wedding for you, my dear—'

'Well, even to give you pleasure, you'll have to wait until I'm good and ready for matrimony, Auntie dear,' she said smartly. 'And it's not going be just yet!'

But she was thankful to know that since the Connors's masked ball was less than a week away now, there would be little chance of Robert pursuing her. And hopefully, there would be plenty of other young ladies at the ball to catch his eye. All she had to do was to be sure to stay aloof, and let him see that she wasn't in the least interested, no matter what he had to offer.

Over the next couple of days, more flowers were delivered to Hartman House, together with several dramatic notes from Robert, to the effect that he wouldn't feel that Lauri had truly forgiven him for his crass behaviour until she said so in person.

He was making far more of the incident at the cove than necessary, thought Lauri, but with new insight into his reasons, she guessed he was seeing it as a convenient excuse to further his cause.

He visited the house just once in the few days before the ball, ostensibly to pay his respects to her elders. None of the Hartman family could fault his charming manner, nor his apparent interest in Lauri.

She didn't trust him one iota, but since she didn't feel it was her business to acquaint her aunt and uncle with the terms of the Connors codicil unless the brothers or Freda did it themselves, she kept her private thoughts to herself. And Robert himself was unaware that she knew of it.

Briefly, Lauri asked herself what difference it would make if she *hadn't* known. Would she have taken this sudden show of affection as genuine? And even more so, would she have responded to it? She certainly didn't think so for a second.

It was all nonsensical and unnecessary, but it provoked her aunt and uncle into laughing comments that if Robert's attentions were anything to go by, then Steven had better watch out for a rival in the matrimonial camp.

'More like a snake in the grass, I'd say,' Lauri murmured beneath her breath.

'What was that, dear?' Helen said.

'I said that none of it cuts any ice with me, Auntie,' she replied sweetly, and then she turned her head away quickly, wishing she had never said the dreaded word, as the hateful connotations swathed into her mind as always.

Ice meant iceberg…and that meant that great and beautiful ship heaving and upending in the ocean…and all those tragic people freezing and dying…

So much detail about the disaster had now been published, that the fatalities were no longer anonymous, but had assumed a strange kind of life and form in her mind: Captain Smith and First Officer

Murdoch...Jack Phillips and Harold Bride, the two Marconi men vainly trying to attract help for the stricken ship. And the poor passengers, some fabulously rich, and some hopefully seeking a new life for their families. Fate made no distinction between those who had perished, or lived to tell the ghastly tale.

There had been so much heartbreaking detail from the survivors and observers that Lauri simply couldn't forget... In her head she could imagine the sounds of the band playing the crazy ragtime music that had finally and symbolically changed its tune to the sombre strains of 'Nearer my God to Thee' as the ship slowly sank into the cold waters of the Atlantic... And everyone now knew that out of over two thousand people on board, more than half had been lost...

'Are you quite well, Lauri?' she heard her uncle's sharp voice as if it came out of a mist. 'You're really shaking, my dear. Do you have a chill?'

'No, Uncle Vernon. I'm just laying ghosts,' she croaked. 'Sorry. It comes over me sometimes.'

'I do understand,' he said sympathetically, and she sensed at once that he did. 'And I know it's foolish to think that an occasion like the Connors's ball will take away the bad memories of other times. But you have two young men who are eager for your attentions, and a loving family here, my love. Many young women would be happy to be so blessed.'

'I know that, and you know how grateful I am—'

'Gratitude is the last thing I want from you,' he said, more briskly. 'So let's hear no more of such nonsense, and do our best to concentrate on looking forward, not back. There's no use in dwelling on things that can't be changed.'

It was a good philosophy, and it echoed her own belief, even if it was sometimes difficult to follow your own advice. But she was young and alive, and she was determined to try.

The night of the ball finally arrived, and as she dressed in her bedroom, declining the help of a maid, Lauri felt both the excitement and the nervousness of the occasion begin to undermine her confidence.

The outfit she had chosen was *so* daring, and she suspected that most of the English guests would be dressed far more conservatively than herself. In fact, the very sight of a saloon dolly might give her away immediately, she thought dubiously now, since it was so very American. Although her aunt had assured her that the British lost their well-known inhibitions on such occasions and would be dressed just as flamboyantly, Lauri secretly doubted it, but she sincerely hoped it would be so.

But how were they supposed to arrive separately, so as to pretend non-acquaintance with one another? She was so jittery by the time the hour was almost here, that she was finding all kinds of difficulties in her mind, and told herself severely to stop it, or she would be a nervous wreck before they even got to Connors Court.

As it happened, Vernon had already made arrival plans.

'I'll drive your aunt and myself in the Wolseley, Lauri, and with her enormous skirts, there'll hardly be room to swing the proverbial kitty,' he said. 'So one of our neighbours has agreed to take you with him and his wife. Does that suit you?'

It did, although she could very easily drive herself. But then again, turning up in her own car would give the game away. Just before the neighbours were due to arrive, and having seen off her aunt and uncle, the final bit of Lauri's preparation was to put on her elaborately sequined mask of silk and feathers, and tease out the bright red wig to surround it. Maisie had insisted on being in on *the piece of most resistance*, as she called it, and gaped when the disguise was complete.

'You look a real picture, miss,' she said admiringly. 'A real out-and-out floosie, if you know what I mean! No offence meant, I'm sure!'

'None taken, Maisie,' Lauri said with a grin, eyeing herself in the bedroom mirror, and seeing the reflection of a brazen hussy that didn't resemble herself in the least. Except in her innermost secret passions, she admitted. 'And I'm well disguised now, at least until the masks are removed at midnight and we have to reveal ourselves—which, I'm told, is the custom at these house parties.'

'Oh yes, so it is, miss,' Maisie said, with a servant's inner knowledge of such occasions. 'Nobody will guess who you are until then—and I daresay the funny way you talk will be thought just right for the part, anyway, you being a colonial person and all.'

'All right, Maisie, I think we'll leave it right there,' Lauri said, laughing now, as the maid began to flounder.

As they both heard the toot of a motor horn, Lauri turned to go down the stairs with her heart beating fast, and she was filled with an excitement that was both thrilling and scary.

Cinderella was going to the ball, she thought fleetingly, *and what was going to happen when the clock struck midnight was anybody's guess...*

The gardens of Connors Court were strewn with Chinese lanterns, and servants leapt to attention whenever a car arrived, to whisk it away to some pre-arranged parking area.

So she needn't have worried about being recognised too soon, thought Lauri, for everyone entered the house on foot, to be greeted by a butler and other servants in the spacious drawing-room. They were each given a glass of champagne, before being ushered into the splendid ballroom where a band was playing soft music. And where everyone was greeted formally by the three people awaiting their guests.

These three were obviously to be identified, since they were the hosts of the occasion. Freda Connors was resplendently regal as Mary Queen of Scots, and the two tall young men beside her were...

Lauri gasped, knowing now why Steven had had that enigmatic smile in his eyes when she said she would know him at once. Because, apart from knowing that Steven and Robert were co-hosts with their aunt, she didn't know him at all. Or at least, she had no idea which of the two flamboyantly garbed highwaymen, dressed identically in every detail, was Steven—and which was Robert.

If it had been their plan to fool everyone, and cause a ripple of delighted excitement among the guests the minute they arrived, it worked admirably. But did one of them recognise her immediately, knowing her anywhere, as he had said he would?

The Master of Ceremonies who introduced the guests to their hosts by their assumed names, leaned towards Lauri. She was completely bemused for a moment, and then remembered what she had decided upon.

'I'm Miss Sapphire,' she murmured, thinking now what an absurd and outrageous name she had chosen on account of her eye colour. *Miss Sapphire*, indeed—right now she thought it sounded less like a saloon dolly than an inmate of a bawdy house—but at least it was a mite less provocative than Miss *Scarlet* might have been, on account of her vibrantly coloured skirt. In any case it was far too late to change her mind, as the MC loudly proclaimed her name.

'Welcome, Miss Sapphire,' Freda Connors said, her voice slightly muffled behind her silver mask. 'I do hope you have a pleasant evening.'

'Thank you, ma'am, I surely hope so too,' Lauri said, her voice higher than usual, with the exaggerated accent of the Alabama gal she had planned on emulating.

Why on earth hadn't she decided on being an elegant southern belle instead, she thought now? But it was too late for that too.

As she walked along the line of her hosts, her hand was clasped in a masculine one, the fingers pressing hers more tightly than was strictly necessary.

'Charmed, Miss Sapphire,' the voice behind the dashing black mask said. 'And I claim the first dance.'

'Thank you, sir,' she murmured, moving along.

Her hand was gripped again, and the voice that spoke to her was the same, and the eyes behind the mask were the same...and she couldn't tell who it was. The second in line would surely be Steven, as being the younger of the two...but then again, they could switch positions and identities at will, to fool everyone...and she was sure they would do so to-night...so she *couldn't* be sure...and she simply panicked.

'Leave a dance or two for me, Miss Sapphire, for I know you'll be much in demand this evening,' the second voice said.

'I surely will, sir,' Lauri said in a strangled voice, relinquishing the hand holding hers and moving into the body of the ballroom with a feeling of disorientation.

She was among strangers, and she had never felt it so acutely, nor so absurdly. In the masked identities, she felt that she knew no one, and in the crush of elaborately costumed guests, she couldn't even see her aunt and uncle yet. Then she did, and the temptation to gravitate towards them was almost irresistible.

But that would destroy the image of mystery she knew she was provoking, for surely a real American girl wouldn't have chosen an American costume. That had been the theory behind her choice, and she thought it must be working, because there was no hint of recognition on anyone's face, even though it was presumably part of the game to try to identify the mystery guests. Just as long as the tarty costume didn't cause Robert to hone in on what he might see as his ultimate conquest...

'My dance, I think,' a voice said in her ear some while later, when all the guests had arrived. By then, she had danced with practically every gentleman in the room, except for the pilgrim and those who were rather too elderly to take their pleasure with an Alabama gal…

She turned swiftly, to find herself in the arms of a dashing highwayman. 'And may I say that you look very beautiful tonight—Miss Sapphire,' he continued.

'Why, thank you, kind sir,' Lauri made herself simper, 'and you certainly look the part of the rogue. I wonder how much in character it really is!'

He laughed, his arms holding her closer than was necessary in the dance. She caught her breath slightly as she felt his fingers gently caressing her spine. 'You'll never know, will you? At least, not until later.'

'And do you know me?' she demanded.

'Ah, that would be telling, wouldn't it? I would hate to spoil the illusion too quickly.'

He whirled her in his arms as the waltz music carried them around the ballroom, and as they danced, the excitement in her grew, and she had already forgotten her earlier bout of awkwardness, and reverted more towards the extroverted young woman she really was, and the part she was playing.

Anyway, she had to act in character. What kind of saloon dolly would she be, if she allowed herself to be shy and retiring? And her brashness had certainly seemed to appeal to the other eager young buckos here. So much for the reputed English reserve, Lauri thought. There was none of it here tonight, and it was refreshing and heady to discover it.

She became aware of someone tapping her highwayman's shoulder, and the next moment she was in someone else's arms. It could almost have been the same ones. The similarity between the brothers was not always striking, except when their anger got the better of them, but in their costumes it was extraordinarily tantalising not to know which was which.

She looked up at her new dance partner provocatively, trying to assess whether he was Robert or Steven by his reaction to the question forming in her mind.

'And which of the highwaymen is likely to steal a lady's heart tonight, I wonder? Would he ply her with yellow roses, and play a waiting game, or simply whisk her away into the night to some secret rendezvous?'

Her companion laughed, and Lauri's heart lurched. She still couldn't choose between them, damn it. She couldn't tell at all, and it was becoming oddly unnerving. It would be good to have the assurance that Steven was looking out for her. And it would be good to know that if this was Robert, she must be on her guard.

'Would a highwayman send yellow roses to a lady, sweetness? I think not, although it's not my experience to behave in quite so roguish manner as my present character would suggest!'

'But perhaps fairly roguishly?' she persisted.

'Perhaps. And then again, perhaps not,' her partner said, as he swung her around even more breathlessly in the waltz.

There was no way she could provoke him into giving himself away, Lauri thought, fuming. And it began to alarm her. She was so sure that she loved Steven, and surely she would be able to know at once in whose arms she was held? The fact that she *didn't* would be enough to make a lesser-minded woman doubt her own feelings...but she was made of stronger stuff, no matter how much the pair of them teased her.

The dance came to an end, and her partner escorted her to the long buffet table for some refreshments and cordial. The time was moving on, and there was less than half an hour to go until midnight. And then she would know for sure...

'Would you care to take a turn around the garden, Miss Sapphire?' he asked when they were replete. 'I promise that your honour will be reasonably safe with me,' he added, with a smile in his voice.

Remembering her role, Lauri laughed. 'Oh, shame on you, sir! I never thought a red-blooded highwayman would be so ungallant as not to indulge in a little flirtation with an Alabama gal!'

He laughed back, squeezing her arm to his as he steered her through the crush of guests. She glimpsed his alter ego in the background, talking animatedly and incongruously with a bishop and a black-garbed Satan, and she still didn't know...

Maybe a stroll in the garden would give her the best clue yet. If he attempted to kiss her, he would have to remove her mask, and his own, and the illusion would be gone. She hoped such a thing wouldn't happen. She realised that she didn't want to know yet, after all, and she regretted her foolishness in provoking him towards a little flirtation.

If this was Robert, she already knew her reaction to a tussle in the garden would be that he was crass and uncouth. And if it was Steven—she drew in her breath, feeling her heart tighten. There was a great sense of romance in being alone with a masked stranger on such a night—albeit with a glimpse of

other strolling couples in the scented evening air—
and she didn't want it spoiled. Not yet. Not until the
witching hour of midnight.

'*So*, my delectable Miss Sapphire, is our party to
your liking?' the soft voice asked. As he leaned towards her, she could smell the whiff of liquor on his
breath, and knew that whoever he was, he had been
drinking well, if not heavily.

So it was Robert—or maybe not. Both the highwayman had been imbibing quite freely during the
evening, like everyone else, and an uneasy thought
had begun to creep into Lauri's mind. If this was
Steven, he could be testing her, to see just how she
would respond to the belief that her garden companion was his brother.

To see if her American integrity, and her scathing
dismissal of riches, could be breached after all, with
the enticement of being Robert's wife and the mistress of this house. But it would only be feasible if
he guessed her own identity, she thought weakly, her
brain starting to ache with all the possibilities.

Of *course* it was an unworthy thought, and Lauri
pushed it furiously from her mind. But thoughts had
a habit of sticking like glue, even when you least
wanted them, and she couldn't quite get rid of this
one.

'You can have no idea how badly I want to kiss
you, Miss Sapphire,' she heard the highwayman say
teasingly now. 'You could hardly expect to appear
in such a delightfully skimpy attire without having
every red-blooded male in the place lusting after
you.'

'Robert, please, don't—' she said, as his arms
closed around her, holding her in a vice-like grip.

By now they had entered one of the small shrubberies, and were out of sight of any onlookers.

'Oh, no, my sweet one, you won't catch me that way. For this evening, I'm the masked highwayman with no name. And I don't propose to destroy the illusion yet. But one kiss won't be missed, even if I have to keep on this damnable mask while I have it. But you must admit that it adds to the excitement of the game.'

Before Lauri could resist him, he had pulled her head close to his, and pressed his mouth to hers. Both their masks left ample room for speaking and eating, and she felt the hot touch of his lips as they parted hers more savagely than she would have chosen, and she felt the tip of his tongue probing hers. He was outrageous, knowing that she could hardly scream out when she was pressed so tightly against him.

Even if she wanted to. Weakly, Lauri wasn't even sure that she did. The evening had been filled with a heady excitement that seemed to culminate in this man's arms, and even though she still didn't know whose arms they were, she could feel her senses swim. She knew the feel and the taste of him…and it surely *had* to be Steven…

The sound of laughter broke the spell she seemed to be momentarily under, and she wrenched herself out of her captor's arms as another couple came into view in the shrubbery. It was a French sailor, escorting a woman she had seen arrive quite late in the evening. She was dressed as a Spanish lady, with a beautiful lace mantilla and mask, and a shimmering turquoise gown.

With her jet-black hair, she would always be striking, but among the rest of the gaudily dressed company, she had been just another guest—until Lauri sensed the sudden stillness in her own companion when the others passed by.

'Do you think you know them?' she asked at once.

To her heightened senses, she realised the mood of recent moments had instantly vanished, and rather than being affronted she was filled with intense curiosity. She hardly thought the French sailor would have been the object of the highwayman's reaction, so it must have been the woman.

It wasn't even a hugely noticeable reaction in her companion, except to someone who seemed aware of every nuance of it, but for Lauri it was very real.

'Perhaps,' was all he said in a strangely intense voice. 'In any case, it's time we went inside, and then we'll all be revealed to one another.'

And why was she so sure that whoever the woman was, this highwayman was going to make very sure he was somewhere near her when the masks were removed? And if he was Steven...

Lauri felt a huge shock of jealousy rush through her veins at that moment, wondering if the woman was someone from his past, someone he had once loved.

She had never assumed that a dynamic man such as Steven would have reached the age of thirty without having prior attachments, and nor would she have expected it. The past was what made people what they were. The important thing was to be part of his future...

Chapter Fourteen

As the oldest friends of the Connors family, the Hartmans were invited to stay the night, as it would be very late when the revelries ended, particularly for Helen. Lauri would have preferred to return home, since the atmosphere was already far too charged for her liking. Not that anyone else noticed it, she acknowledged. And why should they? There were very few here who knew of Robert's needs or intentions.

And once she and her masked companion went back indoors, he disappeared on an errand of his own, and she was still no wiser as to which brother she had been with in the garden. She *should* have known if it was Steven kissing her, she thought uneasily. Didn't love make you aware of everything about the beloved? And if she hadn't been sure, then was she really in love at all?

She dismissed the small query at once, remembering the passion Steven could awaken in her. Remembering the tenderness and the empathy between them...and feeling her heartbeats quicken.

And one thing was sure in her mind. She certainly wasn't in love with Robert, nor ever could be.

A sudden crashing of cymbals from the small orchestra made her jump visibly, and the MC announced in a loud voice that the hour of midnight was just seconds away now, and everyone must prepare to show themselves to the rest of the company. There was much merriment in the final guessing game as the grandfather clock began its ponderous chiming, and then it was time.

The guests dutifully removed their masks and the secret identities were revealed, even if some of the delight and amazement was clearly pretence. Some of the disguises had been just too obvious, while others… Even though Lauri's own hair was still concealed by the brashly coloured wig, one of the adolescent male guests told her he had known who she was all the time. She smiled at him, seeing his embarrassment at daring to speak to her at all.

'No, you didn't!' she teased him. 'You didn't have the faintest idea, any more than I guessed who anyone else was.'

But since she didn't know half of the people here, it was a pretty fair assumption. She tried not to look around too obviously for Steven, but for the moment he was nowhere to be seen. And neither was Robert, although their Aunt Freda was clearly enjoying this part of the proceedings. Lauri turned to the young man again.

'Do you know the identity of the lady dressed as the Spanish señorita?' she asked curiously. 'I don't think I've seen her before.'

He glanced across the room and frowned.

'Haven't a clue,' he said in his precisely educated

voice. 'Could be one of those damned gatecrashers for all we know. Perhaps we should play the sleuth and make enquiries. What do you think? Are you game for it, Miss Hartman?'

She was quite sure she didn't want to play games with him at all, let alone playing the sleuth, and she shook her head.

'It's not for us to question the guests here. Besides, the lady has already found a friend.'

Her heart jolted as she spoke. The tempo of the evening had quickly accelerated with the excitement of identifying the guests, and the crush of people was even greater than before. But in a small gap between them, she could see right across the room to the richly peacock-hued gown of the Spanish lady. And she saw the way one of the Connors brothers was leaning towards her so intently. Even as she watched, he caught the lady's arm and they walked surreptitiously out of the room. Not having seen his face and with both brothers still in their highwaymen outfits, she couldn't tell which of them it was.

It all happened so quickly and so smoothly, and people in the ballroom were chattering nineteen to the dozen, and no one else seemed to have noticed it at all. But Lauri Hartman had noticed, and had been born curious...

All the same, it was more than half an hour before she could slip away from the crush of people who were all crowding around, congratulating one another on their various outfits.

She was still telling herself it was none of her business what Steven, or Robert, was up to with the Spanish lady...except that she knew in her heart that it was. If it was Steven, and he had gone off with her on some amorous encounter, then she couldn't bear to think he had been making a fool of her all this time. And if it was Robert—then somebody had a duty to warn the lady that his intentions weren't totally honourable.

Oh *God*, how pompous that sounded, Lauri thought, despising herself, but knowing darned well that nothing was going to stop her following them out of the ballroom as soon as she got the chance.

Of course, there was another alternative to her swirling thoughts, she realised. The lady may have been quietly escorted away because it was just as the young man had said, and she was an interloper—a gatecrasher. But if that were so, why hadn't the Connors brother returned from escorting her off the property?

And she had to know. She moved silently through the maze of rooms leading off the central corridor, and then a voice spoke close to her ear.

'I've been watching you, saloon gal. Where do you think you're going?'

As she jumped, her skin prickled, knowing she had been caught out in creeping about in a house where she didn't belong. She turned slowly, hot with embarrassment, the way people were when there was no conveniently glib answer on the tip of the tongue. And looked straight into Steven Connors's unmasked face.

Even in the dim corridor lighting, she knew it was him without a shadow of a doubt, and she sent up a small prayer of thanks that it hadn't taken a moment for her to recognise him. But this was his home, and she was still somewhere she had no right to be. He might even think she was taking it all in, with a view to someday soon becoming its mistress. Her breath caught on a huge gulp.

'I needed some air—'

'Oh, yes? In the middle of the house?'

Then he smiled at her and his face lost its quizzical look, and became more like the Steven she knew. 'Or were you doing the same as I was, and tracking down my brother and the mysterious Spanish lady?'

'Who *is* she?' Lauri said, not bothering to deny it.

'Who knows? So why don't we go and find out?'

He took her hand and they moved as joint conspirators towards the closed door of the library, the last room in the corridor now. Steven opened the door quietly, and he and Lauri stood quite still as they saw Robert and the stranger locked together in a passionate embrace. At first, they were totally oblivious to anyone else's presence, but Robert must have seen them out of the corner of his eye, for he sprang away from his companion, and glared angrily at Steven.

'What's this? Are you spying on me now, brother? Or were you and our colonial Miss Sapphire looking for a little hidey-hole for a bit of private sporting yourselves?'

Lauri knew at once why she had never liked him, and never would. He had none of Steven's finesse. He was uncouth and brash, and he shamed her by his insulting words. But Steven ignored the jibe.

'Why don't you introduce us to your companion, Robert?' he said, his innate good manners showing up his brother still more. 'I don't believe I know the lady.'

Robert's companion spoke then, murmuring in a cultured voice, but in the slightly stilted and accented manner of the foreigner. 'Robert, I should not have come here like this, but when I heard about this evening I could not resist taking my place among the masked guests. I should go now—'

'Of course you should have come,' Robert said roughly. 'You have every right to be here.'

In the small silence that followed, Steven spoke more sharply and forcefully.

'Hadn't you better explain that remark?' he demanded, moving across the wood-panelled room towards the couple. Lauri trailed him more discreetly. All right, it *was* none of her business—but it would take more than wild horses to keep her out of earshot now.

She saw Robert put a protective arm around the woman's shoulders, and she leaned her head slightly towards him. They glanced at one another, and although it was so brief a movement before they each looked away, it was an intensely intimate gesture from them both, and one that startled Lauri.

Why she should always have thought the womanising Robert Connors incapable of the deep feelings of other men was neither here nor there at that moment. It was just that, in the present circumstances, she hoped very much that the Spanish lady wasn't being taken for a fool. Right now she looked completely under his spell.

'This is Maria Lorenzo,' Robert said abruptly. 'You may have heard the name, brother.'

Steven said nothing, and then, 'The wine people?'

Robert's laugh held a hint of something like desperation mixed with bravado. 'God, living in your tinpot little world here, you know nothing, do you? *Yes*, the wine people! Maria's father is Garcia

Lorenzo, owner of the richest vineyards in Andalucia, exporter of the best wines in Spain.'

'*Querido,*' they heard Maria murmur again. Robert stopped her from whatever she was about to say.

'No, Maria, since they're so damned curious about my affairs, they should hear it all. It will all come out soon enough, anyway.'

'May we sit down before we hear this exposé?' Steven's voice was scathing, clearly expecting some sordid little tale to emerge. From all she had heard about Robert, Lauri suspected that there had been many as far as he was concerned.

'I think we should.' It was Maria who spoke with quiet dignity then. 'And I hope that what you hear will not condemn me in your eyes.'

As she glanced at Miss Sapphire and then away again, her fathomless eyes were even darker than usual. But Lauri hardly needed to see any expression in them, and she drew in her breath. She was more perceptive than Steven at that moment. It was a look between women. She had seen it before, and although she was no clairvoyant, her heartbeats quickened, almost sensing what was to come.

The leather chairs in the library were not exactly conducive to intimacy, but perhaps that was all to the good, thought Lauri. Nevertheless, as she and Maria sat down, and Steven perched on the arm of her chair, Robert stood behind Maria in a protective stance, his hands on her shoulders. At the movement, Maria's hand move upwards to squeeze his.

'Should I tell it?' she asked, less certainly.

Robert shook his head, sitting on the arm of her chair in the same way that Steven sat on Lauri's. They were so alike in their highwaymen costumes, and yet the difference in them both was so marked now, that Lauri wondered how she could ever have thought them one and the same.

Before Maria could say anything more, Robert began speaking in a clipped voice that Lauri guessed hid his feelings more than any emotional outburst.

'Maria and I have known one another for a long time,' he said. 'She was always the reason why I was lured back to Spain, despite what anyone might have thought of my wanderings. Maria, and my interest in the viticulture, of course. But the Lorenzo family is a proud one, and little short of aristocracy in the Spanish hierarchy. Like many of these old-established families, they don't take kindly to an interloper from another culture until they know him well.'

'I hardly think that would have stopped you,' Steven retorted. 'And if you were so enamoured of Maria, you've certainly spent enough time on other pursuits in the past year or so. I'm sorry if that offends you, Miss Lorenzo, but I know my brother—'

'But not as well as I do,' the woman said softly, stopping Steven in his tracks. She looked up at Robert questioningly, and he nodded.

'The last time I went back to the Lorenzo estate, I was told Maria had gone on an extended European tour with an aunt, and no longer wanted to see me. Each time I went abroad from then on, it was with the sole intention of trying to find her. I couldn't believe she had disappeared with no word of explanation. We had both meant too much to one another.'

If this was showing Robert up in a new light as far as Lauri was concerned, she could see that Steven wasn't convinced. But the more she heard, she more she guessed what was to come.

'I trust you had an enjoyable trip, Miss Lorenzo,' Steven said, clearly not yet seeing what Lauri saw.

Maria gave the ghost of a smile, her voice tremulous, her hands constantly twisting together in embarrassment. She took a deep breath, then the words tumbled out.

'If you mean being booked into a private clinic in Paris under an assumed name with every luxury until—well, until a certain event occurred, then I was certainly comfortable enough, yes.'

Lauri heard Robert take charge now.

'Take that outraged look off your face, brother, and I'll tell you what Maria finds too delicate to say. Yes, she was in a clinic awaiting the birth of her son—*our* son—and I wish to God I had known about it before this night, because he would never have been born out of wedlock, no matter what the Lorenzo family thought.'

'They did what they thought was best for me, Robert,' Maria murmured in distress. 'What they had to do—'

'Good God!'

Steven had leapt to his feet now, glowering at the two of them while Lauri tried to restrain him. He brushed her aside as if she were an irritating insect. 'And you believe this tale, do you?' he went on harshly. 'You don't think it a coincidence that somehow one of your mistresses has got wind of the inheritance, and your need to marry within six months, and has decided to cash in on it?'

Lauri gasped at his brutal words, but before she

could speak, Robert had leapt at him and got him by
the throat.

'You'll retract that statement, you bastard, or I'll
kill you—' he grated.

'Show me the proof of what the woman says, and
I'll gladly do so,' Steven tore out the words.

Everything happened so quickly then that Lauri
was left reeling. One minute they were glaring at one
another like two halves of the same coin, and the
next they were battling it out on the library floor like
savages.

'Stop it,' Lauri screamed, 'unless you want your
guests to hear and witness this disgraceful behaviour.'

She was appalled by what had happened so
quickly, and she couldn't imagine what the elegant
Maria Lorenzo must be thinking... but she could see
how pale she had gone beneath her tawny complex-
ion. Before Lauri could guess what she was about to
do, Maria turned and bolted from the room.

By the time the brothers had hauled themselves to
a standing position, Lauri was near to crying. The
news was both momentous and awful...and there
was so much to think about, because nothing could
possibly be settled in a few moments in the middle
of a masquerade ball.

'Maria—' Robert exclaimed, turning. His voice
ended abruptly. 'Where did she go?'

'Out of your life for good and all, I should think,'
Lauri said, appalled, knowing that this was none of
her business, but making it so.

He brushed past her, almost knocking her over.

'I'm going to find her. Get back to the guests,
Steven,' he snapped, 'and try to look as though

you're enjoying the rest of the ball, because I most certainly am not.'

If anything was meant to indicate the seniority of the brothers, it was his imperative order, Lauri thought furiously. She hated Robert for it. But once he had banged out of the library, she wilted, feeling angry and impotent, and fearful of knowing Steven's true feelings about all this.

In her heart, she didn't doubt Maria's story. There had been too much emotion in the looks that passed between her and Robert for that. And she hardly seemed the kind of woman to invent the existence of a child. The shock and disgrace to a proud Spanish family would never allow her to try such subterfuge. Besides, there would be ways to prove that it was Robert's child, she presumed, dates and occasions...

She licked her dry lips, never having been personally involved in such a situation before, and not wanting to be so now. She didn't dare to look ahead to what the consequences of it all might be. Right now, she was held tightly in Steven's arms, and she didn't dare ask him, either.

'We had best remember the occasion,' he said harshly. 'We have guests in the house, and one of the hosts should show his face, even if the other has temporarily absconded.'

'Steven—'

'Tomorrow, Lauri. We'll thrash it all out tomorrow. For the rest of the night, we'll continue playing our parts. I know my duty, even if my brother finds it convenient to forget it whenever he chooses.'

She didn't remind him that it was already tomorrow, but she knew he was right. The Connors's guests would already be wondering what had happened to them all, and they returned to the ballroom, where the revelry was in full spate, and the noise and chatter were still deafening.

It seemed as if no one had even missed them. What seemed to have taken a lifetime to Lauri, had probably taken no more than half an hour. But it was a half hour that would undoubtedly and drastically change peoples' lives.

The guests began to depart around 2 a.m., and by then, Freda Connors had long since retired to her bed, and so had Lauri's aunt and uncle. There was no sign of Robert or Maria, and Steven bid every guest a formal goodbye. In asking Lauri to share the task, she knew he was setting her up as more than just another guest. She could see the question in more than one person's eyes, but she was also more than ready to do so, knowing that the smiling façade hid a simmering anger against his brother. Robert hadn't only brought disgrace to a Spanish family. It was the Connors's disgrace too.

But by the time the last guest had gone, and they were the only two left in the ballroom, she was suddenly embarrassed at knowing far more of their family troubles than an outsider had a right to know.

'Thank you for your support, my love,' he said abruptly, without the need for explanation.

But tears misted Lauri's eyes. The words were said with dignity, but they managed to put a great distance between them. She had felt so loving towards him, so much a bolster to his need of her, but she sensed that he was too wrapped up in his fury now, to want it. Now wasn't the time.

'We'll talk tomorrow, Steven,' she said, reaching

up to kiss his lips chastely, and resisting the wild urge to pull him to her, and beg him to stay with her tonight. To give each other mutual comfort and love—and to forget all else.

She almost leapt away from him as the thought churned into her head. She was thinking more like one of the bold-eyed women Robert seemed to favour...but at the thought, the image of Maria Lorenzo swept into her head, and she knew instinctively that the word never applied to her. Maria was a lady, and Robert had presumably loved her. That she had loved him too was unquestionable. She had borne his child...

Lauri couldn't begin to guess at the torment and upheaval such a situation must have caused within Maria's own family. And she had never told Robert until now. The question *why not?* trembled in Lauri's mind, but she was too tired to think any more. She needed sleep, and she needed it desperately.

She awoke late in the morning, to find a maid pulling back her curtains. The strong sunlight hurt her eyes, and she shielded them at once. Despite the lateness of the hour when she had gone to bed, she was instantly alert, and it was no time to be lazing in bed, especially when there was something to be done. For a moment, Lauri couldn't think what it was, and then it all flooded back to her. She was going to find out just what Robert Connors's intentions were towards the beautiful Maria.

If Lauri and Steven meant anything to one another—and she knew that they did—then she couldn't let it go now, any more than Steven could. They were all involved.

Once she had bathed and dressed, she went quickly down to the dining-room. Steven was already there with the elders. There was no sign of Robert, and she knew better than to enquire about him in this company.

'Did you sleep well, dear?' Freda asked her, surprisingly bright considering her supposed frailty. And Helen too, looked relaxed and cheerful. It did the old dears good to have a lively social occasion, Lauri thought, as she replied that she had slept very well, thank you.

'We're leaving after breakfast, Lauri,' Vernon said. 'Do you want to come back with us, or do you have other plans?'

'Lauri and I thought we would take a breather this morning,' Steven said, before she could answer. 'I'll bring her back later today, if that's agreeable to everyone.'

She tried to look as if she had known these plans all along. In any case, she would have used every method she could think of to stay...

So, some time later, they set out in Steven's motor for the coast. And she was suddenly tongue-tied, wondering what kind of a night he must have had, when she had gratefully fallen asleep the moment her head hit the pillow, blotting out everything. Some support *she* had been, she thought.

'Did you sleep?' she finally asked.

'What do you think?' he said, tight-lipped.

'I don't know. That's why I asked.'

God, this was awful. They were tossing sentences at one another as if they were playing a game of table-tennis. Stupid, meaningless sentences to fill in time...

'I kept having to fight the urge to come to your bedroom, if you must know,' he answered, his voice still so stormy she could hardly believe she had heard him aright.

She looked sharply at his handsome profile, aware that her heart was racing. Knowing it had been what she wanted too, and that her rush into sleep had been a thankful aid to stop her thinking about him, and wanting him.

'Did you?' she said in a cracked voice.

'And then I thought that one little peccadillo in the family was enough, and I couldn't bring that to your door.'

He spoke harshly, and for a second, Lauri couldn't follow his thoughts, but of course, he meant the child that was already a fact. Robert and Maria's child. She ignored his fury, knowing he had to release his anger in any way that he could, however insulting.

'What do you think will happen, Steven?'

'God knows. I've no idea where he went last night. He certainly didn't come back to the house, at least not to stay, because his bed wasn't slept in.'

'Will he ask Maria to marry him, do you think?'

'Of course. It solves all his problems, doesn't it? And she's not going to say no, otherwise why did she come here in the first place, when she could have left him in blissful ignorance of his son?'

'But I'm sure she's no fortune-hunter, Steven,' Lauri felt bound to say. 'From what I heard last night, her family is considerably wealthier than yours, so it must be love.'

'And you're too damned romantic by half,' he retorted.

* * *

She realised they had arrived at the boatyard as if by a homing instinct, and she knew at once the sense of it. For Steven there was familiarity and security in his business. Here, he was king, for however much longer it lasted…

'My God, he didn't waste much time, did he?' she heard him say angrily.

Lauri's heart sank as she saw Robert and Maria. They were both dressed formally now, so Robert must have come back to the house at some stage during the night. Maria's arm was linked in his, and Robert was pointing out various aspects of the boatyard with a proprietorial and possessive air. It looked so much like an instant and inevitable take-over that Lauri was shocked.

Steven obviously had no defeatist feelings about the situation. He stormed across the sandy ground, leaving her to follow, and wrenched Robert around to face him.

'Come to claim your pound of flesh already, have you?' he said, and turned at once to Maria. 'You do know why he needs a wife, I take it, madam? Or has he conveniently forgotten to tell you?'

'Of course I know why he needs a wife,' she said in her soft, cultured voice. 'Just as I know why I need a husband, and why we both know that it can be no one but each other, no matter who tries to keep us apart.'

'Has someone tried?' Lauri put in quickly.

'My family—Robert's father—'

'What the devil do you mean by that?' Steven snapped. 'How could my father prevent anything from the grave?'

Robert snapped back. 'I would remind you that

you're speaking to a lady, Steven, and to remember your manners.'

'You're a fine one to speak to me about manners! You've always preferred to deal with problems with your fists rather than words,' Steven retorted.

Lauri was alarmed at the way this conversation was going, and also by the fact that many of the boatyard workers had stopped working, and were gathering in small groups, albeit at a respectful distance.

'All right, if that's what you think, come on, then. It's long overdue,' Robert said, shrugging off his coat and tossing it to Maria, and rolling up his sleeves.

'Don't be so bloody undignified, man. I don't want to fight with you. I just want to get this whole thing settled, and to know what you intend to do.'

'Are you welshing on a healthy fist fight, brother?' Robert taunted him. 'Fight me first, if you've the stomach for it—and then we'll talk.'

Lauri could see there was no way Steven intended to back out of this, however childish and ignominious it seemed to her. Robert was truly behaving like a spoiled child, she thought, despite being the elder of the two. But as Steven handed her his coat, she felt ridiculously like a second in an old-fashioned duel.

Before Steven could say anything more, Robert's fist had suddenly jabbed out, and struck him a blow on his cheek, splitting it at once. Lauri gasped as she saw the blood begin to flow. She automatically took a step forward, and Maria moved across and caught at her arm with surprising firmness.

'No. This is for men to settle.'

Lauri was forced to agree, though she couldn't

imagine how the boatyard workers would react to the two owners stealthily circling one another now, like two wildcats eyeing each other up for the kill.

She shouldn't have worried that anyone would intervene. Far from it. Each time one brother struck a vicious blow at the other, there were bellows of encouragement. And when they could draw breath, the two men hurled insults at one another.

'You shame the Connors name,' Steven snarled. 'And you shame the name of Lorenzo as well—'

'That's my business, and it's all been settled.'

'How? By paying her off?'

He was winded then, as Robert punched him in the stomach, and he fell to the ground on his knees for a few seconds. From the small silence from the workers, it was clear which of the brothers they wanted to win this fight, thought Lauri. But she thanked God that they were still keeping a respectful distance, and were too far away to hear the insulting words properly.

There was a wild cheer as Steven swayed to his feet and returned Robert's punch with one of his own, spinning him around until he fell to the ground. And finally it was Robert who went down and stayed down, counted out by a roar from the boatyard workers, who crowded around now to make sure he was well and truly beaten. They didn't know what the fight was about, but they knew who was their champion, and they made their feelings plain.

Lauri saw Maria kneel beside her stricken lover, sobbing and caressing his head in her lap. She turned her flashing dark eyes on to Lauri, standing by helplessly and at a momentary loss.

'This was all so pointless. Our plans have already

been made. But you English! Always so keen to see honour done, no matter how many broken heads are involved.'

'Well, please don't put any blame on me! And what do you mean—your plans have already been made?' Lauri demanded.

But she got no more out of Maria. Robert was starting to come round, and all the Spanish woman's attention was given to her lover. And then she felt Steven's hand on her arm.

'Let's get back to the house and then we'll thrash this whole sorry mess out,' he said authoritatively. He looked down at his brother and, in the perceptive mood Lauri was in, she found the action strangely symbolic.

'You and Maria will follow us there as soon as you feel able. I take it you're capable of driving?' he snapped.

Robert was still capable of giving him a sardonic smile, even though he winced slightly as he did so.

'Anything you can do, brother,' he muttered.

Steven turned away, holding Lauri's arm. Surrounded by the still-cheering workers, they began the drive back to Connors Court. Even though she despised physical violence, Lauri felt inordinately proud of Steven's strength and dignity. Battered and bloodied though he was, he was still his workers' champion—and *hers*, she thought. Always hers.

'Does it hurt?' she asked, almost timidly.

'I'll live,' he said grimly. 'But I'll save the talking until later, if you don't mind.'

His hand briefly covered hers, taking any sting out of his words, and she guessed that his thoughts were

too involved in what the next hour or so would hold
to say anything more.

Freda Connors exclaimed in horror as she saw the
dishevelled state of her nephew.

'What in glory's name has happened, Steven?' she
gasped. 'Have you been set upon by ruffians?'

'You could say that, Aunt,' he said drily, and before he could add any more, they heard the roar of
Robert's motor, and the next minute he and Maria
entered the house.

Freda's face was a picture of disbelief, and at any
other time, Lauri would have registered it minutely,
for the enjoyment of describing it to her aunt and
uncle later. But such a thought was farthest from her
mind now, as Freda obviously saw no significance in
the fact that the two brothers were in a similar state
of disarray.

'Well, whatever's been happening this morning, I
trust that together you saw the ruffians off,' she said
smartly.

'Oh, we did, Aunt,' Steven said. 'Look, can you
arrange for some refreshment for the ladies while
Robert and I attend to ourselves? Then we have serious business to discuss.'

'Of course, my dear,' Freda said, clearly respect-
ing the way he was dictating matters, while Robert's
tongue roamed tenderly around his swollen split lip.

'And perhaps Lauri can tell me what's been happening, and introduce me to your friend, whom I
don't believe I've met,' she added, reverting at once
to being the lady of the house, once the brothers had
disappeared upstairs.

'You have, actually, ma'am,' Lauri said, glad of a

lead. 'Do you remember the mysterious Spanish lady at the ball last evening? This is Señorita Maria Lorenzo, and she is a friend of Robert's.'

A very *close* friend, she added silently. But Freda rose to the occasion as befitted an English lady, and the three of them drank tea and exchanged pleasantries as cosily as if nothing untoward had happened, or was about to happen.

Lauri fended off Freda's questions as to the brothers' appearance by lightly referring to an undignified scuffle with some seamen at the boatyard. In any case, Freda was clearly more intrigued by Maria, and how she had met Robert.

'He has been welcomed in my family,' Maria told her carefully. 'His knowledge of my father's work has impressed him very much.'

Lauri couldn't help wondering just how welcome Robert would be if Señor Lorenzo knew he was the father of Maria's child. Or did he already know? And what had happened to the child? There were still so many unanswered questions...

The brothers joined them, more soberly dressed, and with their wounds tended, and invited the young ladies to join them in the library. Lauri did so with a fast-beating heart. There was no lessening of the almost palpable tension between them. Then Maria nodded encouragingly to Robert, who drew out a folder from his pocket and handed Steven several photographs.

'This is my son. Look at him carefully, and then tell me if there's any doubt in your mind that Maria spoke the truth about his parentage.'

Lauri craned her neck to look at the photographs with Steven, and to any onlooker there could be no doubt at all. The child was about three months old, and he was Robert to the life, but with Maria Lorenzo's flashing dark eyes. The photographs where she held him in her arms clearly established their connection.

'Naturally, I accept it,' Steven said coldly. 'I would not doubt a lady's word. So where is the child now? Has Maria been prepared to leave it so soon?'

'He is called Roberto,' Maria said with quiet dignity. 'He is not an *it*. And he is with my family.'

She stopped, looking uncertainly at Robert now, who took up the story.

'Maria refused to tell the family the name of her child's father at first, and she was sent away with her aunt to Paris, as she told you. The plan was for the child to be adopted, but once Maria saw him, she knew she could never do such a thing. And besides, Roberto would be the heir to the mighty Lorenzo wine empire, and her father dearly wanted a male heir.'

Robert gave a crooked smile. 'Do you begin to realise, brother, that Maria's family is so much richer than ours? If I was offering her marriage to keep this piddling little inheritance, it would be an insult—'

'Robert, please,' Maria said quietly.

'The next plan was for the aunt to bring up the child as her own, but Maria knew she couldn't bear to see him growing up like that. In the end she told her father the truth, and after a terrible confrontation, he demanded that she came to see what I intended to do to put matters right.'

'And what *do* you intend to do about it?'

Robert took Maria's hand and raised it gently to his swollen lips. 'Marry her, of course.'

'So that solves all your problems, doesn't it?' Steven said at last, unable to hide his bitterness.

'Not quite.' Robert stared him out. 'Maria refuses point blank to bring up our son in this cold climate. If I want my son, and my lovely Maria, I'm obliged to live in Spain and take up her father's offer of a partnership in the vineyard in order to secure the inheritance for Roberto. It's a hard life, isn't it, Steven?'

Lauri couldn't believe the mockery in his voice now, and she saw Steven clench his hands as his words seemed to belittle Maria so. But then Robert spoke more testily.

'Oh, for heaven's sake, Steven, stop looking so saintly for once. At least Maria believes in me, and yes, we intend to be married as soon as possible, and I propose to sign everything legally over to you and good riddance to the lot of it. The boatyard never interested me, anyway, and I will be more than happy to thwart Father's manipulative plans. We intend to see the lawyer today, and the sooner we can get everything legally settled, the better I'll be pleased. Besides, I'm anxious to get back to Spain and make the acquaintance of my son.'

For the first time that day, he looked less than sure of himself as he faced Steven's stony face.

'I'm relinquishing everything, Steven, damn it. You've always been the better man for the job, and we both know it. You've cared for the business in a way I never could, so I've no regrets on that score. So do we shake on it—brother?'

Lauri knew Steven couldn't be so churlish as to refuse, and minutes later, the other couple had gone, and she and Steven were alone. He drew her into his arms, clearly too full of varying emotions to say anything for a few moments, and then he looked down into her eyes, his voice husky.

'So it's almost all over. I know him well enough to know he won't go back on his decision, not with all that he has to lose in Spain, and Slater will make sure the legalities are watertight. Robert's got what he really wanted, but I would say we've both won, since I have almost everything I ever wanted as well.'

'Have you? Almost everything?' Lauri whispered, feeling all her nerve-ends jump, and almost afraid to hope he was about to say everything she wanted to hear.

'Almost,' he went on steadily. 'I'm thinking that Maria's family will undoubtedly arrange a big wedding in Spain. These old-established families always insist on an elaborate affair, no matter what the circumstances. Robert has a different need to hasten the wedding now, since he'll want to be with his wife and son. You and I have no such need for such haste, but as I shall be the chief guest on the male side, I would dearly like my fiancée to accompany me to Spain for the wedding.'

'You don't have a fiancée,' Lauri said.

'But I'll do so, if you will just say yes.'

His voice became more intense, more filled with an urgent passion. 'So will you *please* agree to marry me and live with me for ever, my dearest Lauri? I swear I shall go quietly mad if you refuse.'

'Well, I can't have that, so I guess I had better say yes, hadn't I?' she said, in a muffled voice that became even more muffled, and was finally silenced altogether as their mouths met in a long, sweet kiss of promise.

* * * * *

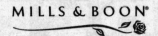

MILLS & BOON®

*M*akes
any time
special

Enjoy a romantic novel from
Mills & Boon®

Presents™ *Enchanted*™ *Temptation*™

Historical Romance™ *Medical Romance*™

FREE

2 BOOKS
AND A SURPRISE GIFT!

would like to take this opportunity to thank you for reading this Mills & Boon® book by
ering you the chance to take TWO more specially selected titles from the Historical Romance™
ies absolutely FREE! We're also making this offer to introduce you to the benefits of
Reader Service™—

★ FREE home delivery ★ FREE gifts and competitions
★ FREE monthly Newsletter ★ Exclusive Reader Service discounts
★ Books available before they're in the shops

epting these FREE books and gift places you under no obligation to buy; you may cancel at
time, even after receiving your free shipment. Simply complete your details below and
urn the entire page to the address below. *You don't even need a stamp!*

ES! Please send me 2 free Historical Romance books and a surprise gift. I understand that
unless you hear from me, I will receive 4 superb new titles every month for just £2.99
h, postage and packing free. I am under no obligation to purchase any books and may cancel
subscription at any time. The free books and gift will be mine to keep in any case.

H9EC

Mrs/Miss/Mr ....Initials ....
BLOCK CAPITALS PLEASE

name..

dress..

....

....Postcode ....

d this whole page to:
READER SERVICE, FREEPOST CN81, CROYDON, CR9 3WZ
re readers please send coupon to: P.O. BOX 4546, DUBLIN 24.)